TRIPTYCH OF A YOUNG WOLF

TRIPTYCH OF A YOUNG WOLF

Ann Allestree

Book Guild Publishing

Sussex, England

First published in Great Britain in 2008 by
The Book Guild Ltd
Pavilion View
19 New Road
Brighton, BN1 1UF

Typeset in Baskerville by
Ellipsis Books Ltd, Glasgow

Printed in Great Britain by
CIP Antony Rowe

A catalogue record for this book is available from
The British Library.

ISBN 978 1 84624 236 6

TO LUKE

our eldest grandson

ACKNOWLEDGEMENTS

Lélia Fournier Le Ber, who shared her knowledge and memories with me when we met on her family island, Porquerolles.

Anne Dominique Ménatory, who continues the work at Parc du Gévaudan in the heart of the Massif Central. This renowned wolf sanctuary, founded in 1958 by her father, Gérard Ménatory, the environmentalist, is an observation centre for the preservation of the species. She gave me her time and views on the ways of wolves.

Laura Vesa, leader of the DiscoveRomania tour group in Bucharest. Her guidance and advice were invaluable.

Dan Marin, our evocative guide through the ravishing terrain of Transylvania and past the footprints and markings of wolf and bear in the mountain forests.

Mark Adlington, wildlife artist, for allowing *Pack Leaders*, from his exhibition *Lost Beasts*, to appear on the jacket.

Hugh Somerville for introductions to his contacts in Romania.

The Aros Hotel in Braşov for its service, comfort and spacious rooms.

Nina Coben for valiant typing in the earlier drafts.

Yvonne Saltoun for the exacting task of translating an overflow of French script into English.

Francis King, CBE, prodigious man of letters, author and critic, for reading the early manuscript.

Andrew Sinclair, distinguished and versatile author and film director, who assured me he was 'eviscerated' by my wolves.

PART ONE
Captive Wolf

1

It was humid. But Madame Veuve was too old to sweat. That trickle down the back of the thighs was now a memory from youth's rounded flesh. She sighed as she lowered her hips into the wicker chair, a bundle of tired bones. Her pigeon toes were placed before her in highly polished black shoes. Thick white hair was coiled high above her miniscule body. The cadaverous face, wreathed in wrinkles, with a nose seemingly hooked to the upper lip, was framed in a dangle of gilded earrings. 'And why not?' shrugged the Comtesse, as she had handed her down these surplus trophies.

Madame Veuve, the *gardienne*, sniffed at the airless evening; it was clogged and hostile with low yellow cloud. She shuffled inside to pour herself a generous glass of red wine from the local 'Domaine de L'Ile' and took up her post again, to savour the overture to a Mediterranean storm. How she hungered for her evening glass of coarse red wine. In her old age it was the young growths she now preferred. The swallows swooped low and the doves were hushed. The breeze became tactile, capricious, blowing up her long skirt and down her neck. Cloud billowed behind the villa, menacing and ready to burst. A warning splatter of rain –

'The balcony! The balcony!' Madame Veuve secured her glass in the kitchen and, pulling on the banisters, levered herself up to the villa's first floor. A dagger of lightning dived through the rooms; the Comtesse's rooms. Madame Veuve edged herself gingerly through the bedroom to the balcony; tugging on the french windows, she locked out the rising wind and turmoil. A violent clap of thunder overhead shook the villa to its foundations. The startled old lady breathed deeply and dragged herself, in the fading evening light, through to the sitting-room and the Comtesse's sofas; to her canapés and her convex gilt-framed mirrors, a retreat of elegance and quiet comforts, with book shelves of Victorian English novels, and Flaubert and Balzac and George Sand. The wall paintings were calming, grey, pale yellows, creams and taupe. It cheered Madame to sit in the Comtesse's room and on the Comtesse's sofas. Despite their emptiness she felt drawn to the rooms. She found them strangely companionable. *Dieu!* How the rain was teeming. She cocked her ear for trouble: for a choked gutter gurgling and spilling from above; for a tree felled or a roof whirled off unceremoniously into the darkening chaos. The thunder became distanced as it growled across the sea to Toulon. Madame limped through to the adjoining bathroom; sky blue walls and steel cabinets. Despite the cavernous white enamel bath this seemed a subdued room; too much blue for Madame's taste. She found it cold and stern and swung open the medicine cupboard to view the Comtesse's pots and bottles with a derisory sniff; half-emptied phials for constipation, indigestion, insomnia stood rejected in a sticky row. The poor woman! A divorcée, alone, and in her fifties already. Madame passed through again into the bedroom with its grand view of the pine forests and a glint of the sea beyond.

The Comtesse's bedroom was an artful concoction of white voile and cream velour. This virginal aspect was dramatically redressed with the skin of a wild cat from the woods, flung casually over the expansive headboard. The floor, thickly covered with a cream woven rug, was adorned with a pair of stuffed wild boar. Madame took a furtive pleasure in flicking her duster hard at their hairy flanks. Yes, she would ask Philomène to help prepare the rooms. She stood for a moment, savouring the peace after the storm, the tentative birdsong, the last of the evening sun, the screen of dripping trees and the fragrance of steaming eucalyptus and myrtle. As though waking from a reverie, Madame Veuve padded down the stairs to recover her glass of wine.

Major (*the sitting-room wall*): 'Did you hear my chandelier tinkling?'

Middle (*the bathroom wall*): 'Pathetic! Were you crying for help? My window nearly blew in with that blast of lightning.'

Minor (*the bedroom wall*): 'Your problems were nothing. My windows were left wide open until Madame Veuve came to shut them. But the infernal damp has got into me; that dull ache creeping down the structure of my inner layer. Tell me, Middle, what was Madame after? She spent a long time fiddling inside your toy cupboards.'

Middle: 'If you must know, Minor, – you who are excessively inquisitive – Madame Veuve muttered that she must bring Philomène to help tidy us all up.'

'Oh! Philomène!' exclaimed Major and Minor in unison. Oh! That she might tidy their books and their cupboards, their sofas and chairs. Oh! To feel again her soft young fingers touching their sides and the brushing past of her taut little rump.

Middle: 'All such bustle and energy makes me tired. The Comtesse uses me hard; showers me with hot and cold; slaps me with her heavy towel and ruins the sight of my mirror with her splatters of toothpaste and her squirts of hairspray. That thick strawberry blonde hair flies into all my orifices, sticking and tickling and clogging . . .'

Major: 'The truth is, Middle, you are a spoilt ninny. You have a pampered life sandwiched between myself and Minor. Soothed with scented vapours, your sweaty little flanks are dusted down in clouds of talcum . . . I must warn you, dear Middle, that if you expect too much from life, you will always be disappointed.'

Middle: 'You are smug and complacent, Major. You have spent your life presiding over voluptuous sofas, nicely bound books clasped to your bosom, fresh air and fresh flowers and the occasional diversion of intelligent conversation. Minor and I even suspect that you have witnessed instances of seductive dalliance.'

Minor: 'In my opinion you are both spoilt. It is I who bears the brunt of the Comtesse when she takes up residence. Constantly I am woken by the whingeing bed springs, and the Comtesse can be indefatigably vocal through the night. You cannot imagine how disturbing this can be; the groaning and the squealing, the faked fainting and panting. My lower flanks tremble so! I have an acute fear of crumbling to the floor.'

Major: 'You have the urge to join in, Minor? But you are powerless. We walls are mere voyeurs of the scene, we must content ourselves with simple satisfactions: I, with my plumped-up cushions; you, with your handsome wild boar and voluptuous hangings; and Middle, with his enviable *coup d'oeil* of the Comtesse lolling in her bath – a vision of rosy skin and silky, blonde hair . . . we all get older and we should remind ourselves of that venerable maxim: that the sign of true maturity is when we learn to accept our limitations.'

Madame Veuve's glass of red wine was nearly emptied. She sat dozing in her basket chair, her wiry little legs stretched out before her, her sharp chin fallen on her chest. She was half-conscious of a substance beside her, a faint and familiar odour, a shadow and then a voice.

'Hello, Grandmamma! It is me, Philomène.' Madame's eyes swivelled to her granddaughter.

'Dearest girl, how wet you are!'

'I was dancing in the rain. Maman, she called me inside but the rain was all about me; in my hair, my body, my feet. And I danced and danced, Grandmamma, in our little yard. I leaned against a wall of rain as it poured down my body in waterfalls over my skin. It made me happy and free and ready for the world . . .'

Madame Veuve gazed on her granddaughter with admiration and alarm. How the child had fast become a woman; beneath that tent of dark hair, her breasts had developed as though by stealth. The nipples pert and prominent through her damp tunic, with the soft flesh set firm above her slender waist. Philomène sat at her grandmother's feet, careless of the wet, and rubbed her wizened little shins.

'You would be how old now, Philomène?'

'Just thirteen, Grandmamma. How good the wet trees smell, the grass, the flowers! You can hear the rivers gurgle? And now the martinet calls, the pipit and the doves? Let us run and dance through the sinking sun, Grandmamma, and breathe in the sea.'

'My little one, but you must return to your mother before twilight.'

'No! No!' the exultant Philomène assured her she had arranged with Maman that she would stay with Grandmamma and see her through the stormy night.

'First refill my glass and find yourself some grenadine.'

7

The lithe young girl soon led the twitching old lady through the clustered heather and the swaying Aleppo pines to the sea. Madame Veuve breathed in the tangy air and spied a bench beside a sandy patch. 'Let us stay a moment.' Madame's soul and heart, shrunk with the passing years, now welled up inside her. How she loved her Philomène, with that pure and bonded love of the first grandchild – her only grandchild.

'What are you thinking of, Grandmamma?'

'How I miss grandpère and . . . papa.' Both lives lost to drink and the sea. Cads and bounders, the two of them: her old black-guard, Louis, and Philomène's papa, Claude. 'It is not so bad, Grandmamma. We are still happy.'

It had been just such another storm. After a drinking bout on a moonless night, on the Toulon quays, father and son had set off for Port-Cros to lurk by the rocks in wait for the return journey of the provisions boat, *Les Îles d'or*. After a delivery to the Hyères Islands, the boat's coffer was full and easily wrenched from its secret panel in the gunwale. The two men had slapped their bellies and chuckled as they watched their quarry leave the island, dipping her hull and lights in the roughening water. But their befuddled bonhomie was snuffed by a savage wave. They were recovered in the grey calm of dawn, their arms outstretched to the sea. Louis and Claude – and Philomène barely three years. The generations of piracy and plunder sank with Madame Veuve's men that night. Those stories, relished on her own grandfather's knee, were gone now and forgotten, along with the whiff of cognac and his cigars, billowing from his wide mouth, his baccy pouches and his pipes . . .

'See the rabbit, Grandmamma! It is sweet, don't you think? It is just such a darling that we need to love and make us happy.' The little grey clutch of fur hopped back into the woods. Madame Veuve again wrenched her mind back to that black and stormy night, when the waves had lashed the rocks of Port-Cros and swallowed her men. The smallest of the Hyères Islands, it rises high above the sea, thickly wooded, green and impenetrable. Madame strained to hear again her grandfather's voice of warning: 'And never believe that this peaceful Mediterranean is always an azure blue without a wrinkle.'

Looking east through the trees, Madame could see the stark fort Langoustier, set proud and commanding above the bay. She patted the girl's knee. 'You are right Philomène. We all need to love and be needed. Let us go now quickly down to the beach before the light fails.' The path had become narrower and was heavily scented with honeysuckle and lavender. Philomène ran joyously on to the sand and dragged her toes through the detritus from the storm.

Branches and twigs from the sheltering pine woods had blown to the shore, where the lapping water was clogged with seaweed. Madame Veuve shuddered. The terror of that cruel springtime mistral, gusting from the north-west and yet . . . Philomène bounded up to her and put her arms round her little waist. 'What is it, Grandmamma? You look sad and lost.'

'Child, I was remembering how the Romans believed that our icy winds would sweep away dirt and disease and leave the sky more blue than before.' Philomène stiffened. Slowly she raised her arm and pointed to the far corner of the storm-strewn beach. Madame followed her gaze; a small grey shape was caught in a nest of seaweed – mammal rather than human. A feral cat? A seal? They walked towards it with apprehension. Madame judged it quite dead . . . and yet . . . Philomène dropped to her knees beside it, passing her hand across the little snout.

9

'It breathes, Grandmamma. What a darling – a newborn puppy dog. We must, must take him home – you agree?' Philomène shivered with cold and excitement in the creeping gloom. She scooped up the prone little bundle into the skirt of her damp dress and strode resolutely back to the villa. Madame stole a sceptical glance at the creature, newborn certainly, with small ears plastered to the head and the eyes shut tight. He would die in the night, no doubt. Philomène paused frequently to peek at him and pet the little treasure snuggled in her skirt. 'I want to kiss his little eyes, Grandmamma, to feed him, love him. And tonight I will sleep with him in my own arms.'

'No, Philomène. He is covered with fleas and his fur is fetid. But you may sponge him down.'

They reached the villa. The moon was rising and the screen of eucalyptus was hushed. Philomène lay her puppy on a rough wool mat on the kitchen floor. It breathed on imperturbably. Madame found a deep cardboard box and padded it with the straw from her last consignment of 'Domaine de L'Ile'. She showed Philomène how to squirt driblets of milk down the creature's throat with a syringe; he was too weak to suck. 'What shall we call him, Grandmamma?'

'Louis,' replied the old woman decisively.

Philomène climbed into her grandmother's spacious bed in the adjoining room and slept immediately. But Madame's mind was still hooked on Louis. 'Louis-Loup,' she murmured with a wry smile in the darkness; for he was a wolf cub. And he would not die in the night. How had he landed on their island? Had he been swept down from the Maures Massif in the storm, secreted on to the Toulon boat and tossed on to their little shore? 'Go with the flow,' she gurgled as she too fell asleep.

*   *   *

10

Minor: 'Are you awake, Middle? There is this furry wet smell – does it come from you? Are your plugs clean?'

Middle: 'Did you hear Philomène? She came to Madame Veuve after the storm and took her for a walk; a long walk. It was nearly dark when they returned and the smell came back with them.'

Major: 'It woke me up. I liked the smell. It suggested to me a rich *bouillabaisse* made from fish heads. I imagined Madame and Philomène warming themselves over steaming mugs at the kitchen table.'

Minor: 'Your rose-tinted spectacles paint improbable pictures, Major. But Middle and I are burdened with a more pedestrian approach to life.'

Middle: 'Quite so. And as you both take pleasure in reminding me, I am squeezed between you my bonhomous Major and my reticent Minor; 'blowing' at the hot air of your arguments with cold douches of my realism.'

Major: 'Middle, your gravitas astounds us. Now what was the dirtiest bath-time you can ever remember?'

Minor: 'It must have been that autumn evening the Comtesse returned from fishing. She flung her moleskin breeches and her sopping socks on to the white bedspread; her undergarments stank.'

Major and Middle: 'Of what?'

Minor: 'Of half fish and half mammal. The Comtesse had happened on a dying seal by the riverbank. She clubbed the poor wretch with her priest and dragged it off to die under a myrtle bush.'

Middle: 'Seals are ambidextrous are they not?'

Major: 'You are in a muddle, Middle. Seals are amphibious.'

Minor: 'Do we now deduce that we have a dead seal in our kitchen sink below?'

Major: 'Or might it be a baby wild boar? They roamed our forests and gave the island its name.'

Minor: '"Porquerolles" – or as some would prefer, we are named from the Celtic "Port Quaides" – the "port of rocks".'

Middle: 'Could we have a rabbit in the sink, waiting to be skinned for lunch?'

Major: 'This speculation on the contents of the sink makes me tired. Let us sleep and dream of things less fanciful – like *raie* or *rouget*.'

2

Philomène sat in the wicker chair spooning up goat's yoghurt with a *biscotte* and globs of myrtle jam. She looked tenderly at the box at her feet; her puppy dog lay replete on his back, his furry legs in the air. She had fed him another syringe of milk and replaced his bedding with fresh straw. She wished he would open his eyes and see the love she had for him. Madame Veuve joined her in the morning sun. A brilliance shone through the trees and garden flowers, rinsed and brightened from the night's heavy storm.

'May I take Louis home, dear Grandmamma? I will nurse him and be sure he is no trouble.'

'Wait a little, my dearest. When his eyes open he will be ready to play with you.'

'When will that be, Grandmamma? This evening? Tomorrow?'

'In ten days. I know his kind. When I was a child, living on the borders of the Maures Massif, we would see these puppies, huddled in the thick vegetation and feeding from their mothers. As they grew they would scavenge in the forests for birds and insects and catch fish in the gorges. We must be patient, Philomène. Soon little Louis will be sucking on your finger. You must go home now to your dear mother. And Philomène . . . listen to me. Do not talk of Louis. He is our secret; just ours.'

The next few days passed for Madame in a limbo state of enchantment. She had a companion. Something to love. Looping raffia round the cub's box, she carried him from room to room, cooing to him and muttering as she swept the Comtesse's parquet floors and wax-polished her commodes and armoires. Sitting on the balcony where she aired the bed linen and calico coverlets, she would rock him in her arms, crooning ceaselessly. He sucked on her fingers and she felt the sharp teeth pricking through his soft pink gum. She searched his tight-fastened eyes as he fed from his bottles. Soon the slits would appear on the sockets and slowly part. Philomène should see that moment. And all too soon their Louis-Loup would leap through these halcyon days of innocence and dependence, like a circus dog through a hoop of fire, and escape them. Madame shuddered, her head caught in her hands. But she would yet enjoy the moment and not fear the unknown.

'Grandmamma, is everything all right? How is Louis?'

'He is quite well, dear Philomène. I wait still for his eyes to open. Do you see how the slits here are parting, like the petals of a folded rose bud. Take him in your arms . . . And now it is happening!'

The girl held fast his little form and stroked his thickening fur. At the sound of her low murmuring Louis half opened his eyes to reveal the pale blue orbs of a wolf cub.

'Bring water in the fish kettle, Philomène, and sponge down Louis; here in the sun. It will help him to empty his bowels.'

Philomène knelt to her task and then rested Louis on the grass beside her. He rolled on to his back and performed. 'Clever boy,'

14

she said indulgently and gently prodded the emptied belly between the wide apart legs. 'Come, see, Grandmamma.'

'It's like they all do,' said Madame knowingly, 'showing off their manhood – males!' She looked down at his pale little belly, vulnerable and exposed. 'Give me the sponge.' With a perfunctory tweak, she passed it over the cub's genitals. Louis drew back his muzzle in an imperceptible grin. 'Soon Louis will defecate standing,' announced Madame. 'We will train him to fertilise the Comtesse's rose bed.'

Philomène picked up her little hero and balanced him on his tottering legs. Briefly he staggered and rolled over. 'Look! Look! Grandmamma.' From his prone position Louis-Loup was sniffing the grass voraciously, poking with his nose and mouth at the juicy greenness.

'He will soon be ready for walks on the leash,' promised Madame Veuve, 'and now let us rest him in his box.'

'When will the Comtesse come, Grandmamma?'

'In the fullness of summer. We must soon get her rooms ready.'

Philomène looked tentatively at the austere old lady and asked in a low voice, 'And Uqqy?'

'And who, child?'

'You know, Grandmamma – that man, Monsieur Uqba, the friend of the Comtesse; the tall dark one with the curly hairs on his chest.'

'Oh,' said Madame Veuve, in a tone of instant disdain, 'that one'.

Minor: 'You saw it on the grass this morning. A real live wolf cub? I view the impact of this savage quadruped on our lives with great foreboding.'

Middle: 'I hope Philomène does not put him in my bath.'

15

Major: 'She would get in an unholy mess with his leaping and floundering that she would have to join him. If you can't beat them, join them, Middle. Minor and I would envy you witnessing such an improbable scene.'

Middle: 'It is time our Madame Veuve cleaned my cupboards and my wall tiles. She has been drooling over this feral foundling for a month now.'

Minor: 'Be thankful for these peaceful days. Already I am bracing my bones for the Comtesse and her nocturnal romps.'

Major: 'I can hear the concealed arousal in your voice, Minor. You and Middle will be pitched on to the master stage of the Comtesse's delights, while I and my books and cushions will be mere gooseberries.'

Middle: 'We will tell all, dear Major. No holds barred. And Minor and I will continue to look pleasant, even if we do not feel it.'

Madame Veuve sat with her customary evening glass of red wine, collecting her thoughts. The rooks and doves were hushed; the green curtain of the eucalyptus hung motionless. Only Louis-Loup stirred the air with his sharp mock attacks on birds and insects. Pawing at the grass, nibbling and licking, he poked his snout at everything by his side. Stabbing his muzzle at sticks and stones and scratching excessively with his claws and milk teeth. A raven flew down to the grass. Louis toddled up from behind, pouncing playfully, nearer and nearer, within a foot of the bird, snapping eagerly. The bird flew off to a far corner and waited to be stalked again. Madame Veuve took a sanguine view of Louis' swift progress, his place in the Comtesse's villa and her own limitations. She pondered on her capacity to feed him. In a few more weeks he would stand nineteen inches at shoulder height with a long, lean body and a ferocious need of raw meat. And she was startled to see that his eyes had turned from blue to tawny yellow, with a black pupil. She could see no love or recognition in those eyes. 'Any direct eye contact with a wolf is a threat,' she had been warned as a child. She pulled an old wine label from her pocket and jotted down a shopping list: one cane whisk, wax polish, washing soda, and to the *boucherie* to discuss horse meat and rabbit. And she would buy a dog leash. The butcher, whose modest establishment was named '*L'Agneau aux deux têtes*', looked on Madame Veuve as a feast or famine client. When the Comtesse took up residence, the villa order was as substantial as it was succulent, but for Madame Veuve alone, the occasional chicken sufficed.

Early next morning she shut the kitchen door behind her, leaving Louis to wander freely through her rooms. His old box was left in a prominent position for clawing and chewing. She set off blithely down the path and along Rue de la Ferme to the village. She found the butcher alone and tending his sawdust floor. She rested her determined chin on the pine counter as he bent his head conspiratorially towards her.

'I have to feed an animal,' murmured Madame Veuve. 'You have rabbit or minced horsemeat today, Monsieur?'

'Certainly, Madame. And I can squeeze some blood out of a duck for you.'

'Yes, Monsieur, but I have little money. I have my earrings. They have value.'

The butcher ushered her into his back room. One of his more regular and respected customers had walked in. Madame Veuve waited for his return, mute and diminutive in a big oak chair. 'Madame,' he came to her expansively, 'would you prefer that I purchase your animal for a good price?'

17

'You are kind, Monsieur, but I love him. There is a rifle in the villa. I could shoot rabbits for him, perhaps, and starlings.'

'What is the species of your animal, Madame?'

'A dog, Monsieur, half mongrel, half pedigree – with a large appetite.' The kindly butcher made up a handsome package of tired rabbits and shredded horsemeat and footed half the modest bill.

Having completed her purchases, Madame Veuve walked purposefully back to the villa. The sun blazed down and burned the backs of her thin legs. She walked fast, keeping to the shade and mindful of her meat. As she neared the garden there was a high-pitched squeal, a child's; it was Philomène. The girl had hurled herself out of the kitchen door, with Louis leaping round her in a mock savage dance, his teeth bared and snapping.

'Philomène! Kneel on the grass, dearest, roll on to your back!' The wolf caught the time-honoured signs of submission; in defence the body is low; and Madame walked slowly towards him. Louis turned to her with his grinning 'play-face' and ambled to the rose bed with lowered tail and ears flattened.

'Grandmamma, he tried to bite my nipple,' sobbed Philomène, exposing her grazed little pink protrusion.

'It is not so bad. We will dab it with Armagnac.'

Philomène, snuggling in her Grandmamma's arms, recounted how she had sauntered through the kitchen garden door, when Louis sprang up to defend his fief. He had chased her into the garden and set up his playful dominance. 'And, Grandmamma, I thought he knew me and loved me.'

'Yes, dear, but he is a wolf and we cannot always understand him. We must never possess him or make him our own. He does not want to hurt you.'

Philomène spied the new leash and jumped up excitedly. 'Can I walk Louis?'

'This evening, child, we will go together, all three.'

'And then shall we talk of the Comtesse and Monsieur Uqba?'

Madame Veuve stewed Louis' rabbit in the afternoon. She added red wine to the water, in equal proportions. The wine would calm him. She would even eat some herself.

3

Christine, the Comtesse de Beaucaire, stepped into the Paris June morning. She had felt boxed in by her apartment in Rue Castiglione. And the concierge, a predatory black heap, had stared at her like a caged owl. In the sun and air the Comtesse's spirits rose. She marvelled at the streets, now reinstated and absorbed with the demands of daily life. Was it a mere month ago? *'La Petite Revolution'*? When the raw strength of student power had kicked against the patriarchal suppressions of Charles de Gaulle. Paris had rocked in chaos as blood boiled against blood. And the Comtesse, in sympathy with this flagrant aggression, had even jogged with student groups at night, singing slogans against the bourgeoisie. To protest was a right, was it not? And the parlous state of no post, no telephone, no petrol had been redressed by an edict that unpaid bills would exact no penalty.

One night the Comtesse had caught sight of her estranged husband, lauding it over a long table at Lipp's Brasserie on Boulevard St Michel. Politics and patriotism had ever fuelled their brief marriage, their ancestral blood firing them with hot-headed valour; and the Comtesse, a descendant of a Maréchal of France . . .

On another adventurous night, she had found herself packed into a bistro with a vociferous gang of radicals; she heard how bodies had been flung in the Seine. Some one hundred students had been thus expediently disposed of by the Special Riot Squad.

But on this sweet and dulcet morning, Paris smiled again and smoothed her lap over each *quartier*. Where she had been wrung and shaken like a rag doll, she now basked in her capacity to enchant afresh. The Comtesse turned in to Rue Cambon. She paused against a stone façade and sniffed the lilies, roses, lavender and thyme from the nearby cart. Familiar wafts of *vanille*, *chocolat* and *choux* pastry stirred from the pâtisserie. From the Auberge du Fruit Défendu rose waves of a simmering *demi-glâce*. Closing her eyes she again recalled the hail of cobblestones on the raised shields of the riot police, the seething exultance of youth gone mad. Flames, the stench of smouldering bitumen, the hiss and splatter of fire hoses, and the explosion of tear gas grenades that had flared the city into a vile playground. Refuse had billowed in street corners and walls were lashed with graffiti.

As she continued on her way, the Comtesse was aware of several men, passing her singly, appraising her with a start of admiration; a fleeting desire, shared and understood. The impact of her green-grey eyes and high-arched brows and that cascade of pale gold hair could be confounding. The Comtesse firmed up her stomach and swung past on swaying hips. Paris! Her true home, where a woman was urged to be a woman and applauded. She found the lingerie shop – Voilettes. Silks and frills and voiles in pastel colours and hot, rich reds, purples and blacks. Cushions, coverlets, tea-gowns and nightgowns. Brassières dripping with silk tassels and bows, bolstered and padded or diaphanous; and the long French knicker burdened with lace, or slips of silk panty to expose each cheek. The Comtesse declined any assistance and took stock from a lilac tub chair. She was searching with Uqba's pleasure in mind; for his visit to Porquerolles. 'I do not like frippery,' he had warned. 'Colours confuse me. Too much choice is a bother.' She could hear him breathing through his teeth; his strong white teeth bared in his wide smile.

'I will buy white today,' she finally informed the *vendeuse*.

The old lady hooked open a high cupboard. 'Cotton!' she announced disparagingly. 'It is all I have in white.'

White cotton, white linen, lawn, lace and muslin. What would be Uqba's choice? She chose swiftly, three white lawn night dresses and a brassière with a whale bone. She must not be late for Antoine. Her hand on the door, she turned: 'Do you have things for men, Madame?'

'Of course, Madame.' The lady spilled a heap of long underpants across her desk. The Comtesse quickly selected a large black pair. 'For your husband, Madame?'

'No, for somebody else's,' replied the Comtesse sharply. The crone cackled with glee and swept up the pants into a smart black box, tied with lilac ribbon.

'My darling Christine, how you defy the years. But you are superb. Stand away that I may devour you in your white and black crêpe with those roses running amok.' It was twenty years since they had first met and he a schoolboy. 'And your skin always so white and clear that we can see black olives course down your throat.' Antoine, so poetic and fanciful. Through the years they had kept close with little words, little rendezvous, advice and innuendoes. Antoine, tall, angular and pale, propelled her to a cavernous cream leather chair and sat on a pouff at her feet. He quickly dispelled her fervour over the recent 'revolution'. 'Revolution? What revolution? The whole world is awash with revolution. Our radios and screens suck up this universal madness. Forget it, my darling Christine. But now I remember your infatuation with your rebellious forbear – Princess Christine Belgiojoso . . .

'I have Sancerre chilled and sparkling water. We will lunch later alfresco.' He moved through the small rooms sinuously and put a glass bowl of black olives before her – 'to enjoy your transparent throat the better.' Christine rolled the flinty, cool wine round her palate. How good it was. Antoine, replanted on his pouff, looked into her eyes. 'I am in love, cherie. So unexpected, crazy, divine, incalculable; from the Bibliothéque; we spend night and day together. I am absurdly contaminated.'

Christine rolled her eyes above the frosted rim of her glass. Antoine looked good. Life was good. What was his name?

'Hubert – he is called Hubert.'

'Is he handsome?'

'Not particularly. Going bald – rather short. He has bad skin and wears glasses. And he likes socks.'

'But why socks?'

'He wears them in bed because he picks his toenails in his sleep.'

'It is not so bad,' murmured Christine consolingly.

'And he finds my pedicure treatment erotic,' confided Antoine.

Over lunch between the stern stone façades of Boulevard Malesherbe, Christine felt secure and confidential. Their corner table was hedged in greenery. Having divulged himself of his aventures, Antoine pressed Christine for her own revelations. 'You are so alluring, Christine, what's going on?' Christine savoured a mouthful of her *rognons aux trois moutardes* – how much to tell? She sighed voluptuously and gulped on her wine.

'It began in Tangier.'

'And it had ended there?' asked Antoine.

'Certainly not!' And Christine embarked on a circumspect summary of her entanglement with Uqba. She described him: tall and swarthy in his loose white robes; with black curling hair tumbling to his shoulder blades. 'His hair is everywhere.' Christine sounded momentarily perplexed.

Antoine, relishing his *tarte de fruits rouges*, mumbled, 'Hair is wonderful. But Christine, my dear one, do not be deceived by a wily Moroccan; at sundown it is a whisky and a little boy that will take his fancy.' They lingered over their espresso. They would meet again . . . Lives moved on in search of life, but friends held on forever.

The Comtesse turned into Place de la Madeleine. The dominant columns of the church beckoned her, Napoleon's '*Temple de la Gloire*'. She stood by the open bronze door, sensing the cool from the lofty domed interior. She entered and passed by the confessionals adorned with engravings of the Crucifixion and the *Mater Misericordia*. Placing her parcel of lingerie at the foot of a side altar, she knelt at the *prie-dieu* alongside. A new page, a new beginning; Uqqy's visit to Porquerolles drew closer. She needed to love again, to open herself wide; her mind and her very legs. She needed to get a life. What was her life about? A heaviness swelled in her abdomen, a yearning and a deep desire. She stood up stiffly and gazed on the group of sculpted angels, ascending from the high altar. She looked to them for a sign, for guidance. 'Love is more important than happiness.' Unknown words seemingly from nowhere. They nudged at her conscience. She stood entranced. As she walked airily down the central nave, a smiling priest handed her the forgotten package of lingerie.

*   *   *

Philomène's brush with Louis-Loup's snapping milk teeth was soon forgotten. The son of the village ironmonger had created a steel-meshed pen at the end of the garden; this, together with walks on the leash, had considerably widened Louis' fief. Madame Veuve had again been ushered by the butcher into his little back room. 'You must never ever leave your animal hungry, Madame – never, never, Madame.' And he had further warned her that Louis must not be left alone. Like all men he would get into mischief. The villagers now looked furtively at Louis on his leash and muttered that he should be muzzled. Madame Veuve, sitting by the kitchen door would see figures and faces through the trees, straining to watch Louis in his pen. He had become a local fascination. His audience watched slavishly as he shoved dirt over his gnawed marrow bones for later recovery; at his busy snout sniffing and snorting; his vigorous scraping of forelegs and hind legs as he scattered his faeces. This inordinate interest in faeces upset Madame Veuve. With his first wrench at the collar, she would let him go, as he dived into some alien mess, rolling ecstatically to cover his neck, his cheeks and his shoulders. One evening she and Philomène had taken Louis to the stream. He had snapped up two fish, and in an orgy of squeals and yelps, had devoured them on the bank, leaving their heads and tails to the last. A family party across the water had been amazed at such unexpected entertainment.

Pottering round the garden with Madame, Louis would nibble on flowers and insects. He would slam and butt playfully against her legs, shoving her aside with mock bites. Sitting on the grass, she would call him and he would come trotting to her, erect with pricked ears. His long, elegant forelegs, the narrow chest and agile body, with a black streak along his tawny back, would halt beside her as he lifted a paw in greeting. Tactile and sociable like his

25

kind, Louis would nuzzle her neck, her ears, her shoulder; snuffling and grunting, he would nudge the corners of her mouth for any stray regurgitations; the cue for Madame to get his dinner.

But she could not hug him; he was never to be a pet; there was no love in those yellow eyes. It had to be enough that he sensed that she loved *him*.

It had been a frenzied week of polishing the parquet floors, wiping down the walls, shaking out the drapes and blinds and then beating the rugs and sofas, to raise even more dust. Philomène had nimbly unhinged the white bedroom voiles, washed them and hung them to dry on the balcony. Her slender hands had become quite blackened with cleaning the brass fire furniture and the silver remnants from the Comtesse's forbear, Princess Belgiojoso. Sitting at the Comtesse's dressing-table, diligently cleaning the heavy gadrooned frame of the big oval mirror, Philomène wondered if the Comtesse was happy. And it surprised her that a lady so distinguished and rich did not have a new piece of glass put in to see herself better. The glass of the old hand mirror was similarly fuzzed. And the bristles in the brushes appeared dry and toasted. She beat the wild cat with her cleaning cloth. A cloud of dust rose but the beast held fast to the headboard. It had been fun cleaning up the bathroom. The Comtesse's pots and bottles had pretty silver lids, but when she and Grandmamma had unscrewed them it was disgusting to see. Stale crusts had clotted the creams, and all the lotions gone thick and brown and sour. They had boiled up extra water and placed everything in the bath, prodding it all with bottle brushes and hand mops. The plug hole had finally gurgled in loud despair at such greasy water. And Philomène had felt tired and Grandmamma propped her up with cushions on the Comtesse's sitting-room sofa. Philomène had picked a novel from the bookcase. It was by

Emile Zola. She hurriedly leafed through the pages for sensual passages: 'His desire, already aroused by the smell of her, was inflamed still further by the way she arched her back to extricate herself from his grasp.'

Madame had bustled in. 'Now, Philomène you must put down that Monsieur Zola. He was a sexual maniac. Go home and wash and put on a simple dress. Tell Mama we are going to the evening service – to commemorate the Stations of the Cross. They were carved one hundred years ago by a young African soldier, with his penknife.'

4

Philomène set off skipping down the lane. What dress could she wear? She had only the one for parties and important occasions; she was seldom invited to either. Her mother had laid it out ready on her bed; of cream seersucker, it had a loosely pleated skirt with a wide blue sash. Philomène loved the sash; the satin slid over her skin as she held it against her cheek. She washed quickly and combed her long, dark hair. Twisting it into thick coils, she threaded through a circlet of her mother's river seed pearls. As she slipped out of their fisherman's cottage, she was conscious of her unusually fine appearance and walked primly to the village square. Sitting beneath a eucalyptus tree, Philomène waited for her Grandmamma. Place D'Armes, once the province of Napoleonic parades and military drums, was the main hub of their village. The wide, sandy space was now flanked and shaded by fine old eucalyptus. A peaceful scene; for the old a place to rest and remember; to warm themselves in the sun or stay cool in the shade; to lay down shopping baskets and exchange village news; to talk of hens and pheasants, farms, artichokes, asparagus, the vines and *La Vendange*.

Four men played a desultory game of pétanque in the far

corner, their hats pushed back on their heads. The iron-clad balls gleamed in the sun as they thudded and rolled heavily on the sand. Philomène gazed on the modest *église Sainte Anne* at the head of the square. The pale yellow Romanesque façade and red-tiled roof supported a simple clock tower. The pediment of the handsome stone doorway had been framed in palm fronds. Philomène could hear singing from inside and then out darted Monsieur le Curé and stood on the church steps. He had chosen to wear a startling purple chasuble with a yellow border. And now Philomène saw people come from across the square in a body. She stood and saw Grandmamma half hidden in a flowered black veil falling to her shoulders. Together they entered the dimmed wood interior.

Madame Veuve led Philomène down the narrow right aisle, where they sat before the side altar. Philomène studied the white marble as she knelt. It was inlaid with a frieze of painted gold olive sprays and sprigs of oak. And she looked intently at the statue of The Virgin alongside. A brilliant blue sash was moulded to hang from her cleavage. It was more beautiful than Philomène's. The two azure tails swung down The Virgin's white skirt and were bordered in shining gold spots. Some nuns filed in to the old chestnut choir stalls. How could they endure their black wool habits falling to their feet on these hot summer days? Their serene faces gave no hint of bodily discomfort. Philomène sighed luxuriously. Madame Veuve rose from her prayers and frowned a little. A baby cried; had the nuns and the priest in purple frightened it? An old dog ambled up the aisle, sniffing and snuffling towards its seated master. Philomène smelt flowers; turning her head she saw tied bunches of lavender and white roses, bound in muslin. A waft of incense swept through the church and then strains from a violin. Two choir boys preceded Monsieur le Curé up the aisle.

One held high the Cross and the other swung the silver incense casket with evident gusto. Philomène sneezed. The odour was strong and spicy like eucalyptus or Grandmamma's camphorated wool underwear or furniture polish. She heard a familiar giggle from a row behind. It was Gervaise. Philomène turned and grinned at her friend; her best friend. Gervaise was wearing a bright pink dress with a wide scooped neckline.

The church was hushed as a young man and a young woman sat before the choir stalls playing their violin and guitar. It was a piece by Paganini, whispered Grandmamma and then there stood a tall, dark young man who sang a romantic Serenade. Philomène watched the yellow red and blue prisms of light from the stained windows make patterns on his white shirt. Monsieur le Curé next mounted the pulpit and set the baby crying again with his loud voice and his flapping purple arms. Grandmamma nudged Philomène in the ribs and pointed to the wood tableau beside them. Philomène studied the carving of Jesus with his eyes closed, slumped in near death, with his loving mother and Mary Magdalen, their arms around him. 'Carved by that young soldier one hundred years ago,' reminded Grandmamma hoarsely. 'And all done with his penknife.'

'We are here to commemorate Joseph.' Monsieur le Curé had launched into his address. 'Not Joseph, the father of Jesus, you understand but the young North African soldier, Joseph Wargnier. We have to bless him for this solo *tour de force* that he embarked upon, one hundred years ago in July 1868. Within thirteen months, Wargnier sculpted from massive blocks of sweet chestnut, and with his own knife, the fourteen tableaux of the Stations of the Cross we see on our walls today.'

There was a brief pause as Monsieur le Curé looked down with pride and satisfaction on his full congregation. It would make an important looking parade around the square. He wondered anxiously if there would be enough Domaine de L'Ile to go round. He gave his final blessing and motioned to the choir boys to pull on the church bells with all their might. The peals rang out to every shore of the island, as the church-goers stepped into the dusk. Each mother and daughter was handed a lavender-scented candle. Fourteen men, chosen for their military proven-ance and stature, led the parade with torches round Place d'Armes. Madame Veuve and Philomène shielded their candles in the light breeze as they followed. Wine and lavender hung on the air. The *boulanger* had baked piles of lavender cake and biscuits. The hotels and cafés edging La Place had laid tables inviting the procession to rest and drink. The first of the season's succulent black olives glistened in little bowls. Philomène had just got her tongue round a slab of goat's cheese on a lavender biscuit when a finger poked at her pearls. She whipped round – 'Gervaise!'

'Are they not amazing?'

'Yes,' agreed Philomène and sniffed her flickering candle.

'I don't mean the pretty candles, I mean the men with the torches. Oh so handsome and strong!'

Madame Veuve looked across warily at Gervaise; what an inappropriate dress to wear to church, nearly tumbling off her; perhaps it was her mother's. 'We must go home now,' she hissed in Philomène's ear and limped stolidly ahead.

'Have you seen Uqba?' Gervaise grinned at her friend.

Philomène put a finger to her lips. 'He will come soon. The Comtesse comes even sooner. We have been cleaning her rooms.' She chased after her Grandmamma. Gervaise was fun and pretty but Philomène sensed she could be wild, more wild than Philomène had ever dared to be. She caught up Grandmamma along the

Rue de la Ferme, a quiet road with colonial villas, shielded by acacia trees, fig, tamarisk and rustling bamboo grass.

'Why did the soldier carve those sad pictures of Jesus?'

'Perhaps he was bored? Or unhappy?'

'Perhaps he was in love?' persisted Philomène.

'Yes, of course, why not?'

'Why was he on Porquerolles, Grandmamma?'

'He was sent to our island to rest his battle wounds. After a year's carving he was recovered and rejoined his African battalion.'

'Then what happened to him?'

'Heavens, Philomène! He soon deserted from the army and became a sculptor at a church near Versailles. And then we can expect he found a pretty wife and had lots of crawling babies.' Madame and Philomène turned off the road towards the villa and the sea.

'And was he dark, Grandmamma, that soldier?'

'Not entirely; a little perhaps.'

'As dark as Uqba?' But Madame Veuve clapped her hand on her heart and fell silent. She shuddered at the mournful howls and piercing yelps coming from the villa. They half ran down the lane.

'Has Louis been hurt, Grandmamma?'

'No, Philomène, but we must be careful, you know. Louis is showing desertion anger. We have been away too long. He may have done some damage.' Louis' growls and barks turned to whimpers as they approached. Madame Veuve murmured to him softly as she unlocked the kitchen door. She motioned to Philomène to stand well back as he sprang out and raced round the garden. He rolled deliriously on the grass before them with yelps of relief. They walked to the house and he followed them in. As Madame turned to close the door, Louis lifted his paw. He was fawning.

Was he guilty? Had his curiosity put the mischief in him? She gave him water and herself a glass of wine. Philomène made herself a hot chocolate drink. They had both grown to love and trust Louis through his first formative weeks. But did he love *them*? Those yellow eyes were inscrutable. Or were they? Madame now understood his body language better. She was also aware of an intuitive intelligence; his grasp of her mood and the next event. Was his acute awareness of Philomène and herself his nearest approximation to love? She knew he could always smell them way up the lane, coming back from the village.

'Grandmamma! Grandmamma! Louis has been naughty in the Comtesse's bedroom!' Philomène rushed in to the kitchen clutching a stuffed wild boar's head. Louis crouched in the corner licking his paws.

'Put the head on the kitchen table, Philomène. We will see to it later.'

Leaning her hand on her granddaughter's shoulder, Madame Veuve limped up the stairs with a heavy heart. Louis followed meekly behind. 'Aargh,' she growled at him – had he done much damage? But it was her fault for not securing the first floor doors. It had been the first time that Louis had plunged into the Comtesse's rooms. Again he snorted his way round the walls, smacking his juicy snout at the dados. He had flung the cushions off the sofa and was now rolling on it. Had he chewed anything?

'Look, Grandmamma, Louis has taken a bite out of the bedroom carpet.' A deep scallop had been roughly severed from its border. It was one of the Comtesse's most valuable possessions, a '*Soumak*' from the Caucasus she had described it. On a red and turquoise field there raged a white monster; half dragon, half phoenix. Madame had never liked it. No wonder it had disturbed Louis so. Had he eaten the piece? Stumbling back through the bathroom, they saw it deposited in the lavatory. Madame Veuve secreted it carefully into her skirt pocket.

'Now please fetch up the boar's head, Philomène.' They placed it back on the steel pike running from the nape of the neck, when suddenly it swivelled and stared at them with its glass eyes upside down. Philomène flopped on to the Comtesse's newly pressed white muslin bed cover.

'Let us use my sash to bandage its head, Grandmamma. It will look pretty. Blue for a boy.' It was a good idea. Philomène's sash would be an effective tourniquet.

'Louis? Where is Louis?' Bored with the Comtesse's rooms, Louis was stretched out again on the kitchen floor. Madame Veuve opened wide the garden door. An owl screech seared the soft night air as Philomène and her exhausted Grandmamma slumped in their wicker chairs.

'The Comtesse comes the day after tomorrow,' announced Madame Veuve.

'And Uqba? He comes too Grandmamma?'

'A little later, for sure.'

Minor: 'We have been witnessing the growing pains of a wolf club and his handlers. He has caused my room unprecedented damage; first in an attempt to eat a boar's head and then in taking a carnivorous chunk from the Comtesse's best carpet.'

Middle. 'I was pleased to see him finally. He looked fun; a fine figure of a young wolf. He smacked his snout at my water-closet and later came back to drop the morsel of carpet in the pan.'

Major: 'Madame Veuve will tighten up any outstanding matters before the Comtesse arrives. Philomène, who is a born romantic, has even sacrificed her blue sash for the boar's neck. And I fear she nurses a secret infatuation for this dago. For a girl of her age she should know less.'

Minor: '"Dago," Major?'

Major: 'In my book, Minor, the tar brush begins in Andalusia.'

Middle: 'I will be pleased to see Uqba again. He is soft spoken and considerate. He likes his baths tepid and so my eyes do not smart and weep.'

Minor: 'Manners maketh marriage.'

Major: 'Come, Minor, we do not anticipate a marriage. For years the Comtesse has kept herself steadily in the fast love lane. Women are made principally for men – not just for husbands.'

Minor: 'We might say that she has reshuffled her lovers, and her husband, with the same consummate ease as the cushions are plumped up and rearranged on your sofa.'

Middle: 'You are both so clever with your wisecracks and witticisms. But the Comtesse is the ultimate survivor. She has enough brains and beauty to sink a battleship.'

Major: 'Or a buttercup?'

5

Scanning the pine forest by the seashore, the Comtesse glimpsed the ochre walls and the faded eau-de-Nil shutters. Her villa beckoned and nodded from across the water. Behind her lay Toulon with its disused shipyards and the blurred peaks of the Massif des Maures rising up beyond. Ahead lay the port of Porquerolles, with its dominant old fort drawing closer. The Comtesse, standing at the helm of the sturdy *Valerian II*, strained to see who might be on the quay to meet her. The furry green arms of the island seemed set to clasp her. She loved her island, the retreat of her alter ego, the provenance of her dreams and illusions, of her love and happiness; her island of peace and paradise, the ultimate . . .

'Madame! Madame La Comtesse!' Gustave, one of the young *vignerons*, stood smiling before her. He motioned to the dogcart and nimble little Rosette pawing at the pier. Her luggage was already stowed and a bunch of her favourite Cardinal Richelieu red roses lay waiting on the seat. 'For you, Madame La Comtesse. From Madame Veuve.'

The Comtesse savoured the little journey through the sleepy lanes and the fragrances of early summer: the tamarisk and broom and lavender. The clamour of cicadas always astonished her. Gustave explained; 'They contract the abdomen four hundred times a second to make their noise.' A cock pheasant with gold and black feathers ran out purposefully before the speedy Rosette, and a hare in the hedge darted back in again. With his crop, Gustave pointed to a cloud of yellow butterflies in the shade of the pine trees. He reined Rosette in to the lane for the villa. The Comtesse gasped. Madame Veuve, diminutive and hunched, was being led towards them by a young wolf. Louis-Loup moved deftly on his elegant legs; his long, agile body shone amber in the evening sun; a black streak ran across his back and down his fore legs. His pricked ears and raised tail denoted an acute awareness of this new arrival. Rosette drew up beside them. Louis shook his head, jerking his body to one side, revealing the whites of his eyes.

'Take care, Louis! Calm yourself!' warned Madame Veuve as she stroked and patted his head. Louis sat and, as the Comtesse gamely stepped down from the cart, he stood and raised his paw. 'What fine manners! What is your name?' The Comtesse patted his neck and shoulder and unfastened his leash. The little party walked the few yards to the villa.

Philomène flounced out of the back door in her cream seersucker and bowed her neat dark head to the Comtesse. 'Put Louis in his pen, Philomène. Would you like tea in your sitting-room, Madame La Comtesse?'

'I will rest here, Madame Veuve, in the breeze. But the garden looks dry and my Richelieu roses half dead; their foliage is withered.'

'We have had no rain for two months, Madame. We had the one heavy storm, which swept up Louis-Loup on to the beach.'

Philomène came out with a tea tray. All the wrong cups and saucers, noted the Comtesse, and that dreadful black tea no doubt.

'Madame La Comtesse. Will you try my lavender tea?'

'*Enchantée*, Philomène. It has been the drink of queens and an old cure for sore heads.'

'Would you like a spoon of eucalyptus honey for a sweeter taste?'

'And what is that you have there, my girl?'

'It is lavender jelly, Madame La Comtesse, to spread on the *pain d'épice*. This bread was served at Court dinners in France in the Middle Ages.' The Comtesse observed Philomène closely. How she had matured in the year; a young woman already. Her hair neatly coiled, off-setting her long slim neck, her breasts full and buoyant, the nipples thrusting at her bodice. What was she saying?

'And your friend – Monsieur Uqba – will he be staying this time, Madame La Comtesse?'

Madame Veuve rapped on the garden table. 'That's enough, Philomène. Please go to Louis and give him his walk.'

The Comtesse lolled back in the wicker chair with closed eyes. Most aggravations in her life were seeded in her own mind. She needed peace and a blank agenda . . . and Uqba. Would he adapt?

'Let us see my rooms, Madame Veuve,' said the Comtesse. Much revived she led the way up the stairs. '*Bien, bien, bien . . .*' She walked through to the bedroom balcony and breathed the tang of salt, of pine and the crushed rosemary and myrtle of the *maquis*. And they would sit here together . . . in the deep silence of the night . . . shared only with the chant of nightingales . . . 'And my big, bad boar, Madame Veuve! Why did you tie him round with a blue ribbon?'

The old lady briefly explained the whole incident. Having made an exemplary repair on the Comtesse's valuable *Soumak*, she did not mention that little area of damage.

'Come, Madame Veuve, let us talk a little.' The Comtesse led Madame to the sofa in the sitting-room.

'You love your Louis-Loup, Madame. And I also have a great penchant for the furry animals. We have a need for animals to give us feelings of tenderness. But take good care, Madame – we must not upset the bourgeoisie.' Madame Veuve nodded sagely, with the villagers in mind. Had the Comtesse plans for a visit from her gentleman friend, Monsieur Uqba, this time?

'But of course', she replied. 'Monsieur Uqba will sleep on the landing. He brings his camp bed. He sleeps by my bedroom to guard me, in the way that his Riffian from the mountains sleeps close to guard him.'

'The Riffian gentleman comes also, Madame?' Madame Veuve remembered him as a profoundly stupid character and a big eater.

'One can never be certain who Monsieur Uqba may include in his entourage . . . his wives have not been invited.'

'Will that be all, Madame?'

'A bottle of Domaine de L'Ile blanc. Thank you, Madame Veuve. That is all.'

Madame Veuve scuttled from the room. It was a long time since she had ingested so much information.

Refreshed from the white wine, the cool night air and the silence, interrupted only by the monotonous call of a huppé bird, the Comtesse woke with the familiar tinkling of her breakfast tray. Madame left it on the butler's table outside her door. She dressed quickly in a light green cheesecloth shift. It was her intent on this first day to get to know Louis-Loup. She wanted to love him. Madame Veuve piloted the Comtesse round the garden and explained the near demise of the Cardinal Richelieu red roses. Louis, accompanying them, sniffed appreciatively at the vestiges of his urine. Madame next informed the Comtesse that Louis-Loup would be full grown at ten months. His new admirer bent to rub his baby ruff and stroked his silky neck. Louis slammed against her legs, butting them with his snout, circling round her, grinning and snapping at the air. 'He is smiling at me, Madame Veuve.'

'It is his "play-face".' And Louis, sensing an audience, stood before the Comtesse and again lifted his paw.

On hearing of Madame Veuve's forays for rabbit, horsemeat and goats' hearts, the Comtesse, shaded by a straw hat pierced with pheasants' tails, took a walk to the butcher with Louis leashed at her side. At *L'Agneau aux deux têtes*, they stood diffidently outside. It was empty save for two clients, and their amiable provider was soon able to usher them through to his back room. They exchanged pleasantries. 'It is kind of you, Monsieur, to concern yourself with my little one. He is handsome, don't you find?'

'But of course, Madame La Comtesse; in fact it is the first time I have seen him. What can I serve you today?'

'It is the régime, Monsieur, you understand. Our friend, the Moroccan, is observing Ramadan. All we need is lamb and chicken. *Quel ennui.*'

'I remember the gentleman. The tall one with the swarthy skin. He will need much meat, at each sundown.'

The butcher was clearly pleased at the prospect. As he shepherded the Comtesse and Louis past a hushed queue at his counter, it was clear that the village had gleaned a notion or two of life at the villa.

As they came out into the square, two young girls stepped in front of them.

'Madame La Comtesse!' Philomène greeted her jubilantly.

'My dear Philomène – who is your friend?'

'Gervaise, Madame.'

'Come soon and see me, the two of you. But for the moment I am walking the wolf and tomorrow we expect our guest Monsieur Uqba, from Tangier.'

'I would be honoured to meet the gentleman, Madame,' volunteered Gervaise.

The Comtesse observed her sharply: the white skin, the deep set azure eyes and the glinting waves of red hair. *'Elle a du chien,'* she warned herself.

That night the Comtesse sat long on her balcony. The tender black air induced thoughts and reverie. Uqba's face loomed into focus: his adoring dark eyes, that attentive incline of the head, his black curls clustering his neck. She shivered and squirmed at the memory of his strong, dark body, his long legs striding through the folds of his *jallaba*. But she shuddered at the memory of Tangier. She had been assured such magic from Uqba's acclaimed paradise. They had touched down at dusk in the October mist. Sky, sea and mountains blotted in a blur. Only the palm trees were visible, spiked to the fading light like menacing sabres. For days she had padded dutifully behind him like a slave girl, with a bangle above her elbow. The narrow streets curled up from the shore to the souks and the steep steps of the Kasbah.

She had picked her way through gutters of squelched fish heads and rotting fruit and slippery pavements. From the small inner courtyards, steam rose continually to the balconies. What were they cooking? she had asked. 'It is *potage garbure*' said Uqba, 'a vegetable, meat soup from all the mutton stock.' It had all added to the pervasive stench. To Uqba's misconceived approval, she bought herself a yashmak and tied it firmly over her nose.

41

She was amazed by the parade of fat women shamelessly swollen under their *jallabas*. Billowing along in swirls of magenta, mustard, flame and indigo, they splashed the dusty boulevards with colour. She remembered again the rickety cafés, the street vendors, the leather and carpet dealers and the shrivelled crone cross-legged beside her reels of silk thread and her hand-dyed shawls.

Was Paul Bowles alive? she had asked as they entered the gate to the Kasbah. 'The pioneer writer? He left New York for Tangier in 1947 and never returned. He has written many Moroccan stories.' Uqba later bought her his renowned first novel – *Sheltering Sky*. It lay beside her bed even now.

The Comtesse fetched herself a shawl and poured another glass of wine. And he had pointed out to her Barbara Hutton's palace, a blazing white terraced confection straddling the flaking ramparts of the Kasbah. 'Some streets she had made wider for her limousines to pass. It is party time when she comes. Many guests, pretty lights and music. She wears a tiara of emeralds, which blaze in the Moroccan moonlight and then in the dawn sun.'

Their afternoon in the Kasbah had been as in a dream. It was so clean and quiet as they went spiralling up and up the shallow stone steps. Uqba had led her from one dazzling courtyard to another, where marble pillars soared to blazing canopies of sky. He sat her down beside a marble fountain enclaved by a fretted screen.

'Your light eyes and skin are beautiful.' He traced her cheek and ear lobe with a finger knuckle and turned to look deep into her eyes. 'Sometimes I fall for a stupidity,' he said, equivocally.

When they returned to his small house in the Medina he told her: 'I import oil. My country is at peace and is family orientated.

But our neighbours are jealous. For why? They are richer. They have oil. But we import our oil. From Russia.' She admired his rooms with the thick, white, sugary walls and arches. Kilims hung from the cornices; their strident and geometric designs made her dizzy. The stone benches and ceramic floors were heaped with more carpets and rugs and padded saddle-bags. It was a welter of colour with blends of blue and red, emerald and saffron. Each shelf and window was adorned with a cache-pot, a water-pipe or a vase, and in one instance a sheathed dagger and a clutch of silver guns. Stretched out on a raft of rugs she sipped submissively on Uqba's approximation of an evening drink; a goat milk-shake with a dash of Pernod. A brass brazier glowed on the low tiled table, encircled with scented candles of vanilla and mock-orange and sandalwood. Uqba's worry beads were heaped to one side: solid balls and ovals of agate, amber, lapis and jade. 'Tribal relics,' he explained, 'like you, my little lark.'

He scooped up a handful of the richly coloured stones and sat beside her. She nestled up to him. 'Uqba, are you a spy?'

'Not yet, dearest lady. When I am approached, I say to them always the same thing. "In the event of hostilities towards our country, I will tell you all I know"!'

They had slept each night in a cavernous cedar chest, coffin-like and inlaid with camel bone and mother of pearl. A heap of goose-down pillows were piled around them, together with sheets of the softest cotton and delicate shawls gleaned from the throat of the ibex. She had curled up, exhausted, with visions of tasselled fez and fretted screen; pie-eyed with pattern and light and shade and the demands on her attention of brilliant mosaics and mosques and souks and mules. Only the mournful yearning of the muezzin troubled her sleep when she would wake to Uqba running his fingers through the skeins of her blonde hair. Her breasts tautened as he smoothed the palm of his hand down her body. He groaned as she guided him down further.

The Comtesse sighed and shook herself with irritation. Where could it all lead? The pine and the eucalyptus would only murmur monotonously to the moon. That first meeting – a year ago – in the Tuileries gardens, in a queue for *citron pressé*. On that brief encounter they had chosen to sit together at a rickety iron table with pierced white chairs. Uqba had looked different in Paris; shorter hair, a cream shirt, a dark jacket and white linen trousers. She had noted his luxuriant chest hair curling to his throat and liked it. His briefcase and shoes were well made. He was on a business visit and they had spent the entire week infatuated with each other. In that late summer Uqba had come to Porquerolles. Their ethnic differences had proved a constant source of surprise. Uqba was used to sweaty steam baths in a hammam; he needed a scrub with pumice and black tar soap; he depended on twice daily wet shaves with mounds of foam. And was there a barber in the village who could trim his nasal hair? The Comtesse giggled weakly at the memory of it all. From the slender resources of her medicine cupboard she had attempted to meet his demands. He would take her to the Ziz valley, he promised, and the Rif mountains and Tan Tan Plage. It had sounded intoxicating. But when she drank wine and smoked her evening Balkan Sobranies, Uqba had raised his newly plucked eyebrows . . .

A series of short explosive yelps and deep snarls were coming from Louis in the kitchen. Would he attack her if she went to him? There was silence; perhaps he had been dreaming. Half-way down the stairs, she stopped and called his name. He whined encouragingly and knocked his weight against the door. The Comtesse opened it wide. Louis sniffed her legs and squirmed on his back before her.

'Silly Billy,' she said and, seeing a saucepan of warmed milk, poured it into his bowl. He lapped greedily and padded after her into the garden. He stalked along the flower-beds and then headed purposefully for her red roses. She led him back to his basket and knelt beside his head. She put her cheek to his. 'A direct gaze is seen as a threat,' she had been warned.

6

At midday the Comtesse hovered on the pier, her eyes glued obsessively on *Valerian II*, slicing through the choppy waves. He had said he would be on the boat. Of course he would be on the boat. And if he was not on the boat, he would be on the tea boat. Was he looking at her even now? She composed herself; with her back to the rail she half turned her head to reveal a serene profile and a halo of blowing curls. She felt a juddering on the jetty and an assortment of chattering day-trippers brushed past her. Where was Uqba? The boat was emptied? The boatman, seeing her prying face, waved his arms akimbo. Her abdomen sank to her toes. She shuffled in an agony of disbelief to the nearby café, Le Bonaparte, and gasped her order for a double Dubonnet *frappé*. She resolved to sit tight for the tea boat like 'patience on a monument'. His plane to Toulon had been late? His bus to the boat? Or had he quite forgotten? Was he even now in Tangier? Marrakesh? Paris? Moscow? In the arms of another? Fondling a new head of silky blonde hair? Lying alongside some delectable lady, fingering the length of her body like some scurrying sand-crab?

'La Comtesse! La Comtesse!'

She started from her seat. It was Philomène and her pretty friend. They were pointing excitedly to a fishing smack heading for the harbour. With still some knots to go, the single-masted sailing boat was battling with the swell. The Comtesse motioned to the two girls to sit with her and asked for iced grenadine. They sat in a row watching the small, proud vessel come closer. Could Uqba be on board? 'It is possible,' said the Comtesse without too much conviction. 'He is unpredictable.' The excitement mounted. A sailing man, drinking anisette, came forward with binoculars. He handed them to the Comtesse. 'It is him! My Uqba! He stands against the mast.' Everybody had a turn with the binoculars and everybody agreed that the tall man in the billowing black shirt was Uqba himself, holding valiantly to the mast.

Closing his eyes to the wind and spray, Uqba savoured the salt on his lips. He breathed deeply on the gusts of sea air; the bromine tang was alluring and calmed him. What was this stupidity? Committing himself to La Christine yet again on her claustrophic prickly green island? It was madness to chase after such a reclusive airhead. But nearing Porquerolles in the blazing early afternoon sun, he was again stirred by its beauty; this antediluvian mammal splayed across the cerulean sea, fused in a savage green. Or was it a vast marine bird, with rings of gold and silver round its claws, which had landed there? He remembered the isle's north coast as tranquil with wide arcs of sand and the south shores rugged with creeks. They would go fishing again in such an inlet where all was intimate and quiet, and the turmoil of seagulls and waves thrashing the rocks was shut out. The port was now less than two knots away. Uqba sensed his space and personal freedom ebbing by the minute. Fort St Agathe, with her thick rounded walls, presided like a formidable matron high above the port below.

'Everything all right?' Uqba called to the skipper. 'Are my goats happy? No seasickness?'

The old sea dog beamed and handed him a heap of sardines wrapped in a copy of *Toulon Matin* – 'For your good lady'.

'You are very kind, my old friend.'

Uqba turned from the mast and glanced behind at the lower deck. The goats were slithering on the boards; his three cherished goats – Fès, Rabat and Blanca. He had not much luggage; a dozen prayer rugs, his water pipe, a pouch of hashish, a set of six white jallabas and six black, a white skull cap and a black. He distrusted any choice of clothes, and black and white were his favourite colours. He felt awkward wearing more than two colours. Now he could see Christine straining to see him – and the little Philomène. How she had matured in a year. There was a friend beside her. They all waved and shouted his name – Uqqy! Uqqy! Ba-ba-ba!' He blew exuberant kisses.

Suddenly he was happy, sure of his girl and wanting his arms around her. The boat juddered as it nudged the bollards alongside the pier. Like a jack-in-the-box, the skipper jumped from the galley with Uqba's two trunks and three goats. Uqba leapt ashore and, clutching his packet of sardines, threw his arms around his Christine. Her relief and happiness was such that his damp shirt impregnated with wafts of goat and fish did nothing to detract from the moment. '*Mon dieu!*' she exclaimed, finally extricating herself. 'Are those goats yours? Philomène, Gervaise, quickly find Gustave and the big *charette.*' Fès, Rabat and Blanca tripped delicately on to the pier and were promptly tethered to the rail. It was decided that the Comtesse and Uqba should go ahead in the dogcart; Gustave would follow with the girls, the goats and Uqba's two leaden trunks.

Christine reined in Rosette to a walking pace. The lane was drowsy with sun and pollen; the doves were hushed, it was their siesta time. And she and Uqba would have their siestas, their time, their love-making, entwined in peace and passion. She snatched a sidelong glance at his head of lustrous hair, his handsome profile and the broad chest pulsating against the damp shirt. When he turned to her his eyes were mischievous and smiling. He leant over and slipped his dark hand through her silk cream shirt. She groaned at the involuntary spasm from her clitoris. Rosette was heading for the ditch. 'Whoa, whoa, Rosie,' cried Uqba. And there was Madame Veuve waiting anxiously ahead.

'Monsieur! Monsieur, you have forgotten your luggage?'

'Enchanté, Madame Veuve, it will arrive soon; this time it comprises three goats for fresh milk and cheese, you understand.' Madame Veuve shot a startled look at the Comtesse.

'Tea on the balcony, Madame Veuve, please. Gustave will see to the goats and luggage.'

Madame Veuve fastened Rosette's reins to the little stable door and, casting an eye on Louis-Loup in his garden pen, she went inside to make the tea.

Uqba and Christine were already on their way upstairs, through the bedroom to the balcony. '*Allah akbar,*' shouted Uqba, and with one bound landed on the plump, capacious whiteness of the bed.

'It is tea-time,' cautioned Christine as he followed her out. Madame Veuve pattered through with the tray; the Porcelain de Paris cups and saucers encircled a lavender sponge cake, sandwiched with myrtle jam. Madame retreated, looking askance at the rumpled muslin bed cover.

'You are perfect in all the ways, my dear little Christine, but you remember I drink my chai from a glass?' Uqba pursed his lips disapprovingly at the rose-leaf tea service.

'Calm down, Uqba. I remember in Tangier, your long glass in its Russian silver container. Tomorrow you will have your chai from a glass; for the present moment I can offer you only a cup or a tooth mug.'

Uqba beamed at her. 'It is the ethnic differences between us. We must be tolerant. I want you now.' Aware of the imminent arrival of Gustave and his motley entourage, Christine evaded his heated gaze. She told him briefly about Louis-Loup. He was appalled. 'If your wolf touches me, a Muslim, I have to wash seven times over.' But it was for the goats Christine was more concerned. She heard the *charette* nearing the villa; the girls' voices and Gustave bidding the pony.

She and Uqba went down to the garden where Philomène and Gervaise, under Gustave's guard, were walking the roped goats to a clearing in the woods. Louis watched from his pen, stiff and erect with his tail raised. A thick ruff formed around his muscular neck; he was maturing fast. As Madame Veuve crossed the lawn towards him, he gave his short yelps of greeting. He rolled on his back as she bent low to fasten his leash for their evening walk. But something stayed her hand. Louis, with the acute olfactory powers of a wolf, had sensed her sudden fear: that he would pull her over and race to the goats. Even Madame Veuve could still detect the pungent whiff of their passing. A tale of her grandfather's flashed through her mind. He would warn that little girls who did not wash would smell of goat – like naughty Henri IV who hated to bathe. Louis stood motionless and rigid as he heard Gustave and the girls emerge from the wood. He danced excitedly as they approached, snapping his teeth with short barks. 'We have tethered the three goats in the clearing,' reported Gustave. 'Would you like me to introduce Louis to them?'

'Yes!' called the Comtesse and Madame Veuve in unison. Gustave checked Louis' leash and walked him to the wood clearing. The Comtesse, Uqba, the two girls and Madame Veuve followed well behind and watched from a distance. Louis sniffed the rough grass as Gustave led him round in a wide berth. Uqba strode proprietorialy towards his prized little herd. They raised their bearded chins from grazing and gazed at him vacantly with simple eyes. The girls joined him and patted each goat on the neck.

'Which is which?' asked Gervaise.

'Fès is the beauty with the black crown on her head. Rabat has the idiotic leer, and Blanca is the miracle goat.'

'Why?' asked Philomène.

'Blanca yields the most luscious milk, beyond the price of pearls. Her cheese is as white and succulent as a young girl's breast.'

Philomène and Gervaise giggled nervously and ran back to the shelter of the Comtesse and Madame, who were returning to the villa. 'It is a lovely evening, girls. Why not stay with the goats a while?'

And so they raced back to Uqba and, pulling him by each hand, showed him the shed in the woods. Their shed. A relic of the last war, under the Italian occupation; a log shelter, half submerged with ground cover. 'This is our secret place, Uqba, where we do secret things.' The two girls caught his hands and danced round him tauntingly. 'We have a special game.'

'Is it naughty?' asked Uqba.

'It's fun,' said Gervaise, 'you can join in.'

'No he can't,' squeaked Philomène. 'Uqba, you can just watch.'

'I think we play this game another day,' said Uqba hurriedly. 'How about having a tea party in your shed one time?'

Oh! Yes! Yes! Yes! And they would make a cake . . .

'I will help you stir the cake,' promised Uqba. 'I have a special ingredient for cakes.'

The two girls set off jubilantly for home. Louis-Loup lay stretched out in his pen after his long walk. And Madame Veuve had added red wine to his sheep hearts.

Uqba was next to be seen draping his prayer rugs over the balcony balustrade. A colourful choice in rich browns and greens, blue and deep wine red, depicting dragons, phoenix, flowers and medallions.

'And this is one for my pretty lady.' He pulled out a roll from the heap of wrappings and threw it open at his Christine's feet. 'A white ground bird carpet – you like?'

'But, Uqba, it is beautiful.' She stared intently at the pretty pink and green birds pecking at blossom sprays.

'It is a classical piece from Anatolia. And now the last, the most sumptuous rug of all to set before your eyes.' It was a rich red and yellow prayer rug and covered the balcony floor. The traditional *mihrab* arch enclosed an ornamental medallion.

'The arch should point to the east, you know that my sweetness?'

'Of course, I remember. But Madame Veuve, when she goes to shake it, she may forget.'

'You tell her to set it down pointing to her friend, in the village – *le boucher, hein*? And now I should bathe in your little blue room. You will scrub me and prod me through all the warm foam? And run your soft pink fingers over me?'

'*Mais comme toujours*,' murmured Christine. She could never decide on these occasions whether she was glad to have a modest bath rather than some double cauldron seething with soap and bubbles. She rose to fill it with the tepid water he preferred.

'Darling,' he called from his encampment on the landing. 'I have a special essence to add. It is Spanish jasmine – most sensual – to mix with a few drops of honeysuckle, French.' Christine, on her knees, turned to see him naked before her. She was shocked anew by his fine strong body with its prodigious cover of curly black hair. Swiftly he lifted her up and pressed her to the wall. Fondling her breasts he undid her shirt, her linen trousers fell to the floor. She kicked off her moccasins and gave way to his arms. Uqba snatched at the bath towels and lay her down. Her nipples tensed as he dabbed them lightly with his tongue; her skin tingled at the brush of his lithe body slipping to her knees. 'Open your thighs,' he urged as he parted the folds of her vulva.

'You are so moist down there.' He stroked and probed her with two fingers as she felt her blood waken. He raised himself to his knees and bent to roll his tongue around her weeping orifice. He was bringing her to a pitch of ecstasy when she heard Madame Veuve, on the landing, put down the supper tray. Whiffs of onion soup strayed over them as he engulfed her. 'Don't stop,' she clamoured; she was nearly there, it was in the bag. She flung her arms around his neck and pulled him down. He rubbed her slowly with the tip of his nose and his lips as she shuddered to her climax.

Uqba stood and grinned happily down at her; his own Christine, tousled and flushed in the foetal position. He was fingering his penis, but before he could plunge it deep inside her, she had knelt before him and taken the membrane into her mouth. With pursed lips and darting tongue and teeth, her fingers drumming on his buttocks and up his soft inner thigh, she was destroying him. He clung to her shoulders, trembling, as he ejaculated, moaning with each gush.

They fell slowly apart and rolled companionably on the bath

towels. Together they slipped into the cool flowered water. Christine retrieved the onion soup. 'Soup should always be taken cold in the bath,' drawled Uqba.

7

It was a jug of warm, frothing goats' milk that woke them in the morning. The peremptory clatter from Madame Veuve's trays never failed to wake Christine. 'Goats' milk should always be taken in bed,' she murmured to her sleepy lover, running her fingers through his curls. Uqba sniffed deeply at her arm pit and then at his mug of milk. 'This is Blanca – she gives the best and whitest milk. Your Gustave is a good milking man. Should we go fishing with him?' Christine thought this is a splendid plan. And they would take Louis, as a way of introducing him to Uqba. Christine had always sensed a strange mystery hanging over the fish creeks on the rugged south coast. The deep and narrow waters were still and clear after the tumult of the breaking waves. The descent down the wooded slopes was scattered with pale asphodel, lilies, lupin and iris. She leapt into some old khaki trousers and coaxed Uqba into something similar. They found him shoes from the boot cupboard. Gustave was waiting on the terrace with an assortment of rods and game bags. Louis stood by his side. He and Uqba gazed on each other quizzically until Madame Veuve ran out and broke the spell. She had sardine baguettes to stow in Gustave's bag. The party crossed the lawn into the woods. Uqba followed slowly as they took a steep, sandy path leading to the sea, through straggling oak and pine. What was he doing here? This crazy scenario; this exotic French siren, the lithe young gamekeeper, and . . . that animal. A wolf! And soon he would have to pat it, even shake its paw. What an erosion of all his ethics. And tomorrow it was Ramadan, which Christine teasingly referred to as 'Ram-it-in'. She turned to him, aglow and golden in the green gloom.

'Are you doing all right, Uqba, my precious?' It seemed to him that all space and light had been drowned by the savage, prickly growth, towered over by predatory eucalyptus and Aleppo pine, their roots lurking in the dry top soil, like starved bones waiting to grab and pull him down. Clumps of feathery brown detritus like coiled boot laces lay in little heaps at his feet. He kept slipping on stones that rolled and slid from under him. A grey film of centuries-old dust tainted leaves and trunks; sinister tunnels skewered through the scrub, where black rats and rabbits raced at night. Oh! For the empty red spaces of the Atlas mountains, where there was no right turn or left. Christine turned to him again and walked back to his side. 'The path gets steeper as we climb down to the cliff edge. Hold on to me.' Uqba wondered when this nightmare would end. 'This inlet has a sacred feeling about it,' explained Christine, quite unperturbed by his obvious misery. 'I expect you will sense it. A fisherman, crossed in love and marriage, erected an altar between the two rocks. We talk softly when we pass. You enjoy yourself, my love?'

But Uqba had slipped on the stones and landed on his bottom in a cloud of hot dust. 'I continue down on my *derrière, chérie*. Is it far?'

Christine bent and ruffled his hair. 'We are almost there.'

A chunk of deep blue sea shone encouragingly through the dim woods. 'Five more minutes, that's all.'

Gustave and Louis had already reached the tantalising target. The young wolf watched Gustave intently as he sorted the rods and reels and nets. Dragging his leash, he padded up the side of the narrow strait, sniffing keenly. And then he jumped in, zig-zagging from side to side, kicking and rolling joyfully. Uqba and Christine had reached the opposite side and were inspecting the rough hewn altar when a crowd of schoolchildren raced in at the end of the creek. Squealing and shouting, dipping their bare legs and toes in the water, they set up a huge commotion. Louis, concealed to his head in the water, had observed them with aston-ishment, before hurtling his nimble body toward them. Gustave yelled curses at him, when a shoal of mackerel leapt like a silver fountain from Louis' paddling paws. He grabbed three in his teeth and swam off happily to the water side to gorge volup-tuously.

The children and their stricken handlers looked on in fasci-nation. 'He won't hurt now,' shouted Gustave. 'He will sleep after his meal.' As he spoke, Louis stood stiff and erect, fixing his yellow eyes on the retreating audience. What would he do next? He swooped again in to the water and snapped up two more fish. 'Rouget,' reported Gustave. With such a surfeit of rich oily fish it was all Louis could do to gulp it down before he slumped in sleep. The rocks around him were spattered with bones and dismembered tails. Christine was sobbing. 'The whole village will hear of this.'

Gustave shrugged. 'Louis did nothing, Madame.'

'But there is this fear of a wolf. And I have a fear for him.'

Uqba was skirting the rocks and looking deep in to the water. 'Louis has left much fish for us, my love.' He threw his arm round her as she joined him. Gustave confirmed that there was dorade, skate and Saint-Pierre. They cast their lines. Gustave stooped to net the catch. Uqba soon collected a silvery pile. He kept his distance from Louis whose wet fur he found malodorous.

'Come, Christine, see the Saint-Pierre.'

Together they caught one and then another. The party was now tired and hungry. Gustave retrieved Madame Veuve's sardine baguettes and lavender biscuits. Christine had stowed a litre of Blanca's milk and a half bottle of Domaine de L'Ile rouge.

Uqba, pleased with his performance, lay on his back, listening to the murmur of the water running out to sea and the foaming waves beyond. And then he pondered gloomily on the return struggle up the cliff. It was arranged that Gustave and Louis should take the short steep route and that Christine and Uqba should make a gradual ascent through the pines. Christine did her best to entertain her treasured Uqba through their shaded path; the occasional butterfly and lizard was pointed out and Gustave's explanation of the cicadas' grating clamour was reiterated. 'Is that so?' marvelled Uqba. 'That little black insect contracts four hundred times a second?'

'We are now coming to a beautiful beach on the tranquil north shore. You like to bathe from the sand, Uqba?'

'I follow you everywhere, my dearest, but I have no bathing paraphernalia. Might it be a naked beach?'

'This one is not. Do you see it below the pine trees? An arc of fine white sand – La Plage d'Argent.'

'Is that the beach from where you abducted Louis?'

'No, that is another still, a small and secretive cove, near the villa. We will go there; just us.'

Minor: 'Bonjour, Major. Middle and I have been so busy on

parade, we have quite forgotten you. The lovers have chosen to entwine themselves in the bath and the bed and the balcony and have spurned your largess and your captivating sofas.'

Major: 'You sound particularly cock-a-hoop, Minor. How is Middle?'

Middle: 'Me, Major? I am in a sensual whirl of jasmine steam, tepid heat, pink limbs and hairy limbs. It is all going on here, Major – and in.'

Minor (in an aside to Major): 'He will soon get tired of it all and get back to complaining.'

Major: 'Good smells from the kitchen these last days. Rouget in brandy butter and almonds one night; grilled sardines another. Yesterday Madame Veuve rescued a packet of *ris de veau* from near putrefaction; doused in red wine and boiled, it truly excelled itself. She consigned it to Louis.'

Middle: 'How is Louis? I have been too steamed up to see out of my window.'

Minor: 'He is growing up. He has a harem.'

Major: 'A harem, Minor?'

Minor: 'Of goats, silly.'

Middle: 'Where are these goats? I have heard their braying.'

Minor: 'They are tethered in the wood clearing. Gustave milks them. Our Moroccan likes to drink their milk warm and frothing.'

Major: 'Some people are intent on making life difficult for others. Tell me, Minor, in your esteemed opinion, is our Comtesse in love with this dago?'

Minor: 'A big question. Love affairs begin and end in the mind with a jumble of body blows in between – would you not agree, Middle?'

Middle: 'Of course my single bath is constricting; tangled up bodies and kicking legs have added to the fun. The Comtesse needs to love and this Uqba is enticingly different; his skin, his dominance, his style. Major would perhaps say he had no style. They are two beings used to playing at love in the fast lane. Now they are stopped short by their ethnic differences.'

Minor: 'They make love with gusto – I assure you, Major. Our dago has an experienced touch. The Comtesse was licking her lips.'

Major: 'You are an incorrigible voyeur, Minor. Tell me, what else was the Comtesse licking?'

Minor: 'A lot of general licking took place. Uqba finally proved himself with a spray of . . .'

Major: 'We cannot subject ourselves, dear Minor, to much more of this.'

Middle: 'I agree with Major. Spilt sperm is beyond the pale.'

Minor: 'Middle has got it in one. The ideal love affair should be based on yearnings and dreams alone.'

Major: 'Oh come! Come! Love is better spent than pent.'

The fishing expedition had induced a pleasant torpor. Uqba made a raft of prayer rugs and cushions on the balcony and tried to persuade Christine to share his water pipe; he had added a few dried leaves of hashish. For their supper, Madame Veuve had cooked the Saint-Pierre with a cod's head to add to the flavour. A card had come up on their tray from Philomène and Gervaise. They had invited Uqba to tea on the very next afternoon, in their shed. Madame Veuve was to allow them space in her kitchen to make a cake. Uqba brandished his summons before Christine. 'But darling that is a wonderful idea. I had planned to desert you anyway, to visit the butcher with Louis.' And was she planning by happy chance that they should eat Louis? Have him chopped up in choice cuts? 'Uqba, you are appalling.'

The following morning, as Uqba proudly inspected Blanca, Fès and Rabat, he set to helping Gustave make cheese. A goat skin had been slung between forked sticks; the empty carcass was stretched full with tossed and chuckling milk. Philomène and Gervaise looked up from their cake making and ran across the lawn to join them. They were soon jerking the milk from side to side to curdle it into yoghurt and cheese. Could Uqba go and taste the cake mixture? 'It is half chocolate, half coffee.' He slipped into the kitchen and crumbled some hashish over the rich brown wetness, stirring it thoroughly. Madame Veuve passed through and looked at him suspiciously. She scooped the mixture into the cake tin and shut it firmly in the centre of the baking oven.

In the early afternoon the Comtesse and Louis set off at a sedate pace for the village. Uqba walked tentatively to his meeting with the girls at their log shelter in the wood. Philomène and Gervaise squeaked with fear and delight as his hefty shoulders filled the entrance. He noticed the must and mould had been swept away. A checked red and white paper cloth, spread across two logs, displayed the chocolate cake and a thick, soft round of Blanca's cheese. He had taken the precaution of bringing along three litres of water.

'So, girls, can I enter your domain?'

Philomène and Gervaise, their long legs revealed to excess beneath their skimpy dresses, stood and ushered him in with mock bows and curtsies. He sat beside them on a rug. 'So this is your secret place?'

'Yes, it is where we do our secret thing; our own secret game.' Gervaise was taunting him; she oozed sex appeal with her red hair and smouldering deep-blue eyes.

'Your game sounds too naughty for me,' said Uqba coyly, 'I'd like to have some cake.'

'We call our game Rub-a-dub,' explained Philomène. 'We lie on our backs beside each other on the rug, and then . . .'

'And then . . .' Gervaise picked up the thread with relish, 'what we do is . . . are you listening, Uqba?'

'Of course, little one.' He threaded his long, dark fingers through her red hair.

'You see that we do not wear panties.'

Philomène and Gervaise promptly pulled up their skirts. 'They would get in the way,' explained Philomène. She continued in a pragmatic monotone. 'Now we stroke our pussies gently up and down. When they get sticky we rub faster and faster, racing each other to the finish.'

Uqba felt momentarily out of his depth. 'And do you rub each other's pussy? Do you want me to join in?'

'No, no, Uqba!' they squeaked. 'You can't play, you haven't got a pussy.'

Gervaise fluttered her slender fingers over her pudenda. 'Tell me about the finish,' asked Uqba warily.

'Well everything happens at once,' started Philomène. Gervaise continued. 'Our thighs are stretched out and tensed and we are trying hard to get there – to get there. Our pussies are bursting with huge expectations – and then a rush of excited feelings jab at the pussy and after the shuddering, it is all over.'

Uqba sighed. 'The "little death" some call it.' The two girls sat cross-legged before him.

'Is Rub-a-dub harmful?' asked Philomène.

Uqba pondered. 'It is a way of discovering your sexual libido, which will turn you both, Gervaise and Philomène, into accomplished lovers. Another time, try it in a warm bath with soapy bubbles. Now let us have our tea.'

They sank their teeth in large portions of the succulent cake and

Blanca's firm cheese. 'Have some water,' urged Uqba and filled a row of paper mugs. The conversation was desultory. The girls soon finished eating and gazed vacuously at Uqba through their dilated pupils. 'Have more water,' he pressed them, 'and then have a little rest.' The girls curled up obediently, dove-tailed like spoons. Uqba gently pulled down their rucked skirts. Their breathing came deep and hard. He watched their breasts rise and fall. The miracle of youth! That translucent skin! Uqba shivered and manoeuvred himself to their side. He eased his hands up the swell of their calves, up their thighs and poked his head up under Gervaise's skirt. He felt quite faint from the heat and hint of her sexual juices. And then he heard voices: Christine and Gustave across the lawn and coming closer. He emerged, flushed, from the log shelter. 'We have been having our tea party,' he called. Christine peered inside.

'Heavens! What has happened? This deep sleep – it is not normal. Philomène! Gervaise! Are you all right?'

'Oh yes, Madame! Everything is fine!' they cried, stirring from their slumber.

The Comtesse's eye fell on the cake. It looked rich and moist. 'A slice for me perhaps?'

'Later, Christine, it would taste better at dinner.' They made their way past Louis, resting in his pen, through the villa and up to their balcony, where Christine confessed she was acutely aware of hostility in the village.

'Madame Prunier, the chocolatier, came out of her shop door, overlooking Place d'Armes, when she saw me pass by with Louis. She looked at us sourly as she patted her false hair piece with her white gloves.'

'I know that lady,' said Uqba. 'Most disagreeable. And she should reserve her white gloves for fingering chocolates and not her dirty hair.'

'Her Belgian chocolates are under suspicion,' continued Christine. The on dit is that they are not made in Belgium, but by a man in a Toulon basement. The "corona" in the box centre, famous for its elixir of Antwerpen liqueur, is a mockery. And the "Marguerite," which boasts "a light Kirsch flavour" has no such thing. For the chopped hazelnuts they substitute pine kernels from the *maquis*.'

'My dear, you and Louis have had a difficult time of it. Try Madame Veuve's eucalyptus tea.'

Christine was not to be defeated: 'And Madame Poisson, the florist, she barred her doorway with clumps of pampas grass. And then that young man "*Aux Journaux*", with the red hair to his waist, pulled an odious face at us. Do you know?' Christine paused to sip her tea. 'I am told that when he cuts it off he sells it to a Toulon Coiffeur . . .'

There were shrieks and giggles below as Philomène and Gervaise skipped and cartwheeled across the lawn. Secreted by a tree trunk was the half-eaten cake. They scattered it over the grass and threw the remainder for Louis.

'They appear to have recovered from your tea party,' observed Christine. 'I have a present for you.' She went into the bedroom and retrieved the black package tied in lilac ribbon.

'What can this be, my Christine? From Paris indeed – and where it all began.' He undid the ribbon eagerly to find the black cotton shorts. 'Black – my favourite.' Christine kissed him as he held them up happily.

'Shall we swim in that secret cove you told me of, where Louis was first discovered half-dead?'

'Tomorrow evening,' promised Christine.

'You are tired, my little one.'

'Yes,' agreed Christine. The bad feeling in the village had tired her.

'Come.' Uqba led her into the bedroom and lay down beside her. 'I will not support rudery from the bourgeoisie.'

'But they have a great fear, Uqba, they are scared to death. They fear for themselves, their babies, their hens and dogs and horses. The wolf species has bad blood. He can be a ruthless hunter. We love Louis. To us he is gentle and courteous. But as he matures and becomes stronger, he will pounce. I see disaster. The village is ready to cast an evil eye.'

'Never fear, dearest. Louis has no reason to feel wild and frustrated. He is tended and fed and exercised. Roll over, I need to unzip your pretty dress.' He stroked her bare shoulders, kissing the length of her back bone; he rubbed his nose in her downy coccyx. 'Shall I massage your back? With my special ginger therapy oil?' He swung his long legs off the bed and rummaged in the bathroom cupboard. Christine rolled over on her back, with her eyes closed and her thighs parted, she waited for his touch.

'You feel sexy?' Uqba was admiring her pliant nudity from the doorway. She teased her clitoris with her finger. In a stroke he was kneeling on the bed massaging her thighs and abdomen with oil. His strong fingers smoothed her slowly, up and down, circling her belly. She turned over and, with her buttocks raised, guided his slippy hand up her vagina. He gasped as he inserted his penis. A long thrust, followed by another and then another. 'Faster, faster, harder, harder,' she pleaded as he jabbed into her. She shook uncontrollably as she was swept along the savage waves of orgasm. Uqba pulled her across the bed, wiping the sweat from her face and heaving neck.

'Was that good?' he asked archly.

'Wonderful, amazing. Try on your new pants.' Uqba reappeared, preening himself in his black Paris bathing shorts. A perfect fit. Christine noted the bulge in his crotch approvingly.

She eased her hands inside and pushed the pants to his knees. Again he was pulsing and erect. 'More, more,' she urged and lay back rapturously.

8

After the strenuous demands on the second day of his visit, Uqba was mollified to have a late supper on the balcony. And he had been reminded by the butcher's afternoon delivery of prime cuts of sheep, that it was the month of Ramadan. Madame Veuve had concocted a thick soup of beans, lentils and lamb – the standard start to the Muslim evening feasting. And the finish too, thought Christine.

'We Muslims eat healthy food in Ramadan,' Uqba told her authoritatively. 'And no drink or foods whatsoever should pass our lips from dawn to dusk. There is no sex allowed and no smoking.'

'Ever again?'

'Would you feel so deprived? My beauty, we may yet make love all night and recover all day.'

'And what else will you be doing or not doing, Uqba? I never see you say your prayers.'

'You are right. I have neglected my faith. Ramadan is a time for Muslims to renew their faith. But you have distracted me. And when a Muslim travels or if he is physically under pressure he may be exempt from fasting.'

'Of course, Uqba, you have been under huge physical demands . . .' Christine giggled.

They snuggled down on a raft of rugs. Uqba sucked hard on his water pipe and threaded in more hashish from his pouch. The evening birdsong had faded and the night sky was pricked with stars.

'Did I tell you I am descended from pirates?' he asked her. He appeared suddenly alien, evil almost, with his sidelong smile and his bubbling hookah. 'From Barbary corsairs, no less. My ancestors raided the Mediterranean shores from Egypt to Algeria. The Berber tribes – the menace of the Moors. We held these coasts to ransom. We savaged your beautiful Iles d'Or; Porquerolles, Port-Cros and Levant. Two hundred years ago your seductive island was ripped apart with fear, pillage and rape. Night and day your inhabitants of Porquerolles were trapped, helpless. These three islands are linked by a line of rocks where pirates lurked unseen, in little boats, watching for plunder. And more than plunder, for kidnapping and ransom.' Uqba stood and paced the balcony. Agitated and sweating, he raked his hair and swabbed his face with the wide sleeve of his *jallaba*.

'Stop, Uqba. If it upsets you to think of these rough times.'

But Uqba continued: 'The land journey from Marseille to Thessalonika was as dangerous as the sea voyage. Coastal communities were torn apart; these shores were not patrolled and at the mercy of the bandits. There was no security for the mainland dwellers. Piracy and plunder was an accepted way of Mediterranean life; the livelihood of the sea. Unpaid ransoms spelled instant slavery. Any captured crews were battened under the hatches to a slow death. I was told these things,' said Uqba apologetically. 'The galley slave was chained naked to a heavy oar with six other men. They were urged on with cruel lashes for some twenty hours at a time.' Christine listened and looked on, horrified and wide-eyed.

'What did they eat?' she asked him fearfully.

'Oh, a few ship's biscuits, vinegar and water, a spoonful of gruel, or stale bread dipped in wine. Death and disease took its toll.'

Madame Veuve was seen standing motionless, as pale as a ghost, in the doorway. Christine looked up. 'Come, Madame Veuve. We are talking of pirates and terrible events of two hundred years ago.' Madame Veuve had overheard a fair amount of Uqba's soliloquy from the landing. 'Sit down!' Christine motioned her a chair. 'And when did all this stop, Uqba?'

Sitting well back in his chair and drawing on his hookah, Uqba appeared in another world. He jumped to attention. 'The age of steam in the early nineteenth century and the improved sea policy . . . and the intervention of Napoleon with his plans of defence. Your village was constructed and your Place d'Armes. The inhabitants were selected from military officers with their families. Now you are guarded by your ancient forts that squat above your shores.'

The Comtesse turned to Madame Veuve. 'Our guest here, Monsieur Uqba, is himself descended from Barbar corsairs.' Madame Veuve remained silent but her face hardly concealed her disapproval.

'I have something to say,' she uttered in her thin, piping voice. She paused. 'My husband was a pirate all around here, and my son; robbers, both of them.' Madame Veuve wiped a tear. There was a brief silence. Madame Veuve had more to say. 'It was my grandfather who talked to me of Anne Bonney. I see her sometimes, high in the trees here, even in the clouds and in the waves of the sea.'

'Thank you, Madame Veuve. We will talk another time about your friend.' The Comtesse rested a hand on the old lady's shoulder. Madame Veuve picked up the dinner tray. She had wished to warn of Louis' rising jealousy, his sexual stirrings . . . but, another time.

Christine turned to Uqba. 'Do we know Anne Bonney?'

'She was a tormentor of my lusty ancestors. Born in Cork around 1700, an Irish girl, illegitimate and reared in Charleston, South Carolina. She married a local sailor, James Bonney. Soon she was strutting round the ships, her ample bosom tumbling from her bodice, her flying blonde hair under a slouch hat. She was seduction enough in her bell-bottomed trousers. And by all accounts, she was brutal too. A brace of pistols were fastened to her tall, strong body, a cutlass, a machete, and a truncheon. As a child she was said to have stabbed to death her English nannie.'

'What a terrible woman,' cried Christine. 'What happened to her?'

'Nobody knows of her end; but she romped through life, killing and robbing and fornicating with pirates. She left James Bonney for a bounder, Jack Rackam, known as "Calico Jack". On board his ship, Bonney conceived a passion for another member of the crew, later to be discovered a woman in disguise. Mary Read and Bonney became good friends and both fell pregnant. Rackam's ship was captured; he was executed. The two girls were tried and spared and gave birth.'

'And what of Anne Bonney and her child?'

'Nobody knows. It is a strange and violent tale. Madame Veuve sees her face in the trees.'

'Let us go down to the garden,' said Christine eagerly, and we can scan the trees tops for Anne Bonney.'

It was a soft night and folded about them like velvet. Christine's white lilies and tobacco plants rocked their scent across the lawn. Louis mewed and yelped excitedly as they walked to his pen. He nuzzled Christine's legs and knees; she lay back on the grass as he ran circles round her, sniffing and licking her face. The moment Uqba sat beside her, Louis growled and butted him. Uqba stretched out his hand to stroke the muscular mane. Louis jerked his head to one side revealing the white of his eye, flattened his ears and bared his teeth. He was jealous; he was becoming a man, thought Uqba wryly.

'Let us visit my goats,' he suggested, and with the abandoned Louis howling, he steered Christine to the woods. Blanca, Fès and Rabat chewed indolently in the moonlit glade. Uqba ran his long fingers through their fleeces. 'Fès, with the black crown of hair, is my favourite.' He put his arms round her long neck and throat. She tossed him aside indignantly.

It was getting late. Christine could see no vestige of the barbarous Anne Bonney, hanging in the trees, and wanted her bed. Uqba, sliding his hand through Fès' fleece, had stirred her.

The next morning, Madame Veuve set off briskly for the village. Louis padded beside her on the leash. Madame Veuve did not especially dislike Monsieur Uqba but she did not like him either. And now this startling revelation that he was from Berber tribes who had plundered the Barbary coasts confirmed her distaste. You could see he had piracy in his blood. But who would have thought it? She rounded on '*L'Agneau aux deux têtes*'. The shop was empty, with the sawdust floor as smooth as a newly raked plage on the Côte d'Azur.

'Come in, Madame Veuve,' and they repaired to Monsieur's back room.

'The Moroccan gentleman, was he happy with the gigot?'

71

'Yes, Monsieur. But always the mutton for Ramadan is so dull. Do you know something? The Comtesse's friend, the Moroccan, is descended from Barbary corsairs!' Madame Veuve almost touched her little knees with her nose as she bent low with her scandalous disclosure. 'We have a pirate in our midst.'

The butcher, drawing a straggling handkerchief from his overall, blew his nose and rubbed his moustache.

'It is not a problem. He has interesting blood. I think Madame Prunier would like to hear the story.' And Madame Veuve knew that there could be no better conveyor of savoury gossip than the chocolatier. 'I will have more horsemeat for Louis here,' she commanded and left through the front shop. A line of customers straining to hear through the back room door straightened up for their butcher.

That afternoon was sultry with the sun cramped in cloud. Uqba lay prone on his rugs in his new black pants. The eucalyptus rattled their dry leaves, panting with a ravenous need of water. He and Christine were to swim in the little cove. He looked idly at the fluttering clematis and bougainvillaea clustered along the iron balcony. He felt stifled with their clinging shade. When Christine would tweak a stray strand into a new tangle, he longed to pull it all away and feel the breezes again.

'Uqba! You look magnificent.' Christine swayed through the bedroom door in an indigo *jallaba*. 'Shall we go? Here is a towelled robe.' It was a short stroll to the cove, through dark pine woods, where Uqba feared for rats and lizards. He did not trust this terrain. Clumps of rosemary, pink oleander and wafts of lavender led down a slope of brushwood to the deserted beach. Uqba noted with distaste the heaps of prickly residue from the woods, and the torpid waves clogged with seaweed. The sun smouldered low in the sky and striped the sea in livid red. Christine threw off her *jallaba* and, cupping her full breasts, pounded into the sea. Uqba followed reluctantly; his long muscular body fell into a rhythmical crawl. He caught her round the waist and eased off her pants, stowing them in his own. 'Uqba! You know it never works in water.'

'Ah! but bodies become so buoyant – your breasts are superb.' They stood up to their necks, fondling each other. The pine woods were inked black as they waded through the water. Christine stopped.

'I feel somebody is prying on us from the woods – your friend Anne Bonney perhaps?' They stood in the water watching the distant trees. Was there a face? Anne Bonney brandishing her bare bosom and her pistols? And then Christine saw him, his eyes blazing in the sinking sun and fixed on them with ferocious attention. Louis-Loup hurled himself from the woods, slithering down the slope and on to the beach. He gained the sea with his elegant swagger. 'Louis, come here, dear one!' called Christine. Uqba turned on his stomach and did a stretch of the crawl – and then another. Through the din of his kicking and the flurry of water in his ears, he heard Christine scream hysterically; and then claws pounced on his back and scratched him deeply. Uqba howled and flailed out with his arms; in a daze he struggled to the shore – Louis was paddling furiously away from him. Christine? Where was she? Crouched by a rock, weeping and shaking her wet head in disbelief! Uqba staggered toward her, ribbons of blood streaming down his shoulder blades.

'Louis – he is jealous, like I told you. Uqba, I am desperately sorry. Louis – he is my baby. He has done a terrible thing.' She flung her arms around her lover and wrapped him in his bathrobe. 'We must go straight to the vet.'

'The vet? But, Christine, my dearest, it is I who have need of a doctor – Louis is fine.' As they dried each other beside a rock, Christine explained to Uqba that everybody went to the vet instead of the bumbling old doctor. He had better drugs, which he knew how to dilute, and naturally he was younger. Not for the first time did Uqba reflect on the idiosyncrasies of his treasured Christine and her crazy island. Where was Louis? They heard muffled steps on the sand and Gustave emerged in the dusk. It was Madame Veuve, he explained, who had been forced by Louis to slip his leash . . .

After a quick change of clothes, Uqba and Christine set off for the vet with Gustave and Rosette, in the dogcart. Louis' claw marks had clotted into round, red beads. Why was it necessary to visit the vet, Uqba again asked plaintively?

'You might get lockjaw,' Christine assured him.

'What is that?'

'Lockjaw is rare but then so are you. It is a rigid spasm of the muscles round the face and neck and can leave the mouth permanently closed.'

'Will we be there soon? I feel a stiffness creeping up on me.' And Uqba became more agitated, opening and shutting his mouth like a hungry shark.

Christine stroked his hand. 'Nearly there,' she comforted him. Rosette trotted up a steep lane – Rue Fort St Agathe – where Gustave reined her in beside a green door.

Uqba read: M. Paul Boudin Vétérinaire, on the brass door plate, and knocked frantically. A disapproving matron in none-too-clean a white overall led them straight to M. Boudin in his small stale parlour. 'My friend,' began the Comtesse, indicating Uqba . . .

'I have lockjaw,' interrupted Uqba, towering over the plump

M. Boudin. He was guided to a burgomaster swivel chair and commanded to say 'aargh'. M. Boudin next whipped his head up Uqba's baggy vest.

'What has happened here? You have met with a wild cat, Monsieur?'

'It was a wolf that assaulted me.'

'My tame wolf,' interjected Christine. 'He was jealous seeing us in the sea together – having fun.'

'And you were doing a high speed crawl, Monsieur? Flat on your stomach, with back and bottom in full view? You know, Madame, Monsieur, your wolf was afraid that Monsieur was drowning. He wanted to revive you with his claws.' With imperceptible speed Monsieur Boudin shot a syringe of penicillin into Uqba's bottom. The patient squealed indignantly.

'All is well, Monsieur – calm yourself.' He turned to the Comtesse. 'Your friend should return here in a week. Your address, Madame?'

'I am La Comtesse de Beaucaire, Monsieur Boudin. We live in the villa at the end of Rue de la Ferme.'

'Ah yes, Madame Veuve's residence,' murmured Monsieur Boudin reverently. The Comtesse guided a stumbling Uqba out into the darkening road. 'And no baths, mind,' they heard their benefactor call after them.

'Is that better, Monsieur?' ventured Gustave. When the Comtesse revealed to him Monsieur Boudin's version of Louis' charitable reaction to Uqba's exposed broad back in the sea, Gustave felt personally exonerated. A vet would always judge an animal above a man.

Two days later, the Comtesse was heard to say to Madame Veuve that she was off to Toulon to retrieve her dignity; to spend time at the coiffeur, to have a manicure and pedicure. Monsieur Uqba would be perfectly comfortable In fact, he had invited Philomène and Gervaise to tea; a light tea in the sitting-room, where they could enjoy the books. With a withering glance at the scorched lawn, her ruined roses and the raw pig's heart being chopped for Louis' supper, the Comtesse was whisked away in the dogcart down to the pier.

9

Major: 'Did you hear the command of the Comtesse today? A tea party is planned midst my sofas, my books and my sparkling chandelier.'

Minor: 'We hope you do not allow matters to get out of hand, Major. Those nymphets, Philomène and Gervaise, are well in with the game of seduction. They exude sex appeal.'

Major: 'My dear Minor, I am a wall of the world. You will not catch me reeking of regrets.'

Middle: 'And you will be tossing them into my bath, Major, I know, when their fingers get sticky. These naughty parties always devolve upon me.'

Minor: 'Talking of devolvement, you heard that Uqba is descended from Berber corsairs?'

Major: 'It is a disgrace that our Comtesse fraternises with such a man. And she, the descendant of a distinguished Maréchal de France.'

Minor: 'Why do we assume a Maréchal to be so distinguished? If that buffoon, Bassompierre, had only insisted that Henri IV shared his carriage on the afternoon of 14 May 1610 . . . Bassompierre's bulk, you may recall, was safely contained in his new coach with heavy glass windows – *le dernier cri*. Whereas Henri proceeded down the crowded narrow streets of Paris in a phaeton open to the winds and his assassination. What a waste.'

Middle: 'With Henri IV our Paris pulsed with life: new bridges, new palaces, houses for the poor; new styles and fashions. It was a golden decade.'

Minor: 'And as for that lunatic Maréchal Foch – always spoiling for a fight.'

Major: 'Despite our reservations over ancient piracy, we should appreciate that such plunder was an accepted means of Mediterranean life. And what characters! The renowned "Black Beard" and "Jambe de Bois" and Captain William Kidd (never known to be under-armed). And do not forget those two outrageous sirens, Mary Read and Anne Bonney. Naturally they were all imbued with their bible – *The Seaman's Monitor* by Josiah Woodward:

May no voice of profane swearing nor obscene speech be heard among you. May no excess of wine or passion betray you, to any indecency or enormity.'

Middle: 'What a load of codswallop. You should be ashamed of yourself, Major. Give me the French army any day.'

Minor: 'We have to remember, Middle, that our Major is a literary man, a most superior person. His mind has wings, whereas ours have wheels.'

Major: 'I am aware, dear friends, that any landmine in my heart could be detonated by an unwary tread. But I can hold my own with these two provocative trollops.'

There was a halting step on the stairs. Madame Veuve paused

on the landing and entered the sitting-room. She carried a white embroidered table-cloth and a cane basket of cups and plates and pearl-handled dessert knives and forks. She slumped on to a sofa and sighed, rubbing her sharp little knees. She must find some flowers from the garden. The room looked neglected. The Comtesse had been too busy in the bedroom and bathroom. Madame Veuve stood up slowly and threw the cloth over the round table in the window. The Comtesse's best Porcelain de Paris tea service was next laid for three.

Catching sight of the wisteria and plumbago festooning the balcony, Madame Veuve snipped at some clusters with the Comtesse's nail scissors and arranged them in a bathroom glass. On a second laborious ascent she brought up a pretty plate of delectable white peaches, a fluted mold of Blanca's milk jelly and a sponge cake layered with heather jam. She hoped that her granddaughter would note all these niceties. Soon they would all arrive, and with an appraising look at her dainty preliminaries, Madame Veuve left the room. An air of listlessness hung over the garden and the woods beyond. The dry soil, the scorched grass and the crumbling vegetation strained for rain. The woods were still, scalded by months of salt sea breezes and slanted sun. The goats were stretched out on crisp, withered leaves. Louis lay inert; he flicked his tail as he heard Madame's step. She opened his pen and he batted her affectionately in the bosom. Her shrinking and his growing had made her withered breasts their natural contact point. He sniffed the close air as though sensing trouble, and followed her quietly to the terrace where they waited for the girls to come. But it was Uqba who arrived the first of the little party. Madame slipped on Louis' leash and there were a few moments of disparate conversation. 'There they are!' Uqba stood up, relieved, and waved his arms, looking magnificent in his white *jallaba.* He gazed on them; the dark one and the red one – with flowers in their hair! And a mound of flowers held between them in a little canopy.

'Here we are, Grandmamma.' Philomène stooped to kiss the silver pumpkin of hair. The two girls rubbed Louis' luxuriant furry neck.

'And a kiss for me?' asked Uqba plaintively.

'You have the two of us and some flowers,' retorted Gervaise.

The little party went up the stairs to the Comtesse's sitting-room, where the girls collapsed giggling on the sofa. Uqba retrieved his water pipe, lightly marinaded with hashish, and a general post-prandial repose ensued.

'How many wives have you, Uqba?' asked Gervaise.

'Three wives; none of them work. And three goats.'

'Are your wives beautiful, Uqba?' chimed in Philomène.

'I do not look at them too much or too closely. And naturally they are well wrapped up; veiled heavily and enveloped in their black *burkas.*'

'Not very pretty,' sympathised Philomène.

'But wives are fun to unwrap,' retaliated Uqba. 'It is all part of our Muslim mystique. Veiled women are a sign of submission and good behaviour.' Uqba took a drag on his pipe. 'But of course my goats are more beautiful – Fès, Blanca and Rabat have such a distinguished bearing.'

'Don't move,' urged Gervaise, kneeling on the sofa beside him. She was threading corn marigolds through his black crochet skullcap.

'And here I have a necklace. Sit still Uqba.' Philomène linked two fragile spears of pink lupin around this throat.

'What else have we for Uqqy?' Gervaise stirred the heap of flowers with a teaspoon.

'Let's have our tea now,' pleaded Uqba and sat down defiantly at the table. The kettle was boiled and he was offered cardamom, juniper or lemon verbena. They all settled for the verbena with a spoonful each of eucalyptus honey. The cake was scrumptious. Madame Veuve had tended them well. Gervaise looped some tangled honeysuckle round Uqba's ears. Philomène took down the Emile Zola from the shelf and read from the sensual passage:

'At once she pressed her lips to his as though to seal his vow, and they kissed . . .' Her voice faded into a fruitful silence.

'I am a little tired, girls,' interrupted Uqba. 'Come and join me for a rest in the bedroom.'

The two girls followed him with their *berceau* of flowers. In a swift flurry Uqba flung off his *jallaba* and lay naked on the muslin bed cover.

'Such an airless afternoon and no birds sing. There will be a storm,' he groaned, and feigned sleep. Philomène and Gervaise giggled.

'You do the feet,' said Gervaise, 'and I will do the wrists and upper arms.'

They both stared dubiously at Uqba's flaccid penis. 'Let's wind the gentian round it. Do you see them? Those blue tassels.' Gervaise lifted them from the pile. 'They look too limp,' said Philomène, 'can't we find something a little more joyous?' Gervaise retrieved some periwinkle.

'Oh yes, much better – the little blue flowers are sweet.' The girls twisted and plaited round Uqba's genitals and found the gentian tassels a malleable option for his exuberant growth of hair.

'Blue suits him round there,' observed Gervaise. Philomène next chose to make him garters and anklets. Gervaise opted for the nipples. They worked quickly from their cache of wild flowers

81

from the woods, delving into anemones – mauve, pink and white with yellow centres – delphinium, iris and yellow rock rose; the deep pink clusters of daphne were threaded between his toes.

There was a sudden snort and Uqba slapped his diaphragm. 'A bath! A bath!' he cried pitiably.

'What a good idea!' exclaimed Philomène. 'Run him a bath – but a tepid one.' Gervaise returned to the bedside with the bottle of saffron oil and the girls rubbed any exposed flesh with firm hands. 'His skin looks quite yellow now,' said Gervaise, 'like he has been embalmed.'

'I have an idea,' murmured Philomène, 'when I gain my baccalaureate, I will work in a funeral parlour.' They looked at their handiwork admiringly.

'And he has a magnificent body; beautifully made,' noted Philomène. There was a tinkling of tea things.

'Philomène! Gervaise! Come at once!' The two girls skipped through to the sitting-room, to confront a disapproving Madame Veuve. 'You must never go into that bedroom. Where is Monsieur Uqba?'

'Come and see, Grandmamma. Monsieur Uqba is exquisite.' Madame Veuve was guided, and not unwillingly, to the apparition of Uqba prone *en pleine fleuri*.

'*Très agréable*. Now you must put Monsieur down before the Comtesse returns.' Uqba stirred at the sound of Madame's nasal timbre and swung his encrusted legs over the bed. Gervaise swiftly smothered his penis with a clutch of marigolds. Madame Veuve walked slowly backwards from the room, as though in the presence of royalty.

'A storm would you say, Madame?' Uqba called after her. 'The air so hot and dry.'

'You are right, Monsieur Uqba. You need to take a bath? The

Comtesse returns soon.' Uqba stood in his full herbaceous glory and strode into the bathroom. The little female party feasted on his firm and hairy buttocks.

Christine breathed in deeply as *Valerian II* steamed off from Toulon. Porquerolles blazed ahead in green and gold under the harsh sun. The captain lifted his chin to the sea and sniffed. 'The mistral has held for three hours already.' As they neared the harbour Christine smelt the sharp, sour acidity of the *pinède* and the dead dust of the *maquis*. Such sun devoured all life. The breeze grew, hot and tearing. Christine walked past the cluster of stalls beside Place d'Armes. Espadrilles, palm hats and juniper walking sticks hung from the awnings; pottery jars of honey, lavender, eucalyptus oil and myrtle jam sat snugly on shelves. Christine found a seat in a crowded café. She needed time alone. Sipping a *citron pressé*, she opened her *Toulon Matin*. There had been a rape in Lyon, a rare sighting of a water spout off St Tropez and murder in Marseille. What devastations! It made her own life seem the epitome of parochial rectitude. She turned the page: 'The first forest fires have swept through Var . . .' Christine was shocked. Var district was close; the lush valley of vineyards, the olive groves, the village flower-beds and vegetable plots – Draguigan, Fréjus, Roquevaire . . . she saw it all pass before her eyes. As she pondered on such ravage and destruction, two *pompiers* circled slowly round Place d'Armes. The café owner stood beside her. His awning flapped recklessly as he stretched out his bare arm to test the breeze. 'The mistral,' he assured her gravely.

'And the *pompiers*?'

'They are on standby for trouble . . . and fires. The mistral can always start a fire.'

The late afternoon sun burned through Christine's shirt as she walked back along Rue de la Ferme. Builders were working on a neighbour's conservatory. Christine peered through their fence and saw random slabs of glass lying about the garden. Madame Veuve and Louis were waiting for her at the gate. Christine clasped Louis round his furry neck; he yelped with pleasure and stabbed her stomach with his snout.

'Louis seems agitated,' warned Madame Veuve, 'it is the mistral; he senses danger.'

Christine felt suddenly tired and walked slowly up the stairs. The wind had increased considerably. Uqba called to her from the bathroom. Waves of silky flower essences and scented steam enveloped her as she neared the landing. Uqba lay languorously in a trough of flowers, his skullcap laced with marigolds and his genitals knotted about in blue petals. Stray blooms drifted around his body like herbs in preparation for a *bouillabaisse*.

'What has become of you, Uqba? Who put you in there?'

'The girls. They put me in every kind of position and then they gave me flower therapy. And you look lovely, my angel, with your curled hair and scarlet nails.'

There was a sudden rip through brushwood; a falling tree, a flash of flames and screams from down the road. Agitated pheasants and partridge squawked as they put up from the wood. The tethered goats whinnied frantically. Uqba dressed quickly. As he raced to the clearing he saw black rats run out for cover. Gustave came towards him. The fire had started up the lane with the mistral blowing from the west. A fine row of eucalyptus leading to the village had gone up in sheets, each leaf bubbling and hissing with oil. A pall of acrid smoke hung over the villa. Louis sniffed convulsively and rubbed his belly against Gustave's shin . . . he had not yet been fed. The three goats hung together, watching

Gustave's every move. He led them to Rosette's stable, where she had been whinnying pitifully. Rabat and Fès were loath to join her but Blanca settled down happily in the straw beside her. Uqba was distracted with fear. Would the fire race down the road and engulf them all? Gustave stood still and raised his arm. 'The plan alarm,' he murmured, 'you hear the announcement from the village? Chains and notices have been set up to guard access to all roads. Bicyclists and pedestrians are forbidden entry. All people to keep clear of the village centre. This is a serious fire.' And Gustave set off purposefully down the road. He had gone only a few metres when the two goats charged after him; past him they raced and into the thick of the blaze. Uqba chased along behind, screaming. Gustave shook his head. His face was smeared with cinders. 'They jumped straight into that blazing myrtle,' he shouted to Uqba in disbelief. And both men detected the unmistakable aroma of roasting fur and flesh. Uqba was shocked. 'Go back to the Comtesse and Madame Veuve and the villa,' urged Gustave, 'I will get news from the village.'

Uqba returned to see Louis leaping up frantically at Rosette's stable door. He shooed him away angrily. His remaining beloved Blanca was still curled up comfortably with Rosette. Louis had loped off into the woods down to the cove. Madame Veuve was joined by Christine in the kitchen doorway. They sniffed at the acrid twilight. Christine ran to Uqba with relief, burying her cheek in his shirt. 'You smell of fire and ashes,' she said.

'There is fire all up the road and through to the village,' he told her.

'What has started it?' asked Madame Veuve.

'A combination of events,' replied Uqba. 'Lack of rain, brittle undergrowth; a broken bottle exposed to the sun can set up a fire. With the mistral blowing, the danger is doubled.' Christine shuddered. She put her hand to her heart and remembered the glass panels spread haphazardly in the nearby garden.

'You hear the bells?' Uqba bowed his head to the village.

'The bells?'

'The bells of the *pompiers*,' explained Uqba. 'The villagers are being ordered to hurry to the jetty with all their belongings.'

'What a nightmare!' cried Christine. 'Where is my Louis?' Her voice was shrill with fear. She was beginning to panic. The mistral was mounting. The distant Aleppo pines could be seen bent almost double in the ferocious gusts. The silvery trunks with their powerful roots grabbed at the sheer rock ledge like tentacles.

'Louis, Monsieur. What has happened to him?' called Madame Veuve. 'Where is he, our precious one?'

Uqba turned to her, 'You have nothing to fear with Louis, Madame. He trotted off down to the cove – well away from the fires. But I have suffered a grave tragedy with the loss of my Rabat and my Fès. They charged down the lane and leapt into a fiercely burning myrtle bush. Little did I suspect that my adored goats would be roasted to their deaths on your peaceful Porquerolles.'

'Uqba, I am sorry – it is all frightful,' exclaimed Christine.

Gustave reappeared, panting. He warned that if the wind should change, they must abandon the villa and go to the cove. What was happening in the village?

'Fishing boats, moored on the beaches, have been burned. Toulon has sent over more men and more hoses to quell the blaze. The little shops – the chocolatier, the florist – all ruined. Madame Prunier went mad with fury. Her boots dripping choco-late, her hair waving loose in the winds, as she ran screaming at the flames. Madame Poisson wanted to save her pair of orange trees, but they caught fire like two torches as she ran along Place d'Armes. The boucherie survived – built in solid stone by the military one hundred years ago.'

'Have the vineyards escaped?'

'Mercifully,' continued Gustave, 'the fire never climbed to that height. The hills of Brégançonnet, the hills of Porquerolles and La Courtade were out of danger.'

'*Dieu, merci,*' squeaked Madame Veuve, 'we all need our Domaine de L'Ile.' Rosette neighed from her stable as Gustave walked towards her and Blanca with a large warm bran mash. And where was Louis? It flashed again on Madame that he had not yet been fed. It was hot and stuffy in the stable with vestiges of smoke and burnt pine. Gustave pushed open the door and drew the two animals and the bran outside on to the grass. The contented herbivores slurped at their shared bowl.

Uqba stirred himself from his garden chair and went to stroke his Blanca lovingly; her woolly neck, her soft pricked ears.

'We love each other my Blanca and your Uqba. You give me your precious milk and when . . .' A strange howl rose from the woods. Louis-Loup in a fury of fur and long legs raced towards them. His yellow eyes blazed as he leapt at Blanca and bit deep into her neck. She bleated helplessly, rolling on her back and waving her legs. Louis pounced to rip open her stomach, making off to the woods with a trail of intestines. Uqba screamed wildly, 'Kill him! Kill him!' But it was the goat that Gustave shot dead.

Madame Veuve hung her head. The words of the butcher came ringing through her head: 'You most never ever leave your animal hungry, Madame – never, never, Madame.'

Christine sobbed quietly. It was Gustave who went to her and put a strong arm around her shoulders. She felt his firm lips moving on her cheek. 'It is nothing. Do not upset yourself,' she heard him murmur. Rosette chomped on her bran and slurped her water until Gustave led her back to her stable. Rolling Blanca up in a horse blanket he wheeled her up the lane to the nearest burning bush.

Where was Uqba?

'Monsieur Uqba? Where are you?' shrilled Madame Veuve.

Christine, a hunched figure in a shawl, half stumbled into the villa. She dragged herself up the stairs, in despair, disorientated, the fragile boundaries of her life now savagely breached. How would he be?

10

There was no sign of Uqba or his prayer rugs; his few belongings had been scooped up into a carpet bag.

'My time here is finished. I am gone – writing – your constant – Uqba – inshallah'

This concise message was scrawled in lipstick on the enamel lip of the bath. She heard Gustave's low, commanding voice in the garden. He had Louis muzzled and on a long leash as they crossed the grass to his pen. Louis whelped and cowered, with his hind legs shaking. Had Gustave whipped him? Madame Veuve put down a light dinner before him.

Each villager would have his story of that late summer fire. But it was the sight of the tall Moroccan bent almost double under his prayer rugs, waving his fluttering white sleeves and calling *'Balek! Balek!* (Make way! Make way!); *Allah Akbar*,' that evoked the most amazement. By ten o'clock the wind had dropped as though terminally exhausted by its wild forces. A wave of quiet swept over the island; high-pitched cries and voices were subdued into silence; a smokescreen of burnt oils, from pine, eucalyptus and juniper caught in the throat; the birds were hushed. Christine looked out of her soot-smeared bedroom window, and wept. Her man had abandoned her and her world. The man who she had believed would open exotic vistas and encircle her with a cordon of love and passion had deserted her. She looked grotesque; her hair fell in thick, greasy tails; her face and neck were streaked with sweat and soot. But she smiled at herself, kindly, in the large silver framed oval mirror. How often must her forebear, Princess Christine Belgiojoso have pondered on her reflection in this same fuzzy glass? Pouring herself a bath with the floral remains of Uqba's questionable tea party, Christine bathed and stumbled into her bed.

Middle: 'Are you stinking of cinders my friends? How are your sofas, Major? You survived the tea party . . . it was Minor that bore the brunt of that episode.'

Minor: 'The Comtesse lay down her head an hour ago. The first calm night that she and I have had for ten days. You know that the dago has been given his congé?'

Major: 'On the contrary – it was our Moroccan who slunk out on our Comtesse – disguising his ignoble act in a heap of dusty old prayer rugs. Love is a mirage, dear Minor, a vanishing flood, permanently baled out by man. Naturally Monsieur Uqba will look on his disappearance as scarcity value; a fine aphrodisiac. And the Comtesse? What is her life but an artful exercise in using up time? She will surely make some convenience of this misfortune. What are your views, Middle?'

Middle: 'It is bad enough if a wife or husband takes to the bottle – but to take to the bible – and all that peeling off shoes five times a day to pray . . . such a hotch-potch of mumbo jumbo, our Comtesse would never begin to keep up.'

Minor: 'And I assure you that when the Comtesse approached the love bed, she had innumerable other duties to keep up.'

Major: 'What do you mean, Minor?'

Minor: 'Pass.'

Major: 'Our Comtesse – always such a modest lady – had no inkling of the jealousy she was stirring up between the two males in her life.'

Minor: 'You mean Uqba and . . . ?'

Major: 'Louis-Loup. He came to adore her. Any extravagant behaviour sparked his need to protect her.'

Middle: 'I have had my own moments of concern. I have seen Louis stand alert in the garden, his ears cocked, his yellow eyes fixed on my window. The Comtesse and Monsieur Uqba were always excessively vocal, you understand. And I have feared that Louis would land in the bath itself, in one superhuman leap.'

Major: 'Mercifully, dear Middle, reality could not compete with your imagination. Let us relish the peace and quiet of the Comtesse home alone.'

Minor: 'She will be restless, worried over her romantic future. She likes to have a hat hung in the boudoir. It is Louis-Loup who will frame her future. Watch my space.'

The Comtesse woke each morning, sedately rested. Her breakfast tray was spirited on to her balcony. Little wicker baskets that secreted croissants in muslin; jams of apricots and myrtle and fig. They were subdued days, with the village, woods and lanes desolated by fire and water; a desultory chorus of hammers and drills and raucous yells rose from the bitter detritus. The Comtesse sat long on her balcony, lethargic, her restless desire quelled a space. Uqba had drained her; her hopes, her dreams, her love. Had she ever loved him? Each morning, Louis looked up at her from his pen. Each afternoon she walked him to the cove where he sat at her feet. On the sixth day after Uqba's departure, Madame Veuve handed her two letters, together with *Toulon Matin*. The central pages exuded fulsome praise as Monsieur le Curé commended the villagers for their discipline in face of the storm. The evacuation of their homes, without complaint, and their orderly file to the jetty. They had observed the 'Plan Alarm' commendably. There could have been no better reflection of *La Gloire de la France*. And there would be a reward . . . The Mayor continued the eulogy . . . thank the Lord! The vineyards, high in the hills, had been untouched by the débacle. His vignerons had even reported a full cellar of great vintages – there would be a party. The Comtesse digested this last with interest. The villa should be represented: Louis-Loup, Gustave, the two girls, herself and Madame Veuve. The party, in the time-honoured Place d'Armes would take place in two nights' time. The surrounding small cafés were already adjusting their awnings.

Madame Prunier, who had restored her demeanour and her choco-late-saturated premises, had also seen the notice. She took Venus, her young white Alsatian along to the butcher. His shop was empty and she and Venus were let into the coveted back room. Any gossip with the butcher was indicative of daily life back to normal. 'What a pleasure, Madame. You appear rejuvenated. All well with Venus? Some baby lambs' hearts for today?' He lowered his voice and Madame Prunier leant expectantly towards his face. Venus snuffled under the door where she had detected a dog in the slowly mounting queue.

'I must not keep you, Madame Prunier, but you have heard of the upheavals at the villa?'

She shrugged and waved her arms extravagantly. 'So be it,' was her succinct comment.

'But we lost the three goats to the fire,' he continued. 'That young dolt Gustave let them burn, and after all the best meats I have been fattening them on.'

'What a disgrace, Monsieur! They all died in the fire? The butcher lowered his voice to a hoarse whisper: 'It was the young wolf – he killed the best of the three . . .'

'Quel ennui, Monsieur, we should be worried for his future.' Venus was snorting hard beneath the door; it was time to go. Madame Prunier clutched at her leash and swept past the Comtesse and Louis-Loup, but not before the two interested parties had exchanged voluptuous sniffs.

Later in the morning, Christine, returned to her balcony, eyed her unopened letter from Uqba. But first she would comb her hair, paint her lips, dab her neck with scent. Sitting on her balcony, she slit the flimsy envelope with a fruit knife. Clearly not a long letter:

Fragrant one, I love you to the end. I have always a hard spot for you. I missed you when I stumbled from you – weighted down with misery and the stench of burning. But love is more important than happiness. We must not count our losses. But your Porquerolles is my loss – a world alien to my own culture and sensibilities; the dust and gloom of your criss-cross woods where every dark corner rounded on another dark corner, with the crunch of insects under my feet and the fear of rats leaping at my throat . . . I suffered, Christine. And to please my queen, I suffered her Louis-Loup. And then I left you and all those secret unhappinesses that I had shielded from you. Yet we remember the fun and games between us – hein? And I have succulent memories of Philomène and Gervaise – so soon to be ravaged by womanhood.

Here I languish in heat. My wives have become lumpy and tumescent; they are like heaving black trampolines. I have no energy to jump on them. It is you I crave and your strong white body that I know so well. Come and see me soon again. Here in my country there is shade and peace; the blue sweep of the Atlas mountains, the rich red soil and the camel to plough it with. Juniper groves, swaying palms, waves of sugar beet and yellow-skinned melons. Across the moorlands and dykes girls canter side-saddle on mules, their veils and skirts billowing, with donkeys swaying behind with their loaded panniers. Come to Fès with me, my dearest, lost Christine. See with me these vivid scenes of life under a sheltering sky. And we will look down from the city wall on the Medina, gold in the evening sun with its roofs of glazed emerald, pierced with minarets. Through giant palm trees and rose terraces and marble courts of frolicking fountains, we will stroll and breathe deeply in the orange groves. And we will love again. Fès possesses you; more than we can even possess each other. The muezzin at darkest dawn, you will find compelling. That winding, spiralling, strong, clear call would tempt my queen to become a Muslim; when all Fès is on tenterhooks and transfixed. In the final silence a cock crows, and then another . . .

But I must leave you ma mignonne to your Provençale life. Think kindly on me, my prized Christine. I now fly to Russia. Only remember: que je t'attends toujours. Je t'embrasse de loin en attendant.

Christine carefully folded the pages back into the envelope and shuddered gently. Never would she be bandaged in black. The bleeding sheep's heads in Tangier market swept through her mind. Yet she remembered the beauty of a fretted marble screen, and elegant fez, a mosaic, a mosque and a mule. Uqba's world was evocative and colourful, but had left her repelled and fearful. The second letter was from Paris, the writing unfamiliar . . . Antoine!

He had led an intoxicating summer with Hubert, his companion with the sock fetish, he reminded her. Their travels and antics had left him jaded; how he would savour a sojourn in her villa! What of her Moroccan? Was his name Uqba – from Tangier? A friend at the Russian consul had mentioned his name to Antoine. It appeared that her hero had a penchant for young girls; nothing paedophilic, she should understand, more poetic. He was also a dab hand at wheedling out more oil from Russia than his brief. And did she know of any village women who had the time and inclination to knit Hubert some socks?

Christine smiled, her head to one side. She might well feel inclined to have Antoine to stay. Philomène and Gervaise would certainly come to no harm with him.

Madame Veuve hovered in the bedroom door. And would the Comtesse be attending the celebration for the vineyards?

'Certainly, Madame Veuve. And you? You could take the two young girls? Tell me, Madame, is Gustave about?'

Gustave was walking Louis; he would soon return. Christine stood and gazed across to the silver screen of eucalyptus. And there she saw them. The frisking young wolf straining on the leash. It was clear that Louis needed more space, more freedom. At barely seven months, he was rearing for life – his own exploratory life – to become adventurous in wide open spaces; to find his own arc of independence. Christine sighed. She must let him go; let go of her love for this playful, rumbustious carnivore. Gustave and Louis looked up at her from the grass below.

He called to her, 'You wish, Madame, that Louis comes to the evening celebrations at Place d'Armes tomorrow?'

'Absolutely.' It was agreed. Gustave would keep him under the strictest control; he would put him on the new chain leash.

The following morning, settled on her balcony, the Comtesse motioned to Madame Veuve to come and sit with her.

'Madame Veuve, I fear for our Louis-Loup. He is heading for trouble, like a youth running into danger.'

Madame Veuve turned her head to the woods and the sun beyond. She recalled in her mind's eye that strange spring twilight when Philomène had seen the defenceless grey shape on the sand. It had become their little Louis; something to love. Now he must have his freedom. She looked down at the palm of her hand, flushed and sore from pulling on the leash. 'Madame, I have to agree with you. He is near full-grown; he should lead a life in the wild. What can we do?'

'We are agreed, Madame Veuve. That is a beginning. I will talk with Gustave.'

'Perhaps, Madame, Monsieur Boudin, the vet could advise you?'

'You understand, Madame Veuve, I do not like so much Monsieur Boudin; I prefer Monsieur *le boucher.*'

'I understand, Madame La Comtesse,' murmured Madame Veuve and left the balcony. And what the old lady had deduced from the Comtesse's preference for the butcher, was her province alone.

Christine leant over her balustrade and sobbed. Her emotions had been seized, twisted and squeezed these last summer weeks. The halcyon days that she had envisaged with Uqba – of swimming, walking, fishing, laughing and loving – had never quite evolved. Oh! But they had had their moments. Now her other love was to lope out of her life. But she had learned from relationships to respect their unique allotted space and that tantamount right to bolt.

11

At six o'clock, Gustave was waiting again beneath her balcony. Rosette, harnessed to the *charette*, her hooves varnished and her mane crimped, stood expectantly. The Comtesse and Madame Veuve leant on Gustave's forearm and stepped up into the worn black leather seats. Louis crept out from beneath the front seat and jumped to the ground. Gustave held him on a long coursing leash as he charged alongside up the road, like a carriage dog. The Comtesse cast an approving eye on her necklace of agate stones as large as plovers' eggs. They glowed gold and red and translucent; a present from Uqba, naturally. She heard his voice: 'Agate has the property to soothe reddened, desert-scanning eyes.' And then 'Voila!' called Gustave as he waved to Philomène and Gervaise on the near corner of Place d'Armes. He motioned them to follow the Square round to Café de la Poste, and drew Louis up into the *charette*. It was arranged that Gustave should stay with him in a quiet corner until the crowd had settled. Christine sensed an implicit awareness between her and Gustave; his tall, slim, sinewy body had set her musing; she saw him on a trapeze, his dark, straight hair swaying above her, the shining eyes, his curling lips. The café terrace set beside *église Sainte Anne* was filling rapidly with villagers eager for a free glass of wine. (It was rumoured that the Mayor had been heavily criticised by the vignerons for his boast of plenty of Domaine de L'Ile – *premier cru.*)

The Comtesse and the girls found a front table wedged in a corner. A game of pétanque was causing excitement; the iron clad balls gleamed in the evening sun as they thudded on the sand. The Comtesse noticed the odious young man from 'Aux Journaux', hunched cross-legged beside Sainte Anne. His head under a tent of red hair, he was playing a guitar; and quite plausibly, the Comtesse had to admit, as he strummed at 'Le Temps des Cerises'. Windows and balconies were looped with lavender and roses and paper decorations. Trestle tables displayed potpourris pungent with herbs and spices; there were lavender bags and bundles and sachets; lavender oils and honey; vinegars and mustard. A brazier close by glowed with the bitter sweet detritus of lavender stalks and dried eucalyptus. The Comtesse breathed in the aromatic fragrances and sipped her wine. It was dusk, and lights swept the square with shadows and secrets. Madame Veuve whispered to herself: 'It is time those girls returned to the table.' And now the Comtesse detected wafts of onions from the *pissaladiera* and the rich tomato stew of the ratatouille. What were Philomène and Gervaise about? 'Here we are!' Laughing with shared jokes, the two girls edged towards them. The *garçon* planted a bottle of white Domaine de L'Ile and *eau minerale* on their table, with a dish of olives. Minutes later the party was joined by Gustave.

But Louis? Was he all right?

'Do not worry, Mesdames. Louis is securely fastened.' Gustave explained how he had attached him in the front of the *charette*, with the new chain, collar and leash, and had left him sleeping. The Comtesse beckoned Gustave to sit beside her and noticed that Madame Prunier was in the adjoining café. Venus sat on the sand at her feet, panting. 'You see that Alsatian dog? A fine specimen, would you not agree?' ventured the Comtesse.

But Gustave pointed out to her the broad chest and short legs and that the Alsatian was a recent breed; but a supremely intelligent dog, he conceded. 'If Louis was stood beside her,' he continued, 'we could compare his slim, narrow frame and long legs with her sturdy bulk.'

There was much cheering and clinking of glasses from the pétanque players and repeated cries of '*Le corso! Le corso!*' A band struck up to welcome a float, swaying with maids in lavender garlands, drawn by two horses from the vineyard. The pretty girls tossed out their bouquets and be-ribboned sprigs and posies to the admiring crowd. The band tuned in with songs of the troubadours, of chivalry and courtly love, as Place d'Armes became crowded with dancers. And then he heard it. Gustave froze. Louis' whimper-howl was unmistakable. Again and again, that wail of pain; of anguish and fear. As Gustave struggled through the crowds to reach the *charette*, the howling stopped. He caught his breath, half-sobbing as he flung himself against the door. Louis' chain collar and leash lay coiled and empty, in the dark. Gustave snatched them up, as a withered crone crept out from the gloom.

'He escaped you, Monsieur. Two boys have let him go. The howls of a wolf are terrible, Monsieur.' She came up close to him; a grey, wizened face of doom. Through her missing teeth, she hissed the French proverb: 'A wolf's tooth worn by a child protects it from night fears.' Gustave shuddered and called to her over his shoulder:

'Wolf skin shoes make children strong and brave.' He heard her morbid cackle. To the villa or back to Place d'Armes? It was then that he heard cries of alarm from the crowd, and their inter-mittent squeals, as though Louis was weaving his swift passage between them, on, on, to the light and music and space of Place d'Armes.

And now where was Gustave? The Comtesse had not been aware of his disappearance. But Madame Veuve had also heard the long doleful whimpers. 'He has gone to get Louis, Madame.' And then Louis was right before them; on Place d'Armes. He was pawing the sand and sniffing it in a mad frenzy. The pétanque players stood aside in a stunned silence. There was a hush from the cafés alongside, when a white Alsatian stepped into the arena. Skittish and playful, Venus backed up towards the young wolf. Louis danced around her and flopped on his front quarters, wagging his luxuriant tail. They set about licking each other's coats; anal sniffing soon followed. Venus, in a *coup de grâce*, lifted her own tail and turned to the side. Louis fell upon her with gratuitous whimpering, moaning and growling. There was an aghast silence from their disparate audience; transfixed with expec-tation, it held its tongue. Venus backed closer, making her mount acceptance clear as Louis with one bound clasped his forelegs in front of her hips.

'Bravo! Bravo!' went up the cry as Louis mounted her with thrust after thrust. He changed his weight, in a rapid dance, from one hind leg to the other. The Comtesse, who was as hypnotised as the rest, was reminded of a golfer, sizing up his ball on the tee. Gustave whispered to her that the thrusting was part of locking into the vagina, to couple the two dogs in a tie. And then there was pandemonium. Madame Prunier screamed for the release of her Venus; and there was a valiant move by some hefty men to wrench the two beasts apart. But Monsieur Boudin, the vet, strode authoritatively on to the square. There was a hush.

'You see these two animals – *in flagrante delicto* – it is a wonderful thing! To be admired! I should explain to you . . .'

'Be quiet, Monsieur Boudin!' shrilled Madame Prunier. 'I am the mother of Venus. It is a catastrophe for her! Especially with a wolf. It is disgusting!'

There was a hiss of water as the *pompiers* discharged their jet sprays on the two animals. But they remained oblivious in their tie. Monsieur Boudin explained to the bemused spectators that Venus and Louis would remain held-fast in their coupling for another ten minutes at the least. He lowered his voice confidentially: 'It is the bitch's sphincter muscle, you understand.' The *pompiers* put down their sprays and Madame Prunier regained her seat; sodden and sobbing she informed all around her that this was the worst night of her life. Her hair piece, dislodged by the soaking, slumped in sympathy down the side of her face.

Gustave, with some cajoling, had eased on Louis' collar as the spent quadrupeds fell apart. He led the wolf across the square and through the silenced crowd, parting before them like the Red Sea. Madame Prunier was ensconced in her seat, steaming with rage, her wet hair and her odiferous Venus. A shocked lull fell over the night's celebrations. The clock tower of Sainte Anne chimed nine o'clock, which prompted an impromptu announcement from the Mayor: 'Animals have no shame. Always happy to celebrate in public under an open sky – even the sexual act. I tell you, we should show animals kindness and sympathy.'

'We are all of us animals!' cried an enthusiast.

'And we share the same joys . . .' conceded another.

'But this wolf could kill and eat a baby in its pram. That would be atrocious . . .' This last drew silence and fear from the villagers, but their attention soon reverted to the onion soup and the strands of melted cheese swaying from their spoons.

Gustave had successfully removed Louis from the lively scene and had run him back to his pen. He stroked him and murmured consolingly; the exhausted animal was soon asleep. Returning to Place d'Armes, he found the Comtesse, Madame Veuve and Philomène, subdued and anxious to leave. And where was Gervaise? She had other things to do, explained Philomène briefly. On return to the villa, they crept across the lawn and looked down lovingly on their fallen hero. Philomène fell to her knees beside him. Madame Veuve went to collect chairs and glasses on the terrace. The Comtesse asked Gustave to open a bottle of wine, subconsciously conferring on him a sophisticated role. Madame Veuve made lavender tea with an optional dash of cognac. What was to be done with Louis-Loup? His behaviour had been normal and healthy although Gustave was compelled to point out that a young wolf, nearing seven months, was rarely so sexually advanced.

'He wants space and excitement, like any young man,' wailed the Comtesse. 'He needs a wide, open air life, the chance to hunt at speed.'

'You are right, Madame.' Gustave looked at her with assurance. 'Louis needs his liberty – and soon.'

'When and how?' the Comtesse sighed deeply. It seemed an intractable problem.

'Listen to the bird,' called Philomène. The party listened, mesmerised by the nightingale.

'He sings for Louis,' said the girl and everybody felt calmer.

'Tomorrow is another day,' advised Gustave sagely. 'I will give you a good idea for Louis' freedom. A captive life for him would be a tragedy.' He stood up from the table and walked away, tall and commanding, without a backward glance, to the front gate. Christine, despite all the evening's harrowing distractions, admired his retreating body.

The next afternoon, Antoine made his surprise entry. Seeing the parched lawn, the brittle woods, the wilted roses and the '*dégagé*' air hanging over the villa, he suggested it might be easier if he stayed at Hôtel de la Poste. A glance at Louis, erect in his pen with pricked ears, had finally decided him. Madame Veuve was dispatched to the butcher to find veal sweetbreads for dinner. It was one of Madame's favourite dishes to prepare. She would wrap each *ris de veau* in larding pork and strips of truffle. And she sensed that Monsieur Antoine would prove more amenable than Monsieur Uqba, and a more suitable influence on the Comtesse. Gustave had also been invited to supper; in his capacity as chief adviser on Louis' future, the Comtesse had explained to her.

Madame Veuve arrived at '*L'Agneau aux deux têtes*', and despite the queue, was sidled off to the back room. The butcher wiped the blood of a rabbit off his hands and stared at Madame Veuve with amazement.

'What a débâcle! Our Louis-Loup! The whole village talks of him. Some of us understand his behaviour, of course, Madame Veuve, but . . .' The butcher blew out his shining red cheeks and, leaning towards her, confided in a low voice that the village wanted Louis away; that his life could be in danger.

'*Dieu!*' cried Madame Veuve and stumbled out to queue for her *ris de veau*.

A similar conversation was taking place between Madame Prunier and Monsieur Boudin, the vet. Venus, resplendent in her white fur, had sauntered archly into the premises. Madame Prunier, nervously patting her newly washed hair piece, followed her charge into Monsieur Boudin's private rooms.

'Good morning, Madame Prunier! And how is your beautiful Venus?'

'Monsieur Boudin. You know perfectly well that my Venus was violated by that dirty wolf. He made an intrusion, Monsieur Boudin, a gross intrusion. For me, it was a disgusting show and completely unacceptable.'

Monsieur Boudin stood up behind his desk to his full modest height. He found Madame Prunier intimidating.

'But, Madame – has it not occured to you that, for Venus, this sexual act was altogether agreeable? Louis-Loup is quite a catch for Venus; a well brought up young man, tutored by Madame Veuve herself – and fed on the best rabbits, lambs' hearts, tripe – I assure you, he is a superb specimen.'

Madame Prunier squirmed in her seat. 'Monsieur Boudin, Louis-Loup is the wrong specimen for my Venus and unsuitable for this village. He is a wolf, she an Alsation. The two are incompatible.'

'Incompatible, why, Madame? *Pour la route de la joyeuse entrée?* I was standing close to their coupling and I assure you, Venus was enjoying herself – enormously – Madame! Finally, there was no danger. Louis is a young wolf. At barely seven months, he appears adult but he has no sexual maturity. Venus is still *intacta*.' Madame Prunier looked piqued. What was the matter with the woman? She looked up at him with an expression of mock tragedy. She had not wished her Venus to become *'pleine'* without her direct guidance, Monsieur Boudin should kindly understand. But now that Venus had availed herself so abundantly, Madame Prunier wished her every happiness. The seasoned vet looked at her closely. Did she now wish her Venus pregnant? 'Madame, we must wait and see. It is possible that for Venus and Louis, we shall witness an immaculate conception after all! He chose not to divulge to Madame Prunier that Venus was on heat on the night of their coupling; his practised sense of smell had made no doubt of that.

Monsieur Boudin finally extended his hand. Madame Prunier had tired him. He suggested she and Venus come back in a week's time. Madame Prunier jutted out her chin and pursed her lips.

'Thank you, Monsieur Boudin; until next week.' As he walked them to the door, he noted Venus was swaying her hindquarters in a provocative manner. 'Take care of Venus outside the home, Madame. We would not wish to encourage more suitors.'

12

Madame Veuve had contrived a ravishing setting for dinner on the balcony. White linen mats with a froth of embroidered borders were adorned with the best silver. The wine glasses shone with her extra polishing. It was a still evening with the tobacco plants and petunias pulsating their scent. The aroma of sweetbreads, wine and herbs stole up the stairs. She had extricated a forgotten faïence bowl from the kitchen cupboard; cramming it to overflowing with white verbena, she placed it in the centre of the sitting-room. Madame Veuve liked Monsieur Antoine. A pity Gustave had been invited to muddy the scene. She caught sight of the Comtesse through the door; tanned from the summer, in a white silk shift and pearls, with her hair scooped up and curled on her head. She looked 'raffinée' thought Madame Veuve, just right for Monsieur Antoine, who she remembered to be a fastidious gentleman. The Comtesse lit tilleul candles in blown glasses around the balcony. Wafts of lime blossom enveloped her as she leant back in her chair, her eyes momentarily closed to the winds of change.

And then Antoine's voice below; his step on the stairs and her peace broken. She sat on languorously as he stepped into the scented bower. 'You look a dream, my dear Christine. You are ethereal tonight. The vicissitudes of your summer have honed you to even greater perfection.'

'That'll do, Antoine, my dear. I have a dry white wine from La Croix-Valmer.' He poured them both a glass.

'We have a third guest?' Antoine glanced at the elegant table setting.

'Yes, my gamekeeper will join us. He is principally my wolf-handler; he is now the most essential man in my life,' confessed Christine provocatively. And as though to dispel any doubt on the matter, Gustave strode through to the balcony. He had shaved well, bathed, and cleaned his fingernails and graciously accepted his glass of wine. A tall good-looking young man; Antoine approved his lean-limbed body and the wave of brown hair that flopped to his forehead.

'How do you do, Monsieur Gustave?'

'Bien, Monsieur,' returned Gustave.

Christine motioned they should all sit. 'It is our Louis-Loup. He has to go.'

Antoine took a long sip of wine.

'A natural progression for a young wolf, my dear. You have clearly been an excellent chaperone through his pup-hood. What has prompted this sanguine assessment?' Christine invited Gustave to explain.

'Monsieur Antoine, you are a clever man and you understand that a healthy wolf does not attack a man. But man is afraid and ignorant. The wolf has no accepted place in the ecological system. Yet everybody is agreed that the wolf has a right to exist . . .'

'Indeed!' interjected Antoine. '*Canis lupus* – a sociable animal; the progenitor of man's best friend; the surrogate mother to the sucklings Romulus and Remus, the fabled founders of Rome.'

'But Louis-Loup can no longer live on Porquerolles. The village has become too tame for his needs; and he has become too erratic for theirs. They sense danger.' Gustave lowered his voice. 'We have had much poaching of *rouget* and mullet from the creeks. And we have had incidents, Monsieur Antoine; a savaged goat, a fucked Alsatian.'

'But it is normal to roam, to fish and to hunt, and totally normal for a young man to chase women and good victuals.'

Antoine's valiant support was interrupted by Madame Veuve and Philomène bearing hot tureens. Philomène lifted the lids with studied aplomb, as veils of delectable steam drew the party to the table. She ran down the stairs, calling 'we need more wine – white and red, Grandmamma.' And as the old lady wrested the corks, Philomène whispered to her hoarsely, 'He is so handsome tonight.'

'Yes, dear; Monsieur Antoine?'

'No, I have eyes only for Gustave – do not mistake me!' She darted up the stairs with the bottles and to snatch another look at her hastily conceived idol. Monsieur Antoine was telling spicy tales of Porquerolles in the olden days. And what ever happened to that rollicking Anne Bonney? And the swarthy corsairs and the rape and pillage and plunder? Christine stirred herself languidly: 'It is said that Anne Bonney can be seen hanging in the tree tops like a Cheshire cat on a moonlit night . . .' She had heard it all before from Uqba.

'Dog comes, cat goes,' murmured Gustave enigmatically, as he leant back in his chair and scoured the moon. He explained to the party how a waxing half moon takes the shape of a 'D' and a waning moon becomes a 'C'. Philomène was offered half a glass of Domaine de L'Ile rouge, diluted with water. She insinuated her slim body beside Gustave and admired his fingers, his wrists, his neck and chin – his nose . . . Christine, seated on the other side, yearned to rub her toes up inside his trouser legs but mercifully restrained herself. Antoine stood to make a flowery exit and Gustave followed. He liked Antoine, and as they walked back along Rue de la Ferme, they talked of Louis-Loup and Gustave's 'grand plan'.

Major: 'Our Louis-Loup has taken a leaf out of his Comtesse's book. Her roller-coaster life has caught up with him.'

Middle: 'That tasty white Alsatian saw him coming and Louis jumped to it.'

Minor: 'Jumped, Middle, or humped?'

Middle: 'Louis-Loup knew what he was about.'

Major: 'But he is sexually mature already? The mix of wolf and Alsatian suggests a heady concoction.'

Minor: 'Your description evokes some rich ragoût – flavoured with aromatic herbs and spices. But now there is talk of our Louis-Loup having to be sent away.'

Middle: 'He needs his space and to be with his own kind.'

Minor: 'And our Comtesse? Where next does she put down her restless feet? With whom will she share her questing heart?'

Major: 'The Comtesse is a well-seasoned juggler of the cards. She will reshuffle the pack, pick up her cards and sort them.'

Minor: 'And then? If they all fall down?'

Middle: 'The Comtesse is a survivor; the descendant of a Maréchal de France, remember. I can see her now, by the woods, talking earnestly to Gustave. They stand close and together . . . so that Louis-Loup does not hear their plans.'

Minor: 'Gustave close to the Comtesse! Now he would need a lot of reshuffling.'

Major: 'Dear friends. I smell remnants of last night's *ris de veau*. Quieten down, I need to dream.'

*   *   *

The following evening, the Comtesse and Gustave went for an evening stroll through the pines. Louis ran between them, nose-stabbing playfully against their legs. 'He is ready for more,' observed Gustave. 'More space, more challenge, more variety. He grasps our mood. He is aware of the need for change.' Gustave looked down at her with a warning look. 'Wolves have an acute awareness of mood and changes around them. It is an extra sensory perception they have.'

'You know so much,' said the Comtesse admiringly. 'What is your plan for him? . . . and for us two,' she murmured in an aside.

They sat beside each other on a fallen tree trunk. Gustave told her of a learning centre for research purposes. An exploratory wolf sanctuary, on Mont Lozère, the highest granite peak in the Massif Central. He explained how it was designed with attention to the mental comfort and rehabilitation needs between wolf and man. 'Louis could contribute to wolf research,' he impressed upon her.

'You have been there?' she asked him, wide-eyed. He knew the keeper. There were nineteen wolves in residence with room for one more. Louis would have the freedom to run through a wide area of trees, clearings, and drinking pools with stone ledges. Climbing rocks and digging dens was encouraged for shelter and retreat. He would be intoxicated with his new life of 'semi-liberté'.

'With his charisma Louis-Loup would soon head the pack.' And so Gustave persuaded the Comtesse how Louis could make his first transitional leap to a life of freedom in the mountain wilds. They sat silent. The Comtesse's knee tingled as it brushed against Gustave's hard thigh. Louis lay stretched at their feet, snapping at flies and leaping up for the first falling autumn leaves. The Comtesse fell on her knees beside him. She rubbed her cheek on the ruff of his muscular mane. 'My happy savage,' she crooned. 'We have all loved you so. You have to get a life.'

Two evenings later, the Comtesse and Antoine returned from a walk to the cove – Louis' cove – to find Madame Veuve sobbing uncontrollably. 'He is finished – Louis is finished – he has been taken away; those men, two of them . . .' The distraught old woman gasped and hiccupped so hideously, the Comtesse feared she would choke. Madame Veuve heaved on a big breath and wheezed out tremulously: 'Louis was given an injection in the neck. Then Gustave . . .' Gustave! Where was Gustave? Madame Veuve explained that he had brought the two men in the dogcart to take Louis away. 'He is off to Toulon,' Gustave had told her 'to re-establish himself.'

That same afternoon an emotive rendezvous had unfolded between Madame Prunier and Monsieur Boudin. Boudin had braced himself beforehand with a substantial lunch at Hôtel de la Poste, aided with a half bottle of Domaine de L'Ile rouge. Madame Prunier had flounced into his private room, flushed and flustered.

'Bonjour, Madame Prunier. How is the beautiful Venus? She is in good health?'

'Not at all, Monsieur Boudin. Venus has become over-active.'

Monsieur Boudin looked alarmed. 'You mean she has found more admirers on Place d'Armes?'

Madame Prunier snorted in disdain. 'Venus is absorbed in her condition. She is *enceinte*.' (Was Madame herself having a phantom pregnancy?)

Leaning across Monsieur Boudin's desk, she told him in hushed tones how Venus had been quiet and withdrawn and had settled herself in a nest of dust and feathers under the bed. Whereupon

Monsieur Boudin stirred himself to rub and prod Venus' stomach. He straightened himself laboriously.

'Yes, you are right, Madame! She has little bumps already. Are you pleased?'

Yes, yes, Madame Prunier was at last happy; and Monsieur Boudin, fortified with his lunch, took it upon himself to pour out his scanty knowledge of 'wolf–dog hybridization'. It amused him how much he appeared to know; Madame Prunier clearly held him with new respect as he recounted how the dog sprang from the wolf. Monsieur Boudin continued, enunciating his words with relish: 'The wolf is the ancestor of all domestic dogs and fresh wolf blood used to be considered beneficial to all breeds – especially Alsatians.' Madame Prunier was delighted with Monsieur Boudin's effusions. 'And the pups?' she asked fearfully.

'The pups?' Monsieur Boudin dug deep in his memory as he recalled the pamphlet in the zoological library. 'But really superb pups, Madame. About five or six: some like the wolf; some like the dog. For example, there was a famous case – rather like your own, Madame – in the Abruzzi mountains. The same! A wolf and an Alsatian. Two pups were born as dogs, completely black, except for white spotting on the legs and chest. The rest were born as wolves, their hair grey and thick.' Madame Prunier shuddered with her conflicting emotions. And then her sanguine senses took a grip. 'Perhaps we might earn a little money?'

Monsieur Boudin extended his hand. 'For both of us, Madame . . . the publicity, the sale of the little ones . . .'

'But Monsieur, I would not wish the Porquerolles be burdened with my unwanted wolf cubs . . .'

'Don't fret Madame, it is very possible that the zoological park . . .' Monsieur Boudin pulled out his pocket-watch and allowed himself ten more minutes' talk on the progeny of Venus. In around sixty-three days Venus would whelp – at the start of December. Venus should perform her functions as a mother for the first month; a box with blankets under a table would give sufficient nestling. And now he would like to see Venus in a month's time for her check up. If she showed any signs of premature whelping – running in little circles, panting, whimpering – Madame was to call Monsieur immediately and he would come to assist. Madame Prunier looked most unnerved at the dramatic role into which her Venus had pitched her. (And what if she herself should start running in circles in a fit of panting and despair, would Monsieur Boudin assist her also?) And if Venus determined on staying in the nest beneath her bed? Madame Prunier saw herself, in her Egyptian lawn nightdress, at dead of night, squeezing under the mattress springs to assist her pretty one with her birth pangs. (And she should set aside a clean chemise in the event of M. Boudin's hasty arrival.) Her eyes gleamed . . .

'Madame Prunier, Madame Prunier – you follow me?' Monsieur Boudin helped his two charges to the door. Madame Prunier had appeared quite dazed with her mixed fortune. Females were so exhausting. He next plucked a lanky youth from the waiting-room, clutching a wicker cage.

13

Antoine was on his way to the villa to take Christine out to dinner. The sweet scent of chimney smoke hung in the evening air, as he walked thoughtfully along Rue de la Ferme. The vendange was underway; and with the horses' dung, the rumble of cart wheels, the sour juices from the wine presses, the familiar Provençale sounds and smells were released. And he thought on the pleasures of autumn and winter to come; in his beloved Paris, with her tree-lined avenues and ordered parterres and parks. He sighed, and he sighed for Christine. He must persuade her to return to Paris. She must not linger in that defunct villa, stumbling through the cold months, wrapped in shawls and disreputable memories. She needed to get a grip on a more conventional life as befitted her distinguished forebears. With his head swollen with sound advice, Antoine stood at the terrace door. Madame Veuve seated primly at the kitchen table with her evening glass of Domaine de L'Ile beckoned him in.

'Antoine!' Christine called from her dressing-table. 'I am a little late – please help yourself.' He poured a glass of cooled Italian vermouth and bit tenderly on a black olive, so succulent and firm; he took another and threw the stones into the twilight. As he was cogitating on the luxury of relieving himself over the balustrade, she wafted in. 'What wonders, my dear Christine, you are truly ravishing this evening.' She swayed towards him in lilac chiffon and sniffed voluptuously at the bowl of white tobacco plants.

'Antoine – it is a special evening for me; to be taken to a restaurant. Where have you decided?'

'But it is for you to choose, my dear. We have the Auberge Chez Maurice, in the village, renowned for the lobster au whisky, or I should take you to Mas du Langoustier; it is their season for pigeon and pheasant. *"Pigeonneau en compote," "Pigeonneau à la diable"* . . .'

Christine listened intently to the delectable alternatives. 'What is that – sauce *diable?*'

Antoine described to her a concoction of mustards, red pepper, eucalyptus honey and wine vinegar . . .

'Perfect! I am starving already.'

Thirty minutes later they were trundling through the darkening pines in a buggy. These sinister woods; how Uqba had feared them – was that him? She had seen a tall figure in white, swaying between two trunks. They dined on the terrace screened by eucalyptus in the light of the rising moon. A floodlit fort was perched high on the distant point. A carafe of chilled Vin Mousseux and a bottle of Domaine de L'Ile rouge awaited them on the table. Antoine observed Christine approvingly; how distinguished she had become. What could be her future? She must not fritter her life away; already past middle age, elderly even, a crone . . .

'How old are you?' he asked abruptly 'It must be a trial for you to be so beautiful.'

Christine, shrugging her shoulders, sipped her white wine and murmured, 'Antoine, I am used to it.' Would she be returning soon to Paris? How would she occupy herself? After the rough

115

and tumble of her summer, Paris would seem tedious? He leaned towards her, talking hurriedly before the appearance of their pigeon, wreathed in its sauces and its retinue. Might she not read and reflect – immerse herself in, for example, Alfred de Musset, the poet of *l'amour* and *la jeunesse*? His '*Scènes de la Vie Privée et Publique des Animaux*' – *magnifique*!

Christine looked blank and disorientated. Antoine, undaunted, tried another tack.

'But of course! The Princess Christine Belgiojoso! Your ancestor – what a history!' He poured out a eulogy of the Princess's beautiful wide eyes, her marble-white skin, her sense of the lugubrious, of the ridiculous – and she was so clever! Balzac even saw her in her tea-gown with ink stains on her fingers. Was she a comedienne? A politico? A poetesse? A joyous beauty? Or quite without humour; cold, spiteful and malicious? The waiter brought to their table *amuse-gueules*; a *timbale de langouste*, set in a ruff of dill and pickled cucumber. Christine took a deep breath and a long draught of wine.

'An extraordinary woman, certainly. She enjoyed young men. And once a corpse was even found in a bedroom cupboard.'

'A corpse?'

'Yes, in her house, near Milan.' Christine talked on vivaciously. Her ancestor, the Princess, was considered as macabre as she was romantic. The male corpse, identifiable as Stelzi, an *amitié amoureux*, was found in a cupboard in good condition. He had been embalmed and dressed in the normal dress for a corpse in a cupboard. As Antoine mused over Christine's alarming tale, she continued: 'It was the cardinal desire of the Princess always to triumph over death. A taxidermist, experienced in stuffing crocodiles but not *au fait* with the human body, was nonetheless persuaded to stuff Stelzi. He was consigned again to the armoire and forgotten, to be finally confronted by a startled gendarme – "*nez-à-nez.*"'

Antoine beamed at Christine, over their pigeon. Now she was talking. Had she been researching the Princess? Absorbing herself in the life of another? Clearly she did not warm to the woman. Antoine had seen a portrait of her, by Henri Lehmann, the society portraitist. He described her to Christine: 'A beautiful, cold, white face, penetrating dark eyes glistening like olives, a faultless nose, wide lips and long fingers. Her thick dark hair parted and coiled up and away from the face.' Christine shuddered. She found La Belgiojoso a disturbing woman.

And her Princess had taken refuge at Porquerolles? enquired Antoine.

'Yes, that is true. In 1830 she escaped to Porquerolles. She had been exhausted by her support for the *Risorgimento*, the Liberation of Italy, and her work in the anti-Austrian movement. She found calm on Porquerolles. With the gentle climate and the joys of nature, she felt revived. But she became bored with the quiet life. She was only twenty-five years old and full of restless youth. After a few months she returned to Paris.' Antoine, engrossed in the tale, wondered where the Princess had stayed on the island. 'It is not known,' said Christine. 'It is a mystery. Perhaps she stayed at my villa. The young woman came and went without a trace. There are many ghosts in our woods,' continued Christine, abstractedly, 'and around our rocks and coves. The corsairs and their molls and Bonaparte's volunteers; soldiers from Africa and America, galley slaves and criminals chained in pairs. And, Antoine . . .' she caught him round the wrist, 'sometimes, I see Uqba swaying in the woods; his dark hair blowing, his white *jallaba* fastened to his body by the wind . . .'

The waiter hovered. Was everything to the Comtesse's pleasure?

She bowed her head and savoured her last mouthfuls. Their glasses were refilled. Antoine was surprised by Christine's anecdotal knowledge of the Princess. Their plates were cleared and the dessert menu proffered. Christine sat back in her chair, marvelling on the full moon; the cicadas, the doves, the murmur from the surrounding guests lulled her to a pleasant lethargy.

'I have another story about the Princess Belgiojoso,' promised Antoine. 'It can accompany our dessert.' With their orange and almond cake and whipped cream, Antoine began: 'Alfred de Musset met your forebear, Christine Belgiojoso around 1836. For the Princess it was a platonic fondness, but she was ever a consummate flirt. For de Musset she was a great impact on his life; he was deeply affected by her. They say that his *amours*, George Sand, Comtesse Marie d'Agoult and all the successive procession of comtesses and marquises, were diminished by comparison.'

'And she was kind to him when he was ill, I believe,' interrupted Christine.

'You are right! In 1840, de Musset became gravely ill with a swollen breast. The Princess visited him on his sick bed and he would allow her to spoon-feed him syrup. But there was an incident that you, Christine, would relish. A near collision between the Prince Belgiojoso and his parted wife – in Paris at a restaurant in Montparnasse; a restaurant frequented for its private rooms. De Musset had chosen the same venue for his intimate lunch with the Princess. When the Prince heard that de Musset was upstairs with an unknown lady, he suggested to the maître d' they might join them. De Musset had trouble keeping the Prince away. When both parties were safely seated in separate rooms, the Princess fled the building.'

'And when did their romantic attachment end?' asked Christine. She remembered de Musset had described it as *'une rapture provoquée'*.

'They parted in 1842. Mortified by her ultimate indifference, de Musset published a poem – it was his flagrant hint at her premature death.

Sur une morte et n'a point réçu
Elle faisait semblant de vivre.
De les mains est tombé le livre
Dans lequel elle n'a rien lu.'*

Antoine quoted to Christine the last verse as they sipped their bitter coffee.

'Tell me, my dear Christine, you have been researching these distinguished characters and their escapades. Will you write a book?' Again he imagined her, absorbed in her studies, off Rue Castiglione, her desk crenellated with the books of her research.

'Perhaps, eventually,' she conceded. But her total commitment now was to Louis-Loup, to visit him, to check on his progress at the wolf research centre.

'It is designed as a learning centre both for wolf and man; to assist their rehabilitation,' she explained briefly. Gustave had already visited him and reported that Louis was noted for his charisma. Christine smiled proudly and lovingly into her coffee. And Antoine wondered if this fleeting show of adoration was for the wolf or the gamekeeper.

It was a week since Louis-Loup had been taken from the villa. To Madame Veuve it had appeared a scandalous abduction. For

* On death and nothing achieved.
Yet she pretended to be alive.
From her hands fell the book.
In which she had not read a thing.

the Comtesse it was a hole in the heart; she was a mother pining for her boy at primary school. The autumn swooped down on Porquerolles. The sand on Place d'Armes was sucked up by the mistral and whirled in eddies. The pétanque balls were boxed up for the winter and the players, throwing their arms in the air, shuffled off for beer at 'Le Bonaparte'. The faded awnings flapped in the querulous gusts and blew their dust over the table tops. Fruit stalls were overturned, their wares tossed across pavements and gutters, to be sniffed at disdainfully by cats and pigeons. The fractious breezes were an irritant; shutters banged, hats and hair were tugged askew and horses shimmied sideways.

Antoine looked from his hotel room on to a grey, puckered sea. A few fishing boats bounced on the scudding water; others were shored up on the beach with sails hauled in. Cicadas had given way to sea gulls; wheeling and screaming, they dived over the port in a dog fight. A serried line of palm trees alongside the jetty waved imperiously. It seemed to Antoine they were bidding him to depart; to let go. In a frenzy he packed his two tan-leather oblong cases with their handles and hinges. He would quit by the afternoon boat. He wrote hastily to Christine, assuring her of his lasting admiration. 'Paris awaits you,' he promised her. He shook his head with mild despair; she was clearly heading for disaster. Chasing after a young wolf, a gamekeeper and that dissolute rogue – the Moroccan – where could it all lead? Holed up with that arcane *gardienne*, slurping on *bouillabaisse* together at the kitchen table; weathering the dark winter nights of dripping trees and that wearisome shuffle of the sea in the cove. He had failed her dismally. He had not persuaded her to return to Paris, to busy herself with literary pursuits. Alfred de Musset! She had spurned him as a subject of research and scrutiny. But he himself, Antoine, would write on de Musset. He would immerse himself in de Musset's exquisite '*Proverbes*', in his romanticism and in his devastating good looks and languor. Such elegance and erudition would prove an agreeable antidote to his chaotic Hubert – Hubert! Collecting his cases, Antoine clattered down the stairs of the Hôtel de la Poste and struggled across Place d'Armes to Le Bonaparte. As he swallowed a large cognac to settle his stomach, he remembered Hubert's request for socks. Swaying through the cluster of stalls, Antoine found a sturdy pair in mustard, purporting to have been knitted in Skegness.

The following morning the Comtesse and her gamekeeper, Gustave, also sailed to Toulon. An exquisite morning – to augur well, they hoped and believed. She felt suspended in a capsule of blue and gold light. She had so much to give: to Louis, to Gustave. As they were driven up high and far beyond to the heart of the bare and bouldered mountain range, she prayed that Louis might still know her. The car stopped finally at the Exploratory Wolf Sanctuary. She was aware of a great silence. Pens of wire netting and steel soared into the chestnut trees. The Comtesse stepped out hesitantly towards new horizons.

PART TWO

En Semi-Liberté

14

I see my lady. She stands by the acclimatisation pens. 'No Dogs Allowed'. She searches for me; Gustave also. He sees me and walks to the transition holding area. I have moved up a pen. I am well settled. My mates watch idly as I stalk to my lady. The wolf's fore paws have five toes but the little toe is not put to the ground. Our hind paws have only four toes. And now I smell her; that indelible smell of her skin and hair and breath. A scrum of joy charges through me. Now she sees me; she wants to touch me, to croon over me. I sashay beside the steel netting, and the keeper slides open the gate. My nostrils widen as I wrinkle my muzzle. My tail wags gently as I raise my paw. My lady squeezes it and I am electrified. I butt and nuzzle her warm waist. It is a lie that a wolf has no love. After time apart, wolves greet each other in an ecstasy. Any separation from a mother induces much hugging and licking on recovery. My lady was my playmate; Madame Veuve was my loving nurse and feeder. There was complicity between us. A *force majeure*.

Now they talk together and look at me. The keeper is pleased. He wants to keep me. I sashay back and forth and scoop hungrily at the salt-lick. The keeper looks closely at my lady and Gustave and says in a slow, clear voice: 'A wolf's protection is a man's protection.' He explains that my new home is a learning centre, a mutual exploratory sanctuary for man and wolf; a place of freedom and peace and runs through the woods; a place of mutual comfort for a wolf's rehabilitation with man. As he speaks, I remember how Madame Veuve would kneel beside me as I lay deep in my box of straw, kissing my closed eyes. When I grew older, she had murmured: 'The wolf signifies both a fear and fascination for men.' The keeper intimates to my departing friends that I will benefit under his care; he lets us walk together through the fir trees and oak. We pass drinking pools and climb to the rocky uplands. I see sheep in a sheltered field below and chestnut cows, their white horns dipped in black. An ancient stone village with its chapel and painted tower is clustered between the steep rock gorges; the river meanders deep and green through shores of whitened shale.

'Louis-Loup will be happy here,' says the Comtesse. She looks to Gustave for assurance. And I know that I have found my feet. They leave me with the keeper; the woods, the rocks, the trees in the wind and the spaces beyond my pen. My winter coat is growing; the thick, gold fur is ruffled and smoothed in the breezes; my back has dark grey marking and my underbelly is white. A ruff protects my neck; to the back of my neck, I can raise a secret tuft of fur in warning. My abundant tail will furl and unfurl, lift and lower, and reflect my mood. We wolves have a distinct de-lineation on the mask, to convey each emotion. The slanting set of the amber eyes is framed and shaded; the ear and the jaw is similarly emphasised. Anger, hunger, intent to attack, are written in clear lines on the face of a wolf.

It is daunting to step into this new world alone. But I am aware of the singular life I have left behind and am ready for the company of my kind. It was the cubs who first introduced me to Marco. As I stood stiff and dazed from my long journey up the hill roads and forests from Toulon, I was knocked to the ground. The two cubs had rolled into me in a ball of fur, nibbling joyously at each other. Chasing and kicking against themselves, they had not noticed me slap in their way. Marco trotted over from the far corner of the pen; he tapped my head with his paw and licked behind my ear, a form of toilettage I was later told and an implicit welcome to the clan. Marco is my good, close friend. He and his father were taken into the reserve, as they escaped poachers in the Italian Alps. He has introduced me to the clan from Mongolia, who were saved from fur trappers, and a few Polish wolves who were donated by zoos. We are a disparate group but there is a distinguishable social order to observe, which Marco explains to me. The dominant alpha couple are the Mongolians, with their four cubs and their four clan subordinates, to include the 'sous-chef' and his female. This beta couple hope for alpha command in three years. The Polish clan numbers eight, leaving Marco and his father and myself, Louis-Loup. Marco-père is permanently hot and fatigued. He is old at twelve years and spends the heat of the day on his back, cooling his genitals. Marco promises me that his father is a formidable howler; his timbre carries over twelve kilometres.

The keepers come with our feed, an agreeable interruption. This evening it is a meat feed. Huge, sumptuous lumps of mutton, pork and beef are thrown to us. The sanctuary is given meat from the slaughterhouse. We are given such a feed three times a week and are tossed dry vitamin biscuits and meaty titbits frequently. It is a strong communication between man and wolf – this tossing and gobbling of feed. And the sanctuary motto – 'Obesity in a wolf does not exist' – is understood.

Marco tells me that we are now ready to be released into the open park; the Mongolian and Polish clans and ourselves. We anticipate this semi-liberté with huge excitement. We will dig a den, find favourite rocks, drink from pools and howl to the moon. The gates are pulled apart and we amble out to the woods and clearings, dazed and curious at this sudden turn in our lives. Marco and I settle in a fringe of fir trees. Before us swoop and swell rough plains where round stone boulders crouch like animals. Marco-père pads up to us. He promises howling practice if the weather holds. Our release from the holding pen has renewed his energies. The sun lowers on the grazing plateaux below, where sheep and goats and their tinkling bells are sheltered by drystone walls. And I strain to see the glinting gold of distant streams. I also note a shepherd's hut; a small, square stone shed with a gaping entrance. I stare at this black hole so far below me. It stands as an open invitation, to me alone; one day, one night, the shed with the black hole will be waiting.

The Mongolian clan trots past us. Marco-père expects they have decided on their settlement. He explains to us the importance of clan hierarchy, and the discipline of manners. Courtesy to the keepers and taking your turn quietly at the feed is paramount. The alpha male and female take first pick; they regurgitate the crushed meat up through the oesophagus for their cubs; all cubs lick and feed from their elders' mouths. Whenever a little one is hungry he will nuzzle a clan member, sucking and nibbling on the lips for nourishment. Two of the Mongolian cubs died, Marco-père tells us; soon after birth. Why? we ask him. How? The mother had been given space by the stream to hollow out a den; a deep hole of soft earth was scooped out from the roots of a fallen tree. She was well protected by a fence and regular visits from a keeper. Marco watched her preparations from the far corner of the holding pen. She panted painfully as her girth grew. Moving in clumsy circles, she drank each evening from the stream; a nursing mother needs much water. She had also saved small pieces of meat thrown to her by the keeper. She had urinated on each morsel, to denote ownership, and buried them separately, in wait for the birth. Six pups were born to her, at irregular intervals through the night. She bit off and ate each umbilical cord. Her long warm tongue was kept busy cleaning the newborn. Marco-père lowered his voice and continued confidentially. 'She later told me that her tongue was so sore and ached as she licked the pups' tummies to help them urinate. Her alpha male had waited beside the den; hour after hour. He did not dare enter; he just waited and waited.'

Why did two of the pups die? 'They were the last born and weak from the start. The moist roots of the fallen tree became infested with lice and other parasites; with all her patience and cajoling, the mother could not come to suckle the pups with her immunising milk. She knew her limitations and she was exhausted. On the third evening she took her two dying scraps and buried them at a small distance. She marked this grave with urine, in the prospect of a small future meal. You could define this sad story as a case of lupine 'natural selection'; a pragmatic example of the survival of the fittest.' Marco-père rolls on to his back. We have tired him with our curiosity. We skulk around the fir trees and drink at a pond. The water is awash with the blood red of the setting sun. The Polish cubs, together with their beta couple, have grouped around us. There is a sense between us all of listening and watching. We wait for a sign from the reserve of wolves across the hills; one single howl, like the call to prayer of a muezzin from his minaret, can start a furore. The cubs frolic, jumping and racing through the tangled orchids. Suddenly, in a body, they sit on all four fluffy legs, stretch up their throats and open mouths wide; a series of wails and whimpers leaves them satisfied. 'It takes a more superior howl to start a chorus,' drawls Marco-père and rolls over on his stomach to watch the dying sun. 'It will not happen tonight – no howling.' As he speaks, a purple cloud sweeps over the fading red bars on the western hills. The air cools, the cicadas quieten, the flies drop. We wolves wait on in the web of our communication. Would there really be no howling tonight? The cloud bundles and spreads; twilight falls and stars are hidden. We retreat to the fir trees.

Over the following days, Marco-père's tongue is loosened; he reminisces and delves back to lupine history. Marco dozes at his father's feet during these legendary forays. For me it is a windfall of culture; my captive short life has barred me from my kind. The seasoned old wolf senses my eagerness to learn more. I am thirsting for new intelligence.

'We have a bad reputation and our destiny is unknown. It is certain that wolves are the victims of malicious myth. Yet we are often portrayed as frustrated losers. We all know of the big bad wolf irresistibly drawn to a farmhouse by the fragrance of the three little pigs. Fired by the thought of their roasted succulence, he plunges his head down the chimney – but they escape him. In *Little Red Ridinghood*, he is seen to swallow the grandmother and her granddaughter and is then killed himself by a hunter. But . . .' At this juncture Marco-père sits tall and continues proudly . . . 'A fifteenth-century panel of a wolf, proffering his paw to Saint Francis of Assisi, redeems him as a saintly power and not to be thwarted.'

'What about the myths?' I ask him. We are stretched out companionably, Marco-père and I, on a rocky knoll, softened with lichen and tufts of grass; it is the highest point in our park.

130

On a distant plateau, we can see the château in its clearing, shrouded by chestnut woods. Sturdy, demure, built three hundred years ago in pale gold stone, the slate roofs and pepper-pot towers gleam softly. Wide parterres of grass stretch all before and a lake curls to the side. I am seized with a sudden desire to have my own lair, to tend my own cubs, to live and hunt as my forebears. The wolf is a familial, social being with every emotional attachment. He is against aggression and killing. Survival is an obsession; for himself and for his young. I have learnt these things.

I see Marco-père rise stiffly on his haunches. He has seen something below. He growls; his menacing muzzle wrinkles. I move away and see a herd of cows tearing across a field; they huddle and tear back again. 'It is the stray dogs. And the wolf is blamed for the loss of livestock,' warns Marco-père.

'Tell me about the myths, Marco-père.' The evening is darkening and getting chill.

'Tomorrow, dear boy. We need the light of day and good feed in our stomachs before embroiling on the grotesque ferocity of 'La Bête du Gévaudan'.

As I nestle down with Marco in our worn dip against the fir trees, he shivers and presses against my stomach.

'We need to make a den for the winter, Marco.'

'What sort of den, Louis?'

'We must be independent of the other wolves, but we should make room for your father; an annexe of sorts.'

'Do we want a den in the bushes, or high in the rocks, or by the stream?'

'Perhaps we should choose a patch where game is to be found.'

'Come, Louis, you mean brown bears, lynx, wild cats?'

'Remember, Marco, we are in the protected park, free from all carnivore predators. But it is in our nature to hunt. We should exercise our fine thoracic cages and nimble paws to stalk the prey and run and run.'

'But Louis, the only reason for a wolf to kill is to quell his hunger and the hunger of his pack. He does not kill for fun.'

'Ah! We must not delude ourselves that the chase is not exhilarating; it is the ultimate in rhythm and sport for our species. And I have seen rabbits and moles in the woods, dear Marco, and squirrels and mice, all crying out to be hunted down; but I am never hungry enough to oblige.'

'As I told you, Louis, we are bred to kill only when hungry. You fancy a den scooped out by the river? A convenient lair for fishing?'

'No, Marco, we will get lice infesting our winter coats. Let us go up to the rocks; the winter breezes will ruffle our thick fur and the snow will spread out in the valleys below.'

'And we will crunch on lizard for supper.'

Frenzied squeals cut through the night. From the far perimeter of the park, sheltered by the mountain ash and its orange cluster berry, they come. It is the Polish cubs who yelp pitifully and the mother who gives short, threatening barks and howls mournfully for help. Marco and I race to the quarter and hang back. Three cubs lie still and bleeding. They have been sorely molested. In the distance I see stray dogs loping down the hill, and I remember how the cattle had been pestered by them, earlier in the evening. The three cubs whimper in severe pain, their demented mother tears round in circles. The keepers arrive. It transpires the dogs had been jumping up at the steel pen and rubbing their flanks against the wire. The cubs poked their muzzles through the netting with excited yips and yelps. Their innocent effort to make friends had ended in disaster. One had his snout severely bitten through; another had both his snout bitten and lost several teeth; the third lost toes from his foreleg. A remarkable act of self-recovery is taking place. Each cub is licking the other's wounds; the third has his severely mauled paw lodged down his mother's throat.

Says the alpha keeper to his helper: 'When a wolf is injured in the wild, he licks himself better; if the wound is out of his reach another wolf helps him. These cubs are settling down well, they have learnt a hard lesson.'

'What's that?' asks the helper. 'To be circumspect rather than gullible,' replies the keeper.

Marco and I tiptoe tentatively towards the group, in a show of our concern. The keeper looks up. We go closer. The mother raises a doleful eye. We slump beside our beleaguered Polish friends. The alpha male now joins his clan and relieves the mother of the bleeding toes.

'They won't harm no more. No tranquillisers needed; no antibiotics,' says the keeper. 'A wolf has an iron constitution, based on natural disciplines. The restraints on his sex life and his stomach are examples to us all.' Marco and I rise to leave this scene of familial comfort and snuffling. Ambling back through damp scrub and the chill of another moonless night, Marco takes it upon himself to quote from the Victorian historian James Froude: 'Wild animals never kill for sport. Man is the only one to whom the torture and death of his fellow creatures is amusing in itself.'

'And don't forget, "man and his stray dogs",' I correct him.

15

All is quiet from the Polish clan as we wake this morning. The Mongolian alpha female has gone to pay her respects. Having lost two of her own cubs, her sympathies are genuine. We learn from her that the little victims are healing well. Marco and I are now determined on digging our den. I persuade him with little difficulty that our new home should be set up high on the mound of rocky outcrops. The distant view of the château and its quicksilver lake is a painting hanging there. We sniff around the crevices and slabs of stone. Marco finds a wide cleft in the rock face. He squeezes through comfortably and reports soft soil beyond. We attack the earth feverishly with muzzles, teeth and forelegs. The excavated earth is heaped behind us. Marco-père catches up with us and guards our widening hole. A screaming buzzard sweeps low over our diggings, fanning his phenomenal wing-span. Next, Marco-père detects a falcon and then a kite. 'These birds of prey sense death and burial with all this earth flying around.' Marco and I work until the sun is high and repair exhausted to our pond. We drink long and rest in the cool grasses. Dozing and drifting into dreams, I suddenly spring to attention. A shot has rung out, two, three, from the grazing fields below. The local farmer has killed two wild dogs, again lurking round his herd. The heavy birds are flopped like black umbrellas over their prey, screeching rapaciously through bloodied beaks. A van drives up to remove the pitted carcasses. 'That is our fate, Louis, if we ever explore the great unknown beyond,' says Marco gravely.

We return to our den and roll down the earth surround. In the early afternoon Marco-père calls, dragging branches of young birch and oak to shelter our bouldered entrance. No – he will not live with us; he has made himself a convenient lair by the stream. It is an evening for our heavy feed. I speculate on what succulent slabs of meat will come our way: mutton, moose, elk? But Marco-père has whetted my appetite with his tales of the big bad wolf and wolverine derring-do. I butt him gently in the ruff. 'Tell me about "La Bête du Gévaudan",' I plead.

'It is an appalling story. A myth, of course, that La Bête was a wolf.' I wait for Marco-père to settle himself on a clean patch of grass.

'The fear of 'La Bête' is still evoked by mothers to check their unruly children. It has been variously described in extravagant detail, by those who have never seen it. The favoured description is of a horrific, black-haired creature with an abnormally long, narrow back, a thick neck with a massive mane to resemble a lion's, and small, sinister, pointed ears, which were too short, far too short for a wolf. Its body was low slung and further worn down with a long curling tail; as long as a – a – a – a . . .'

'A lion's?' I suggest.

'Or a cow's?' shouts Marco from inside the den.

'Its tail was as long as a donkey's,' states Marco-père firmly. 'An intelligent monster, it chose to live under the glorious reign of Louis XIV, the Sun King; it scampered around on its devious missions in the pure air of the Central Massif and no doubt nibbled sumptuously on the forest nuts and strawberries.'

'Yes, yes, father, but what about the atrocities? La Bête ate children, didn't it?'

'I was afraid you would want to know about that. The killings started on 3 July 1764; a girl of fourteen years, in the parish of Gévaudan was devoured without trace. The following month a girl of fifteen years similarly disappeared. At the end of the month, there was yet another victim of fifteen years. It was established that La Bête favoured females and children. It would eat out the heart, drink the blood, tear off the head and take it away with him.'

'What did the farmers and squires do about this? Did they catch it?'

'No, son. First there were rumours that La Bête had been seen and identified; finally it was not caught. Oh, they sent out the beaters and huntsmen on their horses, to track the monster down. There are fine pictures of them in tricorne hats and long boots and handsome jackets with La Bête posed before them, its atrocious fangs opened wide as though to have its temperature taken.' I am intrigued by Marco-père's horrific chronicles. They become worse; an exhaustive document of death. 'The depravation of this animal spread through twenty parishes,' he continues, 'around one hundred and twenty-one are recorded dead with numerous reports of attacks and woundings. In the village of Saint-Juéry, a comely woman, by name Delphine, stepped into her garden on the morning of 6 January 1765. It was ten o'clock and she needed to pick herbs for the pot. La Bête leapt through the hedge, seized her by the neck, devoured first her breasts and then her face . . . oh! There were horrific ravages in that diocese. La Bête was deemed a hyena for its brutal savagery.' Even Marco now

136

listens to these bloody dregs of history. 'On 30 January, in the nearby village of Saint-Just, a woman washing lingerie in the stream was manfully saved by villagers who had seen La Bête padding towards her, its muzzle still dripping with the blood from a girl of fourteen years who had battled bravely.'

'Papa! That's enough.' Marco looks ashamed that his father should emit such lurid sketches. But I want to know more.

'Was La Bête a wolf, Marco-père?'

'Undoubtedly not, dear boy,' claims our venerable storyteller.

'When was it killed?'

'La Bête was finally and decisively killed on 19 June 1767, in the area of Gévaudan itself. The Marquis d'Apchier had mustered his dogs and horses; included in his troop of huntsmen was one Jean Chastel. Still sportive at sixty years, Chastel had the luck to see La Bête pass right before him. It fell at the first shot, wounded in the shoulders. It hardly moved when the dogs were upon it.'

'And then, Marco-père?'

'The Marquis instructed that La Bête be removed immediately for embalming. He wanted to make a presentation to the King. However, the Marquis' instructions were disregarded. La Bête lay for twelve days on view to the curious neighbourhood, the entrails intact where there should have been straw.' Marco-père lowered his tone. 'Louis, dear boy, I do not know if I should add a sombre detail that comes to mind.'

'Oh! Yes, Marco-père, I can take it, tell me!'

'I think for later.'

'No – now – please!'

'To continue the story, Monsieur Gilbert, a servant of the Marquis, was detailed to take La Bête in a crate to Paris and to present it to the King. Due to the seasonal heat and the slowness of the journey, putrefaction set in. On arrival in Paris, at Marquis de la Rochefoucauld's hôtel the King was informed of La Bête's destruction. Monsieur Gilbert was promptly told to bury it.'

'Marco-père, what was that bad bit you said you would keep for later?'

'Aargh, dear Louis. I fear you will become bloodthirsty. When the animal was finally opened up, the half-eaten shoulder of a young girl was found in its stomach, the last interrupted meal before its own death.'

An agreeable odour steals around us. The keeper ambles up with huge chunks of pork and road-killed deer. He watches us fondly as we fill our bellies. We like to see him. It is that rare moment when the wolf can feel close to the man who feeds him. Lying comfortably gorged we return once more to La Bête.

'Father, tell us what kind of animal it was? Did it really exist?'

'My boys, I have to tell you: two hundred years after these appalling attacks and killings, as recorded in parish registers, we still ask questions. "*Tête coupée, poitrine mangée, gorge coupée, peau du crane enlevée, oreille emportée, tête coupée trouvée huit jours après.*" What manner of beast would revel in such bloodlust? We still ask this. This was never the work of a wolf. A fashionable explanation of the day, among the priests and parishes, deemed it the Devil himself. The rumour was that a curse had been set on the people of Gévaudan; La Bête was a werewolf, a man transformed by the Devil and his sorcerers: a "wolf-man", a "*loup-garou*", a "pretend wolf" with a rapacious tendency to track and devour man. It is difficult to divide legend from truth. The whole debate is intractable.' Marco-père is audibly tiring from his morbid narrative. I lower my voice for one last question.

'Do you believe in La Bête, Marco-père?'

'Yes, Louis. Some atrocious animal was at large those three fatal years. My own belief is that this shocking aberration was a hybrid animal, a lynx crossed with a hyena? The hyena is the cruellest and most treacherous of carnivores.'

'Or perhaps it was a wild dog crossed with a wolf? Or a wolf with a panther or a puma?'

'Louis! Stop rabbiting on!' shouts Marco from the den.

We soon drift into sleep. But I wake in the early hours and pad out into the dawn. The stars are fading but in the dwindling moon I look on the distant château below. The lake winks at me in the soft, silver light. And I reflect on my new life – *en semi liberté*; the companionship of my kind and the gradual discovery of the psyche of my species has enriched my energies. And I remember that sea-bound island where every blade of grass had pulsed with life. The voices and activity and the goodness that wafted from Madame's kitchen; the *va et vient* of life at the villa was instant diversion for me. The streams and creeks and the call of the sea became a part of my being. I loved the Comtesse. She accepted me and took my proffered paw. Our relationship was sealed. And I was proud to walk with her to the butcher and see the stares from the queue. Then he came; that big black woolly head, so tall, so strong. I shudder. Has any man been told that a wolf fears the vertical position? I feared that dark man and his meddling with the females. Gustave was my friend and tutor. He showed me how to fish and catch hare, lizards and birds. He would wait patiently while I foraged for the innards. But I disgraced myself in the village square. Hardly did I realise what came over me. I remember the fierce excitement raging through me but I do not remember the girl. Not once in that household was I ever made to feel guilty, not even when I savaged the goat. A wolf's hunger has to be addressed. A wolf's life has to be addressed. Blinded by my birth, half numb from the wet and cold, I could have died that night on the shore. But Philomène found me.

Where was I from? Who brought me there? Who left me? I needed to live. Madame had ideas of my provenance. It does not concern me. Life is a gift; use it well; soon I will go on an adventure of discovery, a secret journey, an escape to the sprawling forests, the rounded hills and the lonely uplands of rock where fir and ash are dwarfed by wind. As I sit quietly in the light of the moon, I hear these things calling to me. I will go and I will come back. Marco is whimpering in his sleep. I go to him and curl up close. It is a good sound den; he will be safe when I am gone.

16

A morning in early December with a promise of sun. I see for miles; from our high mound, the world is a pure oval. My stomach is strong and settled after last night's feed.

'Marco,' I say nonchalantly, 'I am off to see your father; perhaps we will fish in the stream.' I race to a near point in our steel perimeter where I have seen a rickety base strand of wire. With the Devil's determination I scratch and claw at the soil beneath, using my muzzle to knock up the wire. The soil is soft and compliant; it knows my intent; we work together, the soil and I. The keepers stir for another day. With a wild and frenzied shove, I force my body through; through to the wild and beautiful unknown. I am thirsty. I will head for the lake. But first I will visit the shepherd's hut; the small stone shed with the black gaping hole that has always spelt 'enter – welcome'. Tearing through fields of winter wheat, past felled fir and empty grazing land, I reach the hut in triumph. As I stalk up to the black hole there is a vile stench, of something rotting and fetid. I am shocked and enter. An odoriferous being is slumped in a corner of the single room. He coughs and spits through a matted long beard. He clutches a tin from a heap of discarded tins. An air of near combustion hangs over the place; the earth floor is strewn with black feathers, brittle bones and charred kindling. He waves a crook at me. I turn to run and see a dog poised to attack from the entry hole. It leaps at my throat; its blood-curdling yelps and barks follow me across three fields. I slump, severely weakened, in the shelter of a haystack. Things are not always how they seem to be; I now realise there are hurdles to jump in this new open world.

Now, seriously thirsty, I lope for the lake by the château, the first staging post in my quest to break free. Two strange metal objects drone low in the sky; round and around, they search for somebody. I stop dead and lie still in the rough grass. Searching, searching; it is me they want. Squirming fearfully, I gain the nearby chestnut woods. Safe in their shade, I trot down to the lake. I see the water sparkle through the trees; my drink, my water, it is nearly come. I collapse at the rippling edge and drink my fill. As I roll in the grass surround, there is a shot; two shots. A game-keeper on the château terrace is shooting in the air. I race back to the cover of the woods. It is a high price a wolf pays for his freedom. Narrow, sheltered paths slope down to a valley where I see a river and a chance to dream. The sun is high as I sway through tall lush grasses; birds, red-spotted butterflies and drag-onflies dash out at me; creeping flowers, white, yellow and blue, tangle in my fur. The river is clear and bubbles over chalk and pebble. Flopping beside it, I sleep briefly to its murmur. The sun is still high when I wake. All appears still and deserted by man. Why is man frightened of the wolf? Man's fear has maligned the wolf. It is a misinformed and defensive fear. We wolves are shy, diffident creatures and terrified of man's power to shoot and kill. We do not choose to eat him and he would not deign to eat us. Where is the impasse? It is over his livestock: his flocks and his herds. If the wolf is hungry he needs to kill to eat, whereas it is the nature of man to kill for sport. With his stomach bolstered by a good breakfast, he has no need of his deer, his birds and his boar slumped in death. He has no necessity to kill to live. But there is a dignity in a wolf's hunting and a natural balance. The coyote are best culled by the wolf; filthy mongrels, Marco-père calls them, but said to be good feed. I have much to learn of lupine life. Marco-père has prescribed for me a little of the social mores. It revolves around the pack; your place in the pack, your full participation in the time-honoured disciplines and pleasure, and your ascent to alphadom. A strong and intelligent alpha wolf will retire after two or three years; his readiness to relinquish his post to a young male is depended on. I will be such a male. I am told it is rare to meet a lone wolf. We are too sociable and family orientated a species to wittingly stand apart. I remember Marco-père telling me of a young Russian wolf who had lost his female; he howled each day for one month without ceasing. His pack let him be until he had spent his grief and calling. They respected the depths of his misery. Finally he came back to the den.

As I sit and ponder, the sun has slipped behind the rock face and left the river sombre. I wade tentatively over the pebbles. Are there fish? A few early evening gnats whirr in knots above the running water. A trout leaps up and then another. I jump on them and I eat. A clean, fresh feed with the thin blood and juices of a catch running through my teeth. And now I must continue the adventure. I am apprehensive of the challenge ahead. Where will this friendly, chortling river lead me? I lope beside its white shale shore and I smell Madame Veuve's lavender, dying in the winter breezes and the sharp, sweet scent of yellow winter jasmine. Lower and lower down the hills my river leads me. And I look back up the gorge at the soaring pink façades of ravaged rock, clenched each on the other like blunt molars. From their bold contours I can sense phantom towers and round crenellated walls. Church bells ring out in the distance ahead. I hear a dog barking. I will find cover in the town. I smell it clearly and feel the vibrations of man and activity. The river quickens and its bed is now charged with boulders. I am shocked into action. The water is in a ferment of froth and swelling that tumbles in a cascade to join the main river.

The town is almost upon me. I observe it from my bosky hideout of the tall grasses and ferns. Ranged and embedded around the rock face, the houses hug their cliffs possessively. Others cluster the old square, overlooked by the sturdy church, with the bell tolling in its belfry. In a street, spiralling towards the church, a food market closes down; fruit, flowers, cheese, local crafts, bread and honey – I smell it all with every wiry sinew in my body. I slither down the high grass banks and lurk behind a screen of mulberry trees; in an empty moment when all are busy packing their wares, I dive under a cheese table and its cover. I have upset a pyramid of emptied card boxes; there is much cursing from the stall-holder. Poking my nose out, I see an old man sitting astride a stool right beside me. He is painting old houses, flowered balconies and bits of sky and looks wise and at peace. The heat and odour of cheese in my hide-away is stifling. I leap out and knock down tiers of pottery bowls and coffee pots. I scurry on to a hanger of voluminous bedspreads in ugly, bold stripes; another stuffy retreat. Again I lift the hem of my cover and watch humanity mill round: a clutch of teddies hang on a pole; troughs of toffee and liquorice; children drinking from bottles, sucking on ices, chewing, crying, shouting, laughing. And everywhere I see cheap scuffed shoes and boots made from the most inferior

144

skin. So many silly, red, fat faces I see, and heads with dull, greasy hair and heads with no hair. This commonness of man to compare with the distinguished standards of the wolf, is a wonder to me. And now I see in a quiet, dirty corner, a white decimated pigeon, abandoned in a stone trough of petunias; wasps and flies and fleas drain its blood and its pale broken wings. A wolf does not leave such litter.

A cry goes up: 'Les Loups – Les Loups! Libérez-nous des loups!' There is a scuffling of running feet and a clutter of folding tables. The cloths are swept from over me as I dive into the clamouring crowd. Screams of angry fear as I am seen scuttling for my life. Why is man frightened of a wolf? It is the wolf's prerogative to fear man, with an inherited history of fear from down the centuries. A man threatens with his vertical stance and his weapons; the wolf will always be fearful of him. We are a shy and timid species. I run blindly through table legs and chairs, keeping to the cover of the walls. Darting across the old square could be fatal. There are cries of '*Le pompier! Le loup s'en va!* Police!' But I have gained my hiding patch. Dusk is falling as I press my snout and shoulders against the heavy church door. My pale grey and gold pelage merges with the stout wood, heavy with its iron hinges and straps. A great creaking and I fall inside. The gleaming stone flags are cool and comforting to my burning paws. An octagonal font rests on its pedestal beside the back pews. I mount them and see it brimful of water. With what delight I scoop the marble dry with my long, hot tongue. I rest my forelegs along the polished rim, panting and content. Down the side arches and recesses I see flickering red eyes through cages and amble towards them. I must find a den for the night and settle for a darkening small cubicle with a marble block draped in a fine white embroidered cloth. Meals of pretty flowers are placed around. I stretch out exhausted on a red rug beneath. Distant barking from a dog and more church bells do little to disturb my sleep.

I stir at dawn with the odour of humanity. Prone on my rug, feigning death or sleep, I see a priest standing before me, crossing himself with astonishment. He closes the iron grille cautiously and reappears to hang up a notice: '*Prière de ne pas déranger*'. I sense that he is shaken and perplexed as he sits in his vestry. He loosens his collar and makes camomile tea. (It is another hour, he broods anxiously, before his curate will come.) And two heads are better, even if one is a sheep's head. Fillet of wolf *en compote de fenouille*, or 'wolf in roebuck sauce', a sustaining delicacy in the siege of Paris. The priest is ashamed at his gluttonous thoughts in the face of the wolf's good demeanour. What if the wolf is thirsty? But he has already noted the trace of coarse hairs about the emptied font. Does the wolf sense his fear? Or might the wolf fear him, the priest? Shaking and nodding his head, the old man turns on his wireless:

'A wolf is at large in a village on the south banks of the Tarn. St Chély's Saturday market was violently disturbed by a wolf running amok. Nobody was killed. The wolf has not been found – on no account should it be approached. It may be hungry. Lock up your sheep and your children. The police are advising on operations. We hope to recover the wolf before further chaos is incurred.'

My priest is transfixed. He creeps towards me, my body is tensed as I stand and stretch my hind legs. I yawn voluptuously and see him blanch at the wide arc of my molars and canines. Now he hears a familiar clatter behind him; the cleaning girl walks past with bucket and broom. He catches at her wide skirt convulsively. 'But, father! Why do you grab me?' The priest turns her round slowly to face the grille.

'*Comment diable? Mais quelle merveille!*'

I sit placid and expectant in my den of fine linen and flowers. The priest instructs the girl to stand before me, thus hiding me from the early morning communicants. He repairs to the vestry. The girl and I observe each other briefly. We are friends. I sense a complicity. I sashay across the grille and wish a salt-lick was provided. Willing me to stay still, she unfastens the gate and eases through her bucket. Such a deep, cool drink of water she gives me. Her bucket is drained. Now there are shadows, footsteps and low voices, shuffling through the arched church door. A modest and elderly gathering collects in a far corner. The priest's high voice is prompting them to answer, again and again. There is a brief silence. And now the priest lifts his voice to a lofty trill; the communicants reply in a downward spiral, when I, Louis-Loup, let out a hefty howl, to combine artfully with the priest's next supplication. There is a stunned silence and then panic and consternation. I nuzzle the grille and whine for my release. My intuitive young friend opens up and stands aside with her bucket as I shoot out into the rising sun.

'*Le Loup – Le Loup! Quel catastrophe!*' The elderly worshippers stagger fearfully from the church and scan the distant gorge. The priest joins them. '*Soyez tranquilles. Le loup est plein de la grace de Dieu. Il a une grande peur d'homme – voyez enfin!*' Following their priest's gaze, they see me snapping at fish, on a distant bend in the river. A crowd pours in to the old church square. The editor of the publication *Masseloup-Brameloup* flaps his pretty pages. 'Any news of the wolf? A reward!' I can hear the faint warning bells of the *pompiers*, as I plunge on into the woods.

This very evening I will be back in the den with Marco; no exploring, no dilly-dallying on the way. My adventure has served me well; it began in restless curiosity; it will end in experience.

The morning is cold with a pale sun slanting through the stripped beech and oak. Leaves shiver and fall before me. And I remember how Madame Veuve would watch me catch them one by one. A roe deer leaps out ahead and close after him, a doe. When the mists and dark days fall, it will be the yowling stags that hold these forests captive. As I climb higher through rock and root I see figures far below, clambering over white boulders and canoeing in the tough green waters. I am hungry. I do not care for forest nuts and berries and mushrooms. Tonight's evening feed? A road-killed deer? I will be there. The trees are thinning out to uplands and grazing. My cover will soon be gone. I see a farmhouse with bright wooden shutters. There are smells and laughter – intoxicating smells – goulash of goat, sweet peppers, rabbit and anchovy. I do not linger; the forest is well behind me and an immense plateau lies before. The hard ground undulates with scrub and ghoulish white rock. A ruined castle accentuates the desolation. It is a vast and deadly landscape. As I gaze around me I feel a jab in my back right paw. I leap in the air; a small snake swivels out of sight. I find this colossus of rock around me threatening and weird; clustered in chaotic clumps, it appears a deputation to end the world. I see faces on these wind-worn slabs and skulls of animals, scooped out by centuries of rain. Below in the valley, a sprawling herd of sheep is tended by tall herdsmen and black dogs. A field of dying sunflowers hang their heavy, flat heads at me. With the rocky cliff terrain behind me, I will ease down to these plateaux and soon be home with my kind.

I lope on, keeping my eyes skinned for pools of water. I need water. The sun and wind have dried out my eyes and my throat. A long drink from a bubbling valley stream is what I crave. My paw is throbbing; it will soon swell with pain and poison. With the goal of the green valley far below I half tumble and slide down over tufts and boulders, sticky with lichen and the scribble of snails. Down, down, faster and faster. I shut my eyes and scrunch up my body, spinning like a top out of control. A thick tree trunk looms up at me; in a last ditch resort I hurl myself to the side and get caught in its thick and rampant tentacles. I am weak and frightened. A breeze murmurs around me as I doze. Soon again I am following a narrow tangled path and smell water; my excitement gives a new energy. I am in my own country with a clear trout stream bounding before me through a clearing in the woods.

They have seen me: two fishing men. They cry out with an involuntary fear. 'The wolf! The fleeing wolf! It is him!' With my own fears redoubled at their presence I race upstream through sheltering greenery. My paw throbs for attention. I wince and whelp as it touches the icy water. I curl on to my side and suck it and nudge it gingerly with my teeth. Returned to the water, it is soothed and numbed. I drink long and lovingly of the stream. The sun is low and I must hurry. Through the trees I see the familiar rolling hills and grazing pasture. It is as if the château is near. I push on up to the open ground. And yes, it has a smell of home: the cow herds, the sheep, the hay and my friends on the hill. A sudden clatter in the sky – it is those machines again. They are tracking my return up the hill, swooping low above me. My heart contracts hard as a greater danger now gains on me; the wild dogs are closing in on me. I tear up the hill to home, terrified for my life and limb as my heart thuds in my narrow thorax. I hear the monsters screaming like hyenas, baying for my blood and bones. They are gaining and gaining and I smell their savage sweat and saliva. I can see my home; it beckons me. But death screeches before me; my life is done. A sudden rush of noise and air and I am flattened on the grass as a man stands beside me.

'Welcome back, Louis-Loup.' It is my keeper. Again he shouts my name through the roar, hovering above. He indicates to me a net on the ground with meat inside. I jump into safety and sink my teeth into a numbing lump of mutton. As I am hoisted up on board, my sight blurred, my head disorientated, I see the pack of dogs leaping and howling with rage and frustration. Their quarry has escaped again. The hum of the engine and the propellers fades as I lose consciousness.

The following morning I wake from a long sleep. Marco lies beside me. He sees me stir. We are beside the den, shaded from the December sun under our porch of birch leaves. 'You remember, Louis,' he says in a superior tone, 'how I warned you of those stray dogs?'

'What has happened?' I ask him.

'You set off three days ago. In the early morning, you said goodbye to me. You said you were off to fish with père! It was mid-morning before we counted you lost and then your escape hole was found. The police inspector was notified. They whipped up a hill search and saw you, would you believe, sunning yourself by the lake, and then lost you as you careered off into the chestnut trees. What has happened to you, Louis? You have an air of superiority; of the worldly-wise. Did you meet any females?'

'I was too busy keeping abreast of events, dear Marco. The only females of note were the river trout, delicious – one day I will tell you all. Travel is an education. It will take me a lifetime to assimilate all that I have learnt these past three days.'

We hear footsteps. We stand and stretch to see the keeper smiling before us. He kneels beside me and gently touches my back paw. Our resident vet joins him. 'In my opinion,' he says confidentially, 'he has sucked out all the poison; he and his friend, here, will lick it better in days. No necessity for antibiotics in his feed. Infection is rare with a wolf.' And I am a most fortunate wolf. My life has already shown me more men whom I trust than fear.

17

Madame Veuve, happily settled into the dank, dark December days, had set up her own agenda at the villa. There was nobody to cook for, clean for, or care for. The eucalyptus trees, stripped and slaked with rain, stood brave and skinny at the end of the garden. There was no question of Anne Bonney swinging between them, larking around with her cutlass and that silly leer on her face. On sunny days, Madame would swing open the balcony windows and generally open up the villa. The more fresh air, the better after all the goings-on of the summer. She missed her beloved Louis – of course she did. But by now he would be bored and frustrated, cooped up with her. She knew her limitations. The Comtesse had written her a pleasant note. She was enjoying Paris. 'Living more in my mind.' Madame Veuve snorted. But Madame Veuve had no quarrel with her mistress and her rackety life. After all she had been left a generous stack of Domaine de L'Ile, to ease the winter evenings. And Madame Veuve had devised another ploy to jolly along the cold, grey days. Taking a judicious portion from the villa maintenance, she would lunch once a week at Le Bonaparte. It was the pleasure of being served that she valued so much. Sitting in the far window with a view over the port and a pleated wool hat fitted firmly on her head, she resembled some lady detective. It did her good to feel a somebody, just once a week. The young staff showed her a kindly deference and placed periodicals and newspapers beside her. Lost to the world, she would slurp and chew happily from a deep bowl of *moules marinières*. But her eyes and ears were open to all around her.

As she sat in her corner on this quiet December Sunday, she was immersed in a news story in the periodical *Masseloup-Brameloup*. A young wolf cavorting through village markets, howling the responses in a Communion service and finally escaping from the *pompiers* and the police, across the river gorge and last seen to be fishing . . . ! Madame Veuve adjusted her reading glasses. And then? So what? The wolf had finally limped back to his home – some forty kilometres away – and all on a broken hind leg. Gaining his sanctuary, he was threatened by a gang of ferocious dogs. They were set to kill him, to tear him limb from limb, when a helicopter swooped down and snatched up the feisty young wolf in the nick of time. His name was reported as 'Louis-Loup'. Madame Veuve gasped in horror and disbelief. She gulped at her red wine and noted that the periodical was hardly a week old. She frowned over her *moules* and shook her head. Louis, my pet, what will become of you? As she put her hand out listlessly for the day's *Toulon Matin*, a plump and familiar figure, nursing his own glass of wine, came up to her. He was already holding a copy.

'Bonjour, Madame Veuve. You have heard the news? Look!' He pointed his stubby forefinger to an announcement in the 'Brief Comments' section:

A Vénus et Louis-Loup, à domicile Porquerolles, quatre jolis louveteaux; tous en bonnes santés.

Madame Veuve motioned to Monsieur Boudin to sit beside her. She was shaken. He felt like a fleshy cushion beside her, comforting and authoritative.

'What does it mean, Monsieur?'

'It means, dear Madame, that your former charge is now a young father. Due to your extreme care and judicious feeding, Louis-Loup is an especially strong and healthy specimen; his misbehaviour was exceptional.'

'What misbehaviour?' asked Madame Veuve nervously.

'To mount a mature matron like Venus with his own sexual libido scarcely formed was . . .' Monsieur Boudin blew out a deep breath, like a balloon deflating beneath his waistcoat '. . . was,' he continued, '*un tour de force.*' He explained that Venus would be suckling the pups for four weeks under the charge of Madame Prunier. And what then? asked Madame Veuve. Monsieur Boudin had the option of sending all four pups to the same sheltered reserve as their father, he told her. Madame Veuve tensed with sudden excitement and resolve.

'I will have a pup,' she announced. 'I need a life,' she urged. 'The villa dropped dead with Louis' parting.'

Monsieur Boudin assured her that her offer would be well received from Madame Prunier, who had no time or inclination for grooming pups. She was heavily engaged in writing her thesis: *L'Histoire, Culture et Fabrication du Chocolat.* He ordered them both another glass of wine. Madame Veuve, returning to the villa, flushed and smiling, her hat at a raffish tilt, waved a copy of *Toulon Matin* at *L'Agneau aux deux têtes.* The butcher read out the announcement in sonorous tones, as the queue fell to congratulating Madame Veuve. It was as though she had miraculously conceived herself. It was certainly not an occasion for disclosing Louis' other daring adventures.

*   *   *

154

Minor: 'Are you awake, Major, old sod?'

Major: 'I am bored, bored, bored. No smells, no voices, no laughter, no footsteps, no life. The villa has become a morgue.'

Middle: 'You relished the summer *ménage*, Major? Wild behaviour, wild animals, drifts of hashish, tales of rape and pillage and Madame's fishy dishes and her *ris de veau*?'

Minor: 'I think Major would agree that we all miss the Comtesse and the chaotic mismanagement of her affairs.'

Major: 'At least we still have Madame Veuve to feast on.'

Middle: 'Come on, Major. Since when have you cooked up a taste for old bones?'

Minor: 'I think Major means that Madame generates a bit of life and activity. I am told . . . (Minor hangs on his words for greater impact) . . . I am told that Madame Prunier is coming to tea.'

Major: 'When? Why? What about?'

Minor:'Madame Prunier is coming to discuss with Madame Veuve the possibility of her assuming the control of one of Louis-Loup's newborn pups.'

(Major and Middle are stunned. It had come to that? Louis' little skirmish with the blonde Alsatian?)

Major:'It will be good to have another bit of wolf around. I read once that wolf bones, pulverised between stone, with roots and herbs, make an uncommonly good broth.'

From Paris, the Comtesse was also brightened to hear of her Louis' pups; three male and one female. According to Madame Veuve, the female had come out white like her mother, with feathery grey streaks across her little back; two of the males were black with white aprons and the third was of a rufous grey with a thicker fur. Venus, under the chaperonage of Madame Prunier,

155

was weaning her brood. On the advice of M. Boudin, the emerging pups would then be despatched to Louis-Loup's same exploratory sanctuary. However, little Rufous, who bore a more lupine resemblance to his father, would be seconded to Madame Veuve and the comforts of the villa.

The Comtesse's thoughts flew to Gustave and to Philomène. They were becoming *amitiés amoureux*. Of course, Philomène was a charming young girl. And Gustave had even once assured her, the Comtesse, that Philomène was of more than passing interest to him. How distressing! The Comtesse sighed helplessly and crossed her slender hands over her black pearls. But she was enjoying Paris in the winter time. She had turned a page. Indeed Antoine had proffered her a reading list, to include: *The Great Days of Versailles*, *The Sonnets and Songs of Shakespeare*, *The Portrait of a Lady* by Henry James, *The Thoughts of the Emperor Marcus Aurelius Antonius*, *The Art of Kama Sutra* and Dostoevsky's *The Idiot*.

She had taken herself off to a lecture on the birth of archaeology and had joined a tour of Fontainebleau – '*Le Palais Italian des Rois de France*'. Sentimental admirers had taken her to sentimental films: *La Joyeuse Parade*, *Le Bonheur*, *Coeurs Joyeux*. There were suppers at Maxims, Chez Albert and Lapérouse. She had even pleased Antoine with some research from the *Bibliothèque* on his beloved Alfred de Musset: that he had confessed to a confidante – Madame Jaubert – how he had cried his eyes out for a good half-hour over his love for the Princess Belgiojoso. And another touching vignette of de Musset, aged twenty-two years, suddenly taken ill at the Danieli in Venice. A handsome young doctor – Pietro Pagello – was summoned by de Musset's mistress, George Sand. The speculation – '*Et que fit George Sand entre ses deux poêtes?*' – was quickly dispelled by: '*Bah! Vive l'amour quand même!*' The Comtesse had next found some heliographs '*après les dessins de Maillart*': elegant young men, prostrate with love or confused confessions or bouquets of flowers; their heads of flowing curls buried on bosoms or silken laps. And running through this motley collection, de Musset soared with his own head of luxuriant hair – his distinguished features and his reflective pose and expression, poised to perfection on his long, slim body.

Antoine was astonished by her efforts. And Christine knelt in the Madeleine, bought herself gauze confections from 'Voilettes' and yearned for the day when her Comte would come. And Uqba ran like a restless force through her mind and body. She still adored him but swept him from her mind, together with the seeping gutters and odours of Tangier. In anticipation of yet another romance, she took manicures, pedicures and all-over body massages. And, she reminded herself as she walked purposefully along the Faubourg St Honoré, 'You never know who will come out of the lift.'

Louis was non-plussed to hear tell of his four offspring. Gustave and Philomène would journey with them to the exploratory sanctuary in mid-January. He, as their father, was expected to oversee their every move and needs and development. The Mongolian alpha female had already assured Louis of her support; she reminded him of how she had known the sorrow of losing two of her cubs (more to convey her experience rather than any incompetence). Marco-père had also volunteered for duties and, lastly, Marco. Whether Louis was prepared to delegate his precious progeny to Marco was doubtful. After all, he, Louis, had seen more of the world. But his sudden escapade had induced in his fellow species and his keepers a mixed admiration and reserve. Indisputably, their Louis was a leader, a potential alpha, but would he prove over reckless and head his pack into some disaster?

The Polish alphas, seeing the approval of the Mongolian clan, fell in with the conviction that Louis had the charisma, courage and dash to gain his future alphadom.

During the next two weeks, preparations were in hand for the arrival of the three cubs. Marco, not caring to be overrun by Louis' boisterous issue, was feathering a new den down the hill, in the bowl of a willow tree; he had tunnelled out a good shelter. Louis, meanwhile, was bemused to hear that his most wolfish fourth cub had been assigned to Madame Veuve. It was strange to think of his little descendant treading in his very footsteps; fishing and dabbling in the same streams, being guided by Gustave and butting Madame Veuve affectionately in her scrawny bosom. So many sweet and sad frustrations were lodged in his memory.

The Mongolians and the Poles would drop by Louis in the evenings; some to hear of his recent derring-do and others to give advice on the upbringing of his cubs. A veritable *boma* of spruce, old moult and moss now swathed his winter den. The Mongolian alpha male warned him, from his own considerable wisdom and experience, on the dangers of being an irresponsible father. No stepping out of the sanctuary perimeter now; no showing off his cubs to the big, wide beyond. They would be snapped up, savaged, drowned and devoured; swung around like rag dolls by wild dogs, their throats and tummies left bloodied and gaping wide. And what about the fur trappers? Did Louis know their deadly tricks? Young wolf skins seasoned to a parchment made splendid drum skins and soldiers' overcoats and shoes. Their pelts were popular for trimmings and rug linings, and couch throw-overs; the latter were said to induce the sleeper with the stamina of a wolf. Hunting capes, with ears erect, proved excellent camouflage for the sportsman after his game. Marco-père, drawn in to this soliloquy added another savoury detail.

'The tail of a wolf, with the bone removed, can be inserted with a wooden handle. This is an invaluable toy for the trappers and is used like a feather duster, to sweep and smooth the earth clear from signs of wolf traps; wolf scent is another effective cover.' The audience, collected around Louis' den; were momentarily silenced. The Polish alpha male spoke.

'In the Tatra mountains we have space enough for the bear and lynx and wolf to live in harmony. The vast tracts of empty wasteland across the Balkan borders, the Carpathians and the Eastern Alps have protected us.'

'And so did the Jewish race,' hissed his alpha partner. 'It was they who sacrificed their skin for lampshades and drums.'

'Our talk has digressed from Louis and his protection of the cubs. But one more danger springs to mind.' Marco-père thrust forward his head and forelegs. 'It is the poison tactic. Trails of bait – poisoned mice, rabbits, songbirds – can litter the forest floor; hours later the hunters find a string of dead beasts: bears, coyote and wolves. Any cautious quadruped who sniffs only or licks at the poison can take longer to die. The poison lurks in the gut, leading to fur loss and even nakedness in the perishing grip of winter.'

'But man has to kill some wolves to save our species,' reasoned Marco from his corner.

'And we have a right to exist. We are formidable predators. We keep the ecological balance,' argued the Mongolian alpha. 'Five million years ago from the Arctic to Arabia, the wolf was linked with man. We ran with the bulls and bison and never caused harm. And it was we who culled the coyote – that mongrel prairie-wolf – to good effect.'

'The coyote has come a long way south,' remarked a Polish beta minus. 'I heard the keepers complain that they are forming up in packs down the American Eastern Seaboard. One distinguished matriarch was driving home at night from a bridge party and could not get out of her car. Coyotes everywhere, sprawled over her windows, sliding and dangling off the roof . . .' Louis was anxious to settle the debate and retire to his den. Standing and stretching his long, elegant legs, he revived an expression of the Comtesse: 'Plus ça change, plus c'est la même chose,' and the group dispersed.

It is some days after that talk by my den. Our attention is now fixed on two young females who have been taken in by our sanctuary. Sent by the local SPCA they are a pitiful sight; indeed we resident packs are in fear of contamination. The one had clearly been brutalised by stray dogs, her ear bitten off, her tail bitten off, her thigh broken and improperly set. Her coat is shaggy with mange. 'Hook-worm and whip-worm', I heard the keepers call it. She has bites on her muzzle and bites on her feet. The keepers watch her condition attentively. She is fed a specially spiced meat to destroy any bacteria and given a regular supply of marrow bones and cod liver oil. She is a sweet and gentle creature and is recovering. The other female has caused less concern; her condition is less critical: she has sceptic hock sores from 'tick' infestation. The hot summer brought swarms of biting flies to plague her. With the winter cold, her lesions are now drying up and healing well. The keepers have urged us not to lick her hocks.

And now I am to meet my offspring; my three pups will arrive within the week. I am glad to have experienced that daredevil escapade. It has taught me caution in the face of potential danger, the notion that there is peril in every blade of grass; that my strong young body is not infallible. But I sensed a kindness in the men beyond. I will teach my cubs good manners and the law of kindness. Our keeper has arrived with feed; huge lumps of meat from the abattoir and cuts from a road-killed cow. The keeper bends to stroke the two convalescents nearby and then walks towards me as I champ on my portion of flesh and blood.

'Your eyes burn brilliantly at night, Louis – yellow, orange, amber. When your cubs come, it is the duty of us all to help you care for them. They will be hungry at this altitude. They will be nibbling at all your mouths for any morsels that you and the clans may regurgitate.' I rub my body against his long, strong thigh and flop to the ground, my head bowed between my paws; the keeper is my good and kind friend.

'We will find your young fellows some rabbit and mole, and plump little birds. Soon they will be prying for themselves after mice, and dabbling in the stream.' The two convalescent females have made it clear that they will also help me and my cubs. They would be available for den duty, howling practice, rock climbing and general character-forming playtime. But something disturbs me over the female with the sore hocks. She has an unhappy mask; she clings to her friend who in turn is protective. She rests and then reappears as tired as before. She watches me with a mournful eye. She has no energy, no sense of fun. She is unwell. My cubs must now be five weeks old. The keepers expect them any day. They will be strong already with sharp little canines, big, clumsy paws and furry coats. The afternoon is darkening, Marco and I again wait for our feed. It is a 'light' day; small pieces of meat, dry dog food and offal. The land below us is bleak and grey. The folds and hills are swept with wind and rain; the swaying chestnut trees where I took refuge are now stricken skeletons. The cows and their bells are silenced in their shelters. The keeper comes to me and ruffles my mane. 'Your youngsters arrive tomorrow, Louis.' I cannot imagine such an event. How will we ever come to know each other? Love each other? And understand that I am their father? How can I begin to teach them the mysteries and disciplines of a wolf's existence? I feel profoundly ignorant and unequal to the job. And the Comtesse? Will she come too? Gustave? I sleep the night with Marco. His warmth and snuffling comforts me and soothes my apprehension. I wake in the early morning to a strange and muffled quiet. I creep from the den and see an unknown world. A screen of white flakes dances thickly before me. The ground is blanketed white, and white lumps are clotted on the fir trees. A pale sun rises over the far hills, and in the spreading light I see prints on the white ground: a running bird, a hare . . . I run in to Marco, my coat glistening.

'It is snow,' he grunts. 'It falls in winter.' Leaping up, he pushes me outside and we have a tumble in the stuff. The keeper laughs at our noses, tufted white, and gives us biscuits. Suddenly there is a familiar smell just down the hill. I hear that low commanding voice. It is Gustave. A pretty girl stands beside him, her head wrapped round in wool. I could tell those smiling dark eyes anywhere. It is Philomène, my little foundress from the cove. Bending to the three crates, they unshackle each one and ease them through the acclimatisation pen. I watch from a small distance as my three cubs emerge: the two male black and the female white with the grey hoops round her little torso. They scuffle with their footing on the earth floor. 'They were tranquillised for the long train journey,' explains Gustave. A keeper brings them biscuits and sugared water. I tiptoe down the grass bank. Philomène squeals joyously.

'It is Louis, at last! Look, Gustave! How he has became a fine young man!' I nuzzle her soft thigh. She smells the same. She leads me through the gate, where I smell my own. They all three

162

watch me quizzically. Finding their feet and their confidence, they circle round me. The little white sister rolls on to her back before me. It is an act of sheer submission.

18

My two boys and 'Girlie' are a perpetual delight, a delight that is extinguished several times a day. Where are they? What are they up to? Who are they with? Have they escaped? The keepers, aware of my anxiety, follow their whereabouts with a modicum of care.

'Your youngsters are playing by the stream,' they tell me. 'The boys are swinging on the willow branch, Girlie rolls on her back, kicking and yipping.' I love my three cubs. I am a proud father. At six months they will be strong and well enough groomed for the open wilds. Together we will travel the unmarked roads, the forests and mountains. They will learn, as I have had to, the balance of things: the good and the depraved; the kind and the cruel; the days to have not and the nights to devour. Above all, my cubs will stand tall between the lines of lupine disciplines.

It is freezing this early afternoon; the scuffed ground, patched with ice, weeps in the sun. A keeper ambles up to me. His face and his stance pose no troubles. He sits on the boulder beside my den.

'Here you have a panoramic view, Louis-Loup. That château down on the far hill by the chestnut woods. You know it?'

'I did skirt round it a few weeks ago,' I reply archly, 'but I was not invited inside.'

Resumes the keeper: 'It's interesting to learn from the convalescent – she with the infected hocks – that it is haunted.'

'Who haunts it? Wolf or man?'

'Strange to tell – neither.' This improbable dialogue is interrupted by Girlie bounding up, almost obscured by the heaps of snow. She snuggles beside me, licking about my mouth for a stray morsel. She has some tale to share. The keeper moves on.

Girlie is breathless with excitement: 'The château below and its surrounding wood are haunted.' She waves her paw as she speaks. 'Centuries ago, a pretty servant girl at the château had a love affair, either with a man of the family or with a servant. She was full of remorse when a baby was born to her. The lover cast her off. She hung herself in those far woods below. She had first tried to kill her little boy so that he would not be left without her. But he survived and he grew and he wandered so lonely through the woods, for ever searching for his mother, whom he loved and forgave. But if he sees us, man or animal, he turns to stone. And if . . .' Girlie takes a deep breath, 'if anybody touches him in his stone being, he vanishes in a little cloud of dust.'

'My little Girlie, who told you all this?'

'It was the lady with the hocks. She is my friend. She loves me and promises me more stories.'

And it has been noticed that the mournful one has taken on a new breath of life since the arrival of my Girlie.

The following afternoon she again races up to the den. Would I like another story? Before I can waylay her zeal, she pitches into another unlikely tale. Girlie sits on the boulder, the better to command my attention. It was many, many full moons ago, she tells me. There was a joyous wedding party at the ancestral home,

165

for the heir and his new bride. There was feasting and dancing and the handsome young couple were admired by all. The bride looked exquisite in all her white silken finery. As it neared midnight, a guest suggested a game of hide-and-seek. The bride tripped away to a secret place. After a fitting pause the players set off to seek her. She was nowhere to be found; her groom became frantic. He cried out her name, louder and louder and pleaded to her to come back to him. He was distraught. His friends stayed with him all night, searching for his bride; all day they searched and for one whole week. Each room in the mansion was thoroughly rummaged and then the garden surrounds. She was never found. I pat Girlie on her little haunches. She is tensed and hoarse from the excitement of her tale. 'It isn't finished,' she hisses. 'The best bit is to come!' Some years later, a servant found a deep oak chest in a dark corner of the attic. He raised the lid, in idle curiosity; to his horror he saw the rotted bones of the bride in her gown.

'There was a suffocating grey dust everywhere, so the lady with the hocks told me, and a smell of stale sulphur. What had happened was that the bride, so excited in her lovely white dress, had hidden in the chest and left the lid open so she could hear the to-ing and fro-ing of their friends. But suddenly it slammed down on her. She was locked in a tomb. Her calls were not heard. Today there are still cries echoing through the rooms. It is the son and heir, the bridegroom himself, on his long and heart-rending search.'

Girlie curls up into me. 'I am tired,' she says simply. 'I want to sleep.' She is shivering. I am alarmed and lead her into the den. Her eyes are glazed over, her lips and mouth hot and dry. 'Water, water,' she whimpers. I scoop snow into my mouth and dribble it into hers. My darling Girlie is clearly not well. 'Water frightens me – no more water.' She rolls on to her back. There is scuffling outside. It is the boys. They burst in.

'Quiet,' I urge them. How is Girlie? Is she alright? They seem anxious. They had all been down by the river – the lady with the hocks was telling her ghost stories again. She had asked Girlie to lick her sores. Every day Girlie has tended her. Girlie's friend has become a parasite on all their play. Girlie must be warned against the lady. The boys tumble each other in the snow. It will soon be feeding time. The keeper will take a look at my Girlie. But her short bark-howls now signal a threat and alarm. She is squealing with fear on a high note.

I rush into the den; she is severely cramped in her right hind leg. I kneel and rub her with my thorax. I bury my mask in her fragile neck and whimper. But what can this sudden horror be? The keeper eases in down beside us. 'She won't drink,' I tell him. He shakes his head in the gravest concern. Bending to her with a small cloth in his fingers, he wipes saliva from her mouth. As Girlie watches me, her beautiful golden iris swivels back in her head, leaving her vacant and white-eyed. I cry out in anguish as the remaining eye goes dull and her amber gaze fades. And now it is convulsions that take her. I yell to the boys to bring back the keepers, the vet! I dare not kiss my sweetest and most darling daughter. I stand beside her, willing my love and my protection to wrap around her for ever. A paralysis creeps slowly over her small body. The vet and the keeper squeeze into the den and confirm to me that Girlie has rabies. She is unconscious. She will soon die; in her own time. She is now cool to the touch, limp and at peace. Her shrunken little frame soon stiffens. I touch her bushy white tail with love and a special reverence. She lifts it – for me! She has lifted it! It flops from my fingers. I howl and I flee from her death. The boys bar my way and comfort me. They tell me that the lady with the sore hocks has been shot. Now they come again; the keeper and the vet. They bring a green tin box. Away she goes – my baby, my girl, wrapped around and diminished in death. Tomorrow she will be buried in the wild beyond. The boys and I will ride in the keeper's van. We will find a sheltered corner to dig deep. And we will urinate above her, to protect her ground.

I have now stumbled a month through my loss and misery. It is February. Snow billows in on the wind, throwing deep blankets over hill and valley. It has brought a solitude and peace, but little comfort. At night we hear strangled moans; by dawn identified as stray dogs, starved and frozen. The herdsman with the cart comes by; he jumps down to his knees in snow and shovels up the clinging bodies, fused in death. I watch the early sunlight lick the icicles that hang long and thick from our high perimeter gates. Like bones suspended from femoral heads, blazing and weeping. The keepers come in hard hats and thrash them with rods. 'When icicles melt and snap, they can break a man's neck,' I hear them warn. My boys follow the keepers round; there is always something interesting to learn, and the chance of a biscuit. We had a bad moment when the willow branch on which they swing cracked and pitched them into the river. One hit his head on the stone bed; the rush of cold water nearly did for him; his brother knocked him back into consciousness. I am aware of my inadequacy as a father and teacher. This ice white landscape of snow and whining wind that brings aching pads, sore eyes and breathlessness, depresses me. And I mourn my furry white Girlie. I am in a state of abject grief.

I should take my boys to a bigger world beyond. The three of us must move on. The keepers are intuitive to our needs and I see them now. They are on their knees closely inspecting sores on each of my boys' anuses.

'It is the snow finch and the mountain sparrow who are to blame. They are starving and peck at the anus for the faeces,' reports one.

'It is the miserable weather,' concludes the other. And man and wolf long for the spring: the juicy young grasses and chuckling rivers; the song thrushes and the jumping trout.

The evenings become lighter, with a pale sun fading on the western hills. The keepers encourage the cubs in their foraging and diving into the undergrowth. They have become too fast for the hares and lose the scent. Leaping in the air and stabbing the earth with their snouts, they chase each other in the dwindling snow. Snapping his milk teeth and play-biting, one creeps up to rush and charge provocatively; the other fixes with staring eyes and tears off at speed, inviting more chase. They compete with each other's agility all day long and not least with their new-found vocal cords. The whimpering and growling, the snarling with bared teeth; the wider the mouth, the louder the snarl. All such tricks they learn between themselves. One clear evening Marco-père takes them to a high point on the reserve and orders: 'Ears back, heads held up. Breathe out with mouths slightly open, your lips drawn forward.' Their first efforts at howling are commendable enough. The keeper joins in. A low call from Marco-père, a quick rise, to end in a slow fall; the boys now practise in the fir trees. 'Howling is your voice to the world; your world,' explains Marco-père, you will have a sad voice, a happy voice, a play voice and . . . a lone voice. If ever you are lost in the wild, you must howl and howl and be guided homewards to the answering pack.'

I have spent these winter months moping and miserable. I am

still afraid and nervous of my responsibilities. Where will it all lead? My boys are a remarkable pair. They have socialised well with the clans and the keepers. They have respected my lassitude, my loss. It was right that I should nurse my grief. And they had understood. But spring is now evident each day. I smell the pungent sap seeping through spruce and fir. The breeze ruffles my coat and blows sounds from the clear valley streams. I listen for the song of the warblers, the curlew and the sandpipers nested already in the reed beds. I have regained my appetite. My zest for life streams through my being. I feel whole.

I walk into the evening sun. My boys nuzzle me, bumping their chests against my shoulder. They have something to tell their father. The keeper has named them – Nicu and Titu. I sniff appreciatively as the keeper walks up the hill with their feed. 'Liver of roe-deer for Nicu and Titu,' he announces. 'And for Louis – a big surprise.' He throws me pork and moose and is pleased to see me eat. 'Louis,' he calls and sits on a near bench. I drag up my desiccated shoulder of pork and slump beside him.

'We are sending you and the boys away,' announces the keeper with no preamble. I am so surprised I am momentarily dazed. I swallow hard on my meat. The keeper continues briskly, 'You and your Nicu and Titu will go to the forests and valleys of Transylvania; to hunt and to live and to survive. Your robust natures call for a wider show.'

The young keeper, rammed up on a narrow bench in the guard's van, looked down on his cargo. It was a stifling afternoon, to make any man curse his own sweat. Opening the van door, the Gare du Nord clasped him in a warm wave; stale coffee, garlic and Gauloise hung about the rails in a stubborn haze. Soon they would be off on this night train to München. He pulled the three crates out on to the platform. 'Such good boys. What fine travellers you are. Curled up as calm as cabbages.'

A porter came by with water. And then a most elegant lady; not so young and neither so old. She stood before the crates in a red silk dress with white spots and a tilted pillbox hat. There was a scuffling and much attention for the lady and her shining red stiletto shoes.

'What have we here? Lynx? Lion cubs?' As she bent to poke in a finger, she gasped and screamed. 'But, it is my Louis-Loup, my darling, my treasure!' The keeper placed the crate back in the van and called to the lady to follow. Louis rolled stiffly out as the Comtesse pushed a bowl of water to him. He circled her tentatively as she knelt before him. He flopped beside her and put his head on her silken lap. 'Oh, my Louis, my sweetest darling. You were always my love.' Louis nuzzled against her lap and, with a supreme sense of timing, sat tall in front of her and gave her his paw. The keeper next lifted in the crates for Nicu and Titu. He let them loose in the van. He explained to the lady that the train was soon off to Romania.

'Romania! What is there to do in that country?'

'It is for the wolves,' explained the keeper. 'The call of the wild.'

'But of course – for these darling cubs the woods and fields of Transylvania will be a paradise.'

Stepping over the two black frisking young wolves, the Comtesse left the guard's van. As the whistle blew she called her adieus to Louis, choking on her love and tears.

The young keeper felt quite overcome with events. As the train coiled out from the banlieu boredom of Paris, he sat to attention. His charges were dozing already. What an adventure this was, a challenging assignment. Born and bred in the Massif

Central, he had never been further. The empty, undulating plains of his youth, with their rocky white outcrops had been drama enough. He shuddered gently at the afternoon's session with the young medic. Why were his charges not radio-collared? 'They must have further rabies injections – have they been de-loused? All that sticky thick hair. Nobody wants a scene at München,' warned the medic. 'The Germans have always paid particular attention to hair . . .'

The keeper had felt strangely threatened as they were led into a cell-like, windowless clinic. The three young wolves were promptly vaccinated. A stained bathing receptacle was next filled with cool disinfected water. The keeper was ordered to dip them, one by one, into the liquid. The unfortunate medic was liberally sprayed as they each pranced out and shook themselves.

But now the keeper could settle back and enjoy the ride. The guardsman had brought him *brioche* and gruyere and a jug of rough red wine. He devoured the passing panorama of rural France: the sweep of the northern plains, the oak woods, the apple orchards in full white blossom; the flashed vignettes of the timber-framed barns and farmhouses, the cows, the horses, the curling rivers and the bell tower and turrets of a distant church. He watched the evening sun steal its benediction across this ordered land. Epernay, Champillon and Chalons sur Marne, where the train swept irreverently past its Gothic spires, ducal courtyards and Romanesque façades and streaked into the heart of Champagne country. Every southern slope bristled with the green shoots of vines, the sturdy little branches upheld to the skies.

The guardsman came in with water and dried dogs' food and an offer of horse blankets for himself and the wolves. Night was falling swiftly now. And had the keeper seen the Champagne slopes? May was a dangerous time for the budding grapes, the guardsman told him. A frost could kill and hailstones were a hazard. They would arrive at München at sunrise. The train, hissing and galloping through the dusk, swallowed up track and dived through tunnels. The keeper released the wolves from their crates and talked to them softly about vines and steeples and rivers and ruins. Then Louis, Nicu and Titu and the keeper snuggled down all together on a raft of blankets. Dawn came bathing the rich Bavarian soil with liquid gold. The silhouette of München against the snow-powdered Alps was a miracle; cupolas and clock-towers and pepper-pot turrets pointed to the blue sky in a triumph and left the keeper dazed. Slowly and majestically the train loped past vistas of the grandest white and gold façades, pistachio green palaces and rose-pink churches. Again the keeper sighed. He was lucky to see the like. He divided up the weisswurst and pig trotters, and he and the wolves ate with relish. Titu veered away from the light beer on the keeper's breath and, in a fit of high jinks after their long night, there ensued fun and ragging: licking and smelling of mouths and manes and legs and feet and much running and chasing and knocking about.

By four o'clock they would arrive at Budapest. The keeper turned once more to the *tableau vivant* through his window. The rolling plains climbed to more distant mountains and trout streams, tumbling with the meltwater. Crops of green winter wheat, flowering blue saffron, lime trees and willow in crinkled new leaf, flashed past them. Wood houses with sharp-pitched roofs loomed above barns, hens and horses, dogs and logs. The keeper and the wolves dozed through the warm afternoon. They were woken by the guardsman, urging them to be ready for their change over at Budapest. They steamed past another magnetic setting of forts and castles and seven bridges slung across the Danube. (And why was the water brown and not blue? the keeper wondered.) The guardsman helped him out with the crates and wheeled them to a quiet corner of their next platform for Bucharest. At six o'clock they were off again. The Hungarian landscape stretched all soberly before: valleys and bald plains, relieved by expanses of sunflower and maize. And the keeper thought, with a shiver, of those Jews in trucks. An early night called. They would arrive at Bucharest at eight o'clock in the morning. The keeper slept badly, with tales remembered of gypsies dangling from the roof and clambering in through windows, after a sleeper's money and passport.

He was woken by a deluge of tongues and spittle. He lay still, savouring this ambivalent pleasure. Today he must release the three boys into the foothills of the Carpathians; from a tamed life to the savage wilds. He was gripped with a futile misery. He loved his charges; he had tended them at the exploratory park and matched his own development with theirs. He put up his arms and a frenzy of fur and paws and yelps and a buffeting of heads forced him to sit.

The train was jogging gently towards Bucharest. The wolves sensed the end to their long journey, the completion of one life and the start of another; a life with their kind, to be accepted and understood; to belong. The keeper felt strangely in awe and admiration of them; they knew where their life was going. The guardsman hurried in with a dram of țuică and urged the keeper to knock it back. The fiery plum brandy blazed a trail down his gullet. The wolves crowded round the guardsman as he threw them portions of salt moist cheese from the shepherds' camps. The keeper looked out warily on the baleful conglomerate of Bucharest: statues and fountains and pedimented mansions with pillared balconies; the Russian churches, all onion-domed; and the interminable scourge of Stalin's concrete legacy; the Square of Union with its vast central fountain, long dry from dust and revolution.

'Bucharest! Bucharest!' The train slid slowly into the Gara de Nord. The guardsman glanced at the keeper's ticket. Ah! to Braşov! A further journey and a different train, to take two hours or even three hours. 'The Braşov train is slow and unreliable. So slow that doors are left open to assist passengers to jump off at their personal convenience. In these "personal" trains you can relax and enjoy the view.' The guardsman embroidered with further relish on the idiosyncrasies of the cheap 'personal' trains. 'There could be short stops or long stops, at each country station. Any miscalculation in a passenger's jump is easily righted; he may run forwards or backwards, at a leisurely pace, to regain his seat.' The genial guardsman insisted on ferrying the party across to their correct platform; with a fond slap on the keeper's bowed shoulders, he thrust on him a second tot of ţuică. The little party was soon settled in its new guard's van with its broad wooden aperture opened wide. They would be off within the hour.

Their guard looked confident, if a little askance, at the young carnivores, sniffing and prowling at his feet. He did not expect trouble on the journey, he assured the keeper meaningfully. The train soon jerked into action. The keeper settled once more into his spectator role as they trundled through wide plains of wheat and rye and maize. The potato harvest had begun and horse-drawn wagons were piled high with the green leaf and weed for animal feed. The keeper watched young men scything the hay meadows and strained to hear the rhythmic swish of their strokes; others turned the hay to dry out on the one side and then the other. Hay, the main winter fodder, would finally be pitchforked into conical stacks. The keeper, leaning out of the van, was almost smothered with the heat and chaff and the scent of hay; he heard the men singing as they swung their blades. Steep wooded cliffs, rivers, canyons and dense forest lured the train to the foothills of the southern Carpathians. To the west lay a smudged silhouette of the Wallachian hills. The train slowed and stopped abruptly on the outskirts of the mountain town of Sinaia. 'The pearl of the Carpathians,' he had been told.

A sudden rush and flutter and a tumbling through the gaping aperture of the guard's van sent the wolves in a frenzy. With unrestrained curiosity, they set to sniffing up the full long skirts of two young girls. An astonished silence, when the intruding graces screamed lustily. The guardsman burst in and hustled them through the train. Louis, Titu and Nicu crept to their corner, rubbing their snouts and licking on paws. Shouts and remonstrating were heard and the keeper saw the girls thrust unceremoniously on to the platform where they rejoined a colourful group of women with robust babies in their arms. The train lurched out of Sinaia alongside the broad river Prahova, where enchanted fairytale castles and monasteries, and an aura of Edwardian grandeur emanated from the noble villas in this fabled mountain resort.

The keeper's reverie was interrupted by the guardsman. Louis, Nicu and Titu rose to attention, expecting food. Their host lavished them with praise. They had shown commendable control with those beggar women. Crime was a hazard in these mountain towns, he explained. The skiing and hiking in the South Buçeği mountains enticed many travellers, and the slopes were considered the most stunning challenge.

'Check the weather before you set out,' he warned the keeper. 'Leave no litter; your footprints only are acceptable and do not be tempted to pick the flowers.' The train had made good time, he told them. 'At twelve noon we will reach Braşov. I will help you over to the Zarneşti train.'

'Zarneşti? Where is Zarneşti? Braşov is our final destination!' The keeper was seriously alarmed. The guardsman looked at him sceptically. 'You can't go letting out wolves at Braşov, my friend, Zarneşti is the place for you. You are more suited to Zarneşti. It lies at the foot of the Piatra Craiuliu ridge; a more gentle climb than the sheer drops of the Buçeği range.' The keeper shuddered. All he had intended to do in this wild and unfathomable land of Transylvania was to safely release the young wolves and finally collapse in a medieval square with a bottle of red wine, a plate of meat barbecued over apple wood, and those potato dough-nuts with a plum inside. The wolves were now engaged in snorting up the guardsman's wide trouser legs. 'I get them food,' he promised and returned with goat meat, bread, cheese and water.

Braşov was nearly upon them, when the keeper was startled to see a huge, dark bear, on its hind legs and chained in a village side road. He had read that it was a lucrative ploy to cajole any returning hunters and hikers to be photographed alongside such a furry beast. A sheer horizon of mountain forest now loomed, with the medieval church towers and pitched red-tiled roofs of Braşov encircled below. The keeper looked on intently. He could discern the medieval German markings he had read about; the baroque façades, the timber-framed homes. The keeper liked the medieval period; it was home from home; his own tarn gorges and hill tops bristled with such old barns and houses. (But that Count Dracula and his barbarous son Vlad, the Impaler, had claimed no place in his childhood story books.) Braşov! They had arrived. Louis, Nicu and Titu went grudgingly to their cages and flopped down. It was hot and airless. 'You will find cooler air at

Zarneşti,' promised the guardsman and bundled off the crates in his luggage cart.

'Welcome to Transylvania!' he screeched above the platform bustle. 'Beyond the forest!' An easy enough deduction from the Latin but the keeper could see no way forward beyond Braşov, which appeared totally surrounded by towering forest.

The last train: jerky, with a poky van and small window. The keeper released the wolves. About an hour's journey, the young guard had told him. He brought in a bowl of water and then another. He was training to be a forester in the Piatra Craiuliu mountains. He would thin the trees by hand; there was no digging machinery here.

'The forest floor is then left strong and undisturbed,' he said. He loved wolves. He lay down on the dusty boards as they clambered over him with dripping mouths. 'They are no danger to a man,' he assured the keeper. 'They deserve a better image. And we must pray for the puppies; they are the future of the species.' He knelt on all fours; Louis, Titu and Nicu jumped over him, knocked him about and rolled on their backs. They yelped and yipped joyously as the guardsman tickled their pink downy stomachs. As the train chugged out of Braşov, past the green lung of the central park, the keeper noticed an imposing statue, set high on a plinth of rich, red marble. He nudged the guardsman.

'What is it?' And the wolves crowded round the window to take a look. Louis barked. It was a wolf.

'A legend from near one thousand years. There are many such statues in our Romanian cities of the she-wolf suckling Romulus and Remus. Seven hundred years ago, the original bronze statue had stood in the portico to Rome's Palazzo dei Conservatori. In them days,' concluded the guardsman, 'it was water came out of her teats and people washed their hands under her.' The train had paused and the keeper stared at the wolf's wide-open mouth. Perhaps she was panting from the rigours of expressing milk. He noted she had eight full teats; the baby twins had mouths tilted back and chubby little hands upturned to catch the flow. One sat with plump legs outstretched and the other knelt on one knee. The keeper breathed in deeply and sighed. He remembered that old tale: the illegitimate twin sons of the virgin Rhea Silvia and her lover Mars, the god of war; how they were condemned to death and flung into the Tiber. Washed ashore, their pitiful cries had been heard by the nursing she-wolf. And when she finally ran dry she left the babes in a cave on the Palatine Hill. 'Romulus and Remus,' called out the keeper to his wolves. 'The legendary founders of Rome, and thanks be to the she-wolf who nurtured them.'

It was cooler in the van.

'The breezes from the mountain,' called the guardsman. 'Zarneşti is near upon us.' A small mountain town was spreading out from the Carpathian foothills; the sturdy stucco houses, washed in rose, lemon and palest blue, had walnut trees and cherry blossom in their gardens. The train rumbled past rustic avenues of chestnut and silver birch. Many trees had whitened lower trunks. The lime from the mountains was smeared over to keep the parasites away, explained the guardsman. Horses trotted by pulling heavy wagons. 'A horse cart is what you need now. It will take you to the open ground at the start of the forest. You let go your wolves and it is a fine, new life they start; wild and real.' The keeper nodded distractedly. He could not believe that his engaging cargo would soon be gone, irrefutably vanished into a world of savagery and survival.

At Zarneşti, the young guardsman seized a wagon and a pair of horses for the wolf party. A barrel-vaulted canvas roof enabled the wolves to leave their cages. The wagoner barred their exit with a sheep's hurdle.

'Nice horses,' volunteered the keeper, more in query than statement; he was wary of horses. The wagon-driver sat in wooden concentration as they trotted along the white limestone lanes of Zarneşti. In an old tweed cap and leather waistcoat with his sinewy arms, he appeared more than competent. As if sensing the keeper's apprehension, he waved a hunting crop at the horses' heads.

'The red tassels – you see them? Fixed to the bridle headstalls?' The keeper leaned forward, holding fast to his plank seat; the thick red tassels swung merrily. 'They guard us from the evil eye,' he was informed. 'No disaster will become of us. And where do I take you, young man? You wish to release these innocent young wolves into the wild unknown?'

The keeper felt wretched; a traitor even.

'It has come to that. They need their liberty; it is their rightful heritage. Wolves must procreate. They are a distinguished species.'

'And endangered too.' The wagoner nodded ruefully. 'It is still a bad time for wolves in Romania. There are wolf-traps and random poisoning in the forests and much searching for wolf dens and killing of pups.' The wagoner's tongue was loosed on his captive audience. 'Naturally, the bear, boar and deer are prone to these perils, but they are more savvy. Today, in the late sixties, our dictator is anxious to preserve the bears. He is a trophy hunter and likes also to shoot red deer and chamois; horns, antlers, boar tusks and bear rugs are all part of the sport. A sportsman needs the forests teeming with game and so our dictator now reduces traps and poisons. But I tell you, young man, pray for the puppies.' It was the same warning given to him by the young forester guarding them on the Zarneşti train. 'And we have the Orient here,' continued the garrulous wagoner. 'They value the bear claws for necklaces. The sound of claws rattling round the neck induces healing from the ursine spirit. And they value the paws; bear paw soup is a great delicacy. The meat of the left paw is sweetest as it is used to handle the honey extract from the beehives.'

The keeper, befuddled with such a glut of information, stared down at Louis-Loup. The wolf held his head to one side as he watched his keeper; he listened for a sign. The end of the road? The start of the unknown? And yes – new responsibilities. Who spoke? Man or wolf? Louis turned and nuzzled his dozing cubs. 'Louis,' called the keeper softly, his throat constricted and tears welled in his eyes . . . a sudden lurch flung him to the floor. The horses had plunged into the ditch, heaving the wagon into a topsy-turvy near overturn. They had seen a pack of stray dogs running towards the road. The trusty driver pulled mightily on the reins, and in a body the startled horses yanked themselves up on the road again. The keeper, hurled from side to side, had held his seat firmly, with arms wide apart. He urged the wolves to quieten down. They were growling accusingly at each other. (And which one of us was to blame for this wayward débâcle?)

'We soon say goodbye to your wolves.' The driver indicated a twin-peaked mountain; the wooded foothills swooped to the hay meadows, with the Carpathian range undulating far beyond. He turned the horses off the rough road. They cropped the lush spring grass. The wolves stood expectantly, sniffing curiously, licking their lips, their ears pricked.

The keeper groaned. 'I never gave them a last feed.'

'Never fear, they will have a banquet waiting in these forests; trout, pheasant, black woodpecker, roe-deer, and high up the mountain crags they will find chamois. I can take you . . .'

There was an anguished bark-howl from Louis; all pent up patience had snapped. Leaping into the wagon, the driver released the wolves. The three jumped ecstatically on to the grass and raced to the woods.

'Louis-Loup! Nicu! Titu! Come back to me! Say goodbye!' The keeper ached to see a final glimpse: the eternal image of their lean backs, tails held high, streaking off into a free-range world. The green gloom of the fir trees wrapped around them; it was daunting to dwell on their passage. The keeper crumpled on his hard seat, his head in his hands, his eyes again smarting with tears. 'We never said goodbye!' he called, half-choked with his grief. 'They leapt away from me. They never turned in their track, to check that I was there, to roll in submission, to howl out their love . . .'

The sturdy wagoner edged up to his distraught traveller and handed him a cup of pine syrup. 'Knock it back,' he commanded. 'It has healing properties. You wish me to take you a walk through these woods? Early evening is a pleasant time.' He guided his horses across the grass approach to the trees and tethered their forelegs. The keeper was led like a lamb; naturally he was intrigued to see the habitat of his late charges. 'These valleys and hay meadows by the south Carpathians are the pride of Romania. The forests are a miracle – you will see. Come!' They entered a world where flora and fauna held sway. All was tranquil here; every species could burrow, grow or hide in its own time and space. Ancient, rearing tree roots and limestone boulders were swathed in moss. The forest floor was spongy to the tread and crunched with fir cones and needles. The keeper identified dock leaves and coltsfoot and dead nettle, with its soft, pink flower.

'The brown bear scours these woods in the autumn; for mushrooms and beech nuts, cranberries and bilberries. Primarily a vegan, he still likes the odd deer and ungulate. He dens all winter, feeding off his accumulated glut. See here!' The wagoner stepped aside. He slapped the soft bark of a spruce tree and pointed to dents on the trunk, from where resin weeped.

'A bear bite – and look higher – that long level gash is his scratch. He is marking his territory. Rubbing his great body against the tree is another caution. Bears bite on the bark to strengthen their teeth and then claw their way up. Your boys would have smelt these territorial scent markers. They will soon learn the mores of the forest world.' The keeper had fallen silent. He was treasuring these last moments in the forest. A thrush sang exultantly above the murmured trill of a stream.

'Much fish?' he asked the wagoner.

'Buckets,' the man assured him. 'Your boys will survive.'

PART THREE
Clan Life – Romania

19

As the three wolves tore across the meadow, they were seized with frantic joy. Freedom had been thrown to them as a gift; they caught it head-on with heart and limb. Plunging into the dim, green, trackless forests, they bounded on without seeing or hearing; but the scents engulfed them. They loped higher and higher up the mountains, beneath lofty archways of beech trees and ash, and over limestone boulders clustered with a yellow herb that smelt sharp and medicinal. 'Wood sage,' Louis called to his boys, and then, 'here we have the Grass of Parnassus, the white star that threads through the reeds.' And he thought how he must stop this nature trail; it was of blood and bones and carnivore and prey that he must tell his Nicu and Titu. They settled by a chortling stream to eat and drink. 'Trout and silver grayling prefer the cold mountain water; running over rocks, it is full of oxygen and charges the blood. As the sun dips, they will leap for the mayfly and you boys must jump for your feed.' Titu had already set his eyes on a young fish; idling above its camouflage of mottled brown stones, it swayed its tail. Titu leapt at the water and plunged his snout into his first catch. With the fish clenched in his teeth, he paraded the dripping trophy before his father. There was a crackling of undergrowth and snapping of branches. The three wolves stood, ears pricked, rigid and alert. Two black mountain goats sped past through the forest shadows. But in their wake a large bear emerged and stared fixedly at the wolves. Nicu raised a paw.

'Don't move,' warned Louis. 'If she has cubs around, we are in danger.'

The bear ambled up to a juniper tree and rubbed her hefty, dark flank against the trunk. She snorted deeply at the bark.

'It's elk's saliva she smells,' hissed Louis. 'And she leaves her own scent mark with her fur. She is marking her territory.'

The bear looked up accusingly. There was only the stream and some one hundred yards between them. Slowly, she stood on her hind legs, menacing in her majestic height, her massive forearms opened wide as though to hug them.

'Turn slowly and fall in column behind me,' commanded Louis, and he led them away in a slow walk.

After some distance they found another stream and continued their feeding. Explained Louis: 'The bear is the ruling species of these Carpathian mountains. One clout from those powerful arms and he can maul and claw you to death; he could crush your ribcage and break your neck.' Titu, now gorged on grayling, nodded sagely at his father's commentary. In the forest only a few hours and they had seen the lot . . . 'The bear is a clumsy runner,' continued Louis, 'and can't climb trees.'

Nicu cried: 'Father! I see bear cubs and they are climbing a tree!' He was pointing to a thicket of spruce where four golden cubs were gamboling high up in the dense foliage. Louis explained: 'They are having tooth and claw practice; scratching and digging their teeth into that soft, spicy wood. You just watch them come down.' And bottoms first, clinging and sliding, they reached the foot of the trunk. So, thought Nicu, bears come down bottom first and cats and rats head first – but the wolf is fastest of all.

'Come, boys, that mother will be looking for her cubs. We must find a night place.'

'What is this black, shiny stuff, father?' Titu was prodding with his paw at bear droppings.

'That is scat.' Louis led them down through the forest to a small, clear-cut, free of animal markings. Nicu found a lump of something decayed to clench in his lower jaw. He placed it proudly at Louis' feet. 'And that is a rotten old foot pad, shed by a bear, sometime back in March. Inedible.'

'And what is scat, father?' Titu asked.

'Scat is more interesting. That pat of little black rounds you saw was the excreta of a bear; the few bone particles of his feed were wrapped in fur, to protect his rectal canal; that is nature's way with the bear's digestion. In the autumn you will see strawberry seeds, raspberry and apple pips in the bear's scat. The bear eats little meat; he is more omnivorous. But he could take on a horse or a roe-deer.'

'And could he eat us wolves?' Nicu and Titu were curled round each other at the foot of a thick beech tree.

'Unlikely; we consist of muscle and our palates are incompatible.' He noticed a fallen trunk, clawed and weakened by a bear. It was seething with insects in the wide cracks. 'And eat fresh grass to clear out the parasites,' he warned. 'Tomorrow we will make a big feed,' he promised. As they lay cushioned in the long summer grass, on their first night in the mountain forest, it was clear to Louis there was much exploring needed before they could start denning. Naturally he would want to be part of a wolf pack, laired higher up in the rocky ranges. But first he wanted to feel his ground, to initiate Titu and Nicu in the dangers of the wild. He wanted to stalk these south Carpathians in his own time. To lope through orchids and lilies, across alpine plateaux, through orchards, vineyards, lakes and rivers and then higher to the rocks and ridges, the forest glades and the yellow poppy flower. He would keep his boys close in these forays. Any straying on to unfamiliar land could lead to their starvation or death. 'Pray for the puppies,' both the young forester and horse driver had cautioned him. He must soon settle with his kind; find a pack that would accept them into their close unit and share their territory, their hunting and, all importantly, their feed. But for a few precious days, he would relish the independence with his boys, their joint discoveries and shocks and triumphs. The night was still, with a rising moon. Louis heard scuffling, scratching and faint tapping to suggest the forest floor was teeming with nocturnal life. An owl swooped past their tree and perched in another. Louis gazed at the large, flat face with the hooked nose and staring eyes; the fringe of feathers framing its broad head shivered as it let rip a screeching hoot. Bright pinpricks of tiny eyes darted through the far bushes; martens, Louis guessed: pine martens and beech martens favoured these mountain forests. There was rapid rustling as a roe-deer hurtled past. Who was chasing who? The solitary lynx? As fleet as a pocket tiger, it skimmed after the deer. Louis slept finally; but a sense of dark secrets, the supernatural and a parade of sanguineous apparitions dodged his dreams.

The wolves woke to the sound of wood sawing; and to thirst and hunger. Titu caught a brown rabbit and Nicu demolished a mole.

'Fall into line,' ordered Louis as he picked their path beside a mountain stream. The sawing was intermittent, broken with men's shouts; they heard a tree crack sharply and crash to the ground.

Louis motioned the boys to stalk and not be seen. Crouched in the wild grass, edging the clear-cuts they watched the men work. Sections of spruce, supported in horse racks, were being sawed by hand. There was a trailer in the woods, which puffed smoke from a wood stove; a warm retreat for the men at day's end. Louis counted six of them. One looked so thin and hunched that Louis wished him dead as an alternative. As though struck by this sensory warning, the gnome's gimlet eye cut through Louis' cover like a sword. There was no mistaking he was a wolf-killer. He had smelt them, felt them.

'Fetch me my sniper rifle,' he snarled. Fingering the adjustable tube lovingly, he raised it to the woods, scanning to the left and right. 'Scarpered!' The wolf-killer spat venomously. He was surprised to have seen wolves by these alpine meadows; stalking at low level for livestock? It was the season for the herds to come up from the valley for fresh grazing. He must be away now sussing out pups in their dens, and smashing their little skulls with the axe. He would lay around the lair a ring of dainty poisoned portions; bayonet them as they slept, or even gun the lot of them, the she-wolf and all, holed up in the den. Where was the silencer? Torch? Nightstick? The little wolf-killer patted his pockets, fat with his orders for pelts, pulled down his cap and set off higher up the woods.

Louis, Nicu and Titu had observed his every movement. 'Enemy number one,' growled Louis. They watched the loggers lock up their corrugated cabin and trundle down to the valleys in their horse and cart. Their load of beech and spruce logs was stacked in neat cylindrical cuts. Louis did not trust the wolfer further than the next tree. He kept his boys close. The evening was still and warm. They fed on baby brown trout and field mice. Louis had planned an early night; they would wake in the early hours and move through darkness, higher up the mountain forests. They curled up in a juniper glade where the aromatic oil from the cones induced deep sleep. But Louis was woken to the screaming calls and yowling of a wolf; such a shrill and piercing cry; the pain and pleading ate into his groin. He lay on his back in a helpless strait-jacket of fear. From the brilliant moon, high above the trees, he gauged the hour past midnight. The boys woke and, as one, they stalked cautiously through the forest up to the source of anguish. White fluffy thistles, huge in the moonlight, flanked their way like bowing phantoms. Louis sensed a stealthy tread following behind but saw nothing. He had heard tell of phantom black dogs on these moonlit forest tracks. Then in a thicket they saw a she-wolf, lunging and jumping in the air; her neck was caught in a lasso of wire attached to a tree. With each thrust her screams became weaker and more hoarse. The wolves looked on helplessly at this scene of exceptional horror and backed into the trees. From the shadows, two cautious forest wardens closed in on her. Louis heard them muttering.

'See that spool on the neck snare? It tightens and locks and takes the skin off the throat; cuts into the air passages.'

'Is she done for?'

As the two men approached, the wolf feigned death, slumping up against the tree trunk. One supported her body as the other cut the wire. The wolf fell to the ground, stunned and motionless. The wardens knelt to rub down her back and her hind legs. They pushed down gently on her prone body with thin, soft shoes. She bounded away.

'It is that little wolf-killer at work; purging the wolves for the autumn bear hunting. The 'Big Cheese' decrees the brown bear be protected for sport.' Said the other: 'Time not spent hunting is wasted, they say. It's the sport of kings.'

Louis and the cubs had seen it all: the evil and the good. Louis was again riven with morbid sensations: a suffocating premonition that something bad was about to happen. In the tree beside them, a branch snapped. Louis smelt the skin and breath of a human. Looking down at them from the tree was the wolf-killer, his rifle visible through the leaves.

'I will soon find her pups. Beware of my traps. Buzz off you bumpkins.'

The three wolves sprinted up the mountain. And as they tore from that malevolent scene, Louis knew that the odour emanating from the tree had been that of a woman. The wolf-killer was a *she*.

'Tell us about the wolf-killer, father – our enemy number one.' They were resting through the day in a deserted rock hole; some long-seasoned wolf den scattered with whitened bones and the skulls of sheep and goats.

'The wolf-killer wants to kill off our species. She has the tacit approval of the needy shepherds and the rich hunters. She seeks out and kills the pups in their dens; until guns and poison are outlawed, our wolf population will waste away. Where are you off to, Nicu?'

'I smell something interesting.' From out of the rocky recess, he dragged out the skull of a deer with the brain intact. They next found mashed fungus beetles in the bole of a tree.

'Listen carefully to your father. Do not run ahead of me. We have much to learn and fear in these forests. Traps and poison. Remember? There is peril in every blade of grass. Stop shunting that skull around, Nicu. Bring it here. You know the old myth? "When baby is ill, pass his bottle of milk through a wolf's skull and chase the illness away". And have you heard of leg-hold traps? Foot snares? Cage traps? But the worst danger, dear young boys, come close, the worst danger is the lure.'

'Is that a type of wild cat, father?'

'No, Titu, it is the intoxicating smell of wolf urine, or lynx scat. If you tiptoe to take a deeper gulp – wham!'

The boys jumped.

'If your paw triggers a foot snare, a wire loop will spring up and close around your paw. Biting through this snare wire is a lengthy task. But if your leg is trapped in jaws of steel, you can do nothing but wait on your fate.'

Nicu and Titu cowered before their father in abject fear.

'Most probably a forest warden or gamekeeper will collar you. He will inject your hind muscle with a tranquilliser. He will release you from the trap and, while you are in a befuddled state, he will fit you out with a collar.'

'But we have never had collars!' cried the cubs.

'Your freedom is your own precious right. Keep it. A leather radio collar is heavy and cumbersome; lapped with two steel plates and nuts and bolts and a Perspex bubble, it transmits your every move to men fielding wolf research. Now quiet please. An afternoon nap before we move on.'

'But we are always moving on,' said Titu querulously. 'What are we moving on to?'

It was late dusk before Louis led his cubs up to the forest glade. He had again been plagued by the sense of being followed; of being weighted down on his tracks. Yet he could see and smell nothing and the boys bounded ahead. 'Titu! Nicu! Stay close to me.' He had smelt the irresistible tang of rotting flesh; a dead horse? An ox? The cubs danced up at Louis impatiently. Across the glade beside a stream, strung high around the trunk of a tree, could be seen the half-devoured carcass of a horse. Left by the game wardens to fatten the bears? Or was this a bear bait site for shooting bears or any other carnivore? They tore into the sweet flesh and, in minutes, had taken their fill. Scattered skulls of dogs and sheep, horse shoulder bones and cattle tibia, glared white in the rising moon. It was a place of death and feasting. And the wolves smelt trouble. The wolf-killer's presence had been masked by the dense putrefaction. There was heavy breathing in the branches above. They darted up the chortling river.

'Your bellies will fleece better with your feed digested. You young gluttons!' The high screech and crazy laughter of enemy number one ricocheted through the trees. Fear gave them wings as they fled along the river bank; but they were soon barred. Trotting towards them was another bear. They leapt into the water. With growls, bared teeth and angry, chomping jaws, the beast rose on its hind legs. It snorted hard at them and blew and puffed and panted. Clearly it suspected them of feeding on its bait. The wolves flew on, hugging the river until Louis called a halt; he had another tactic.

'We will fan out back through the woods, in good sight of each other, and return to the bear site. It is the wolf-killer we need to lead astray. She saw our escape route.'

As he spoke, a single shot rang out from the feeding site, followed by roars of wild pain and squealing. The wolves tensed; the nearby crackling of undergrowth signified a severely wounded mammal charging its attacker. Louis motioned his cubs further into the wood. He assumed the wolfer would chase after her prey for a final shot and the spoils. But enemy number one had hurtled up a tree. A second shot at the rampaging bear and it was felled. An alerted warden came running up. He yelled in scorn at the wolf-killer.

'You murderous little dolt. You are a menace in these forests, you filthy felon. Don't you know to shoot a bear on the side or across the back? Shooting at him full frontal has led to a vile death. Whatever tree you are up, get out and stay out.'

The wolves hung back, well camouflaged in the night shadows. A second warden came, and Louis and the cubs listened hard to their talk. They watched intently as the two men approached the bear; a silenced, dead beast.

'That wolfer should be shot. Fancy helping herself to such a colossus – and with no special licence. She should keep to wolves; wolves have no protection order yet; they have a bad deal, wolves: traps, strychnine, bad will, greedy poachers.' They reached the bear, deflated in death with the warm blood marking its final rest. They disembowelled it and the young man was stationed by the grim hulk, to wait for a cart. Louis was in a quandary: the wolf-killer would have escaped up the river. He guided his cubs back down to the bear feeding site; another helping of horse would settle their stomachs. The three wolves anticipated, with relish, some more feed, and stalked cautiously to their goal. They stood on the edge of the clearing. All was silent; no bird or tree stirred. Louis led the way in a slow skulk. As he neared the ravaged, dark mass of the hanging carcass, he smelt the poison: rat poison mixed with lime. He whipped round and herded the cubs back to the woods.

'What would happen if we fed on that smelly stuff?' asked Nicu.

'If you feed on such poison you will have a painful death. When your stomach digests such abomination, it will haemorrhage; you will have bursts of internal bleeding and the most agonising torture. We will now take an easterly direction and stay clear of the enemy. There were vestiges of her body smell around the poisoned horse meat. She is a devil.'

'She? Father?'

196

'Yes, she is a *she* wolf-killer; a witch.'

The wolves woke to their fourth day in the forest; a day for denning, decided Louis, and for initiating the cubs in a kill. They had climbed to the higher mountain forests and were still shielded by beech woods and spruce, a dense cover that yielded a variety of small prey: rabbit, hare, wild fowl and game birds. If they mounted higher to the rough and rocky pinnacles, their cover would be weakened. This was now the time and place to settle, to be aware of wolf territory and existing clans, to rigidly respect their privacy. Every species marked its habitat limitations. It was a matter of tolerance and trust; an accepted *force majeure*. How to make himself and his cubs known? wondered Louis. He had heard not one howl. Spring and summer was not a busy time for howling. Nicu and Titu came to him to hear the day's plan.

'We have to introduce ourselves,' announced Louis; 'do you remember, boys, the howling practice you were given by Marco-père? We will go to the river where our call will travel more clearly. My strong adult howl should be heard eight kilometres by man and even further by wolves. We can alert the whole upper forest in our need to communicate. We must listen hard for an answering voice; our days of roaming alone must now end. We need the protection of a clan's acceptance. The cry of a lone wolf,' continued Louis solemnly, 'means a stranger to the community. It does not induce welcome or even sympathy from the surrounding packs. They have to husband their own feeding lands and their growing young. It will be clear to any wolf that heeds our calls that we are misfits in the habitat.'

Titu and Nicu blinked at their father in astonishment. They had always been led to feel infinitely desirable. Louis looked tenderly into their lustrous amber eyes.

'Do you see well in the dark?' he asked them.

Very sharply, they assured him, in black and white.

'If your vision was ever reduced and your powers to detect odour diminished, it is your howl that can lead you to safety. Before we begin I have a comforting myth to tell: St Peter the apostle comes each winter to the forest to distribute food for the wolves. A shepherd climbs a tree to check that not one of his sheep will be caught and eaten. Each wolf comes for his share of sheep and deer. Finally there is no sheep left for a limping wolf. The shepherd sacrifices himself.'

'And I have a tale.' Nicu sat tall on his haunches: '"Dracula" means 'Devil' or 'Dragon'; and every weird and evil thought that ever was is whirled around in the horseshoe of the Carpathians.'

'And mine too,' called Titu: 'Birds have made nests in the skulls of Dracula's victims. The Carpathians still echo to screams and rattling chains; to werewolves and whining mosquitoes.'

'You are a couple of literary sophisticates,' said Louis in surprise. 'We must now attempt a howl. Let us stand.' The wolves lined the riverbank, facing upstream. Again Louis reminded his boys of the hidden motives of a howl: the call of a lone wolf seeking a clan; a lost wolf seeking his clan; the call of a pack inciting play; or a fight. A rousing hunting call; a claim of territorial territory. 'And . . .'

'And what?' asked Nicu and Titu, standing close to their father, attentive and subdued.

'And a mating call; not yet applicable.'

And what was their own howl to convey?

'We will convey that we are a willing, able trio, new on the scene; that we seek acceptance by the lupine forestry body and a clan; that we will be an asset to the community.'

'Wolves need each other, don't they, father? They like to belong.' Titu looked to Louis for reassurance.

198

'To belong in groups, Titu, Nicu; to understand each other's needs and feelings without explaining. We will find our clan. Never fear.'

Louis took his stance on the bank. With head up and ears back he released a few plaintive moans. Next, with all the resonance he could muster, Louis' vocal chords opened with a modest baritone that swelled to a high register, falling to silence. Again and again he howled for a minute at a time. The cubs looked on in awe until Louis butted them into action. On the fifth call, Titu and Nicu joined in with their high, thin timbre as their father rolled out his deep call, soaring to a ghostly height, to drop deep in to the quivering woods. The distant silences following each bout were disappointing. The cubs moaned despairingly to their father.

'No clans want to know us. They don't want to let us in. They don't need us. Their feed is too small to share.'

Louis explained that a midday in May was not the most evocative moment to howl; that early summer was not the season to hunt in a pack; that the older wolves liked to hunt their feed alone, on a choice of smaller creatures: marmot, squirrel, rabbit and fish, and with their worn out teeth preferred to eat more slowly than the younger ones. There was a crashing through the trees; Louis smelt roe-deer leaping towards them full tilt. She clattered into the river, as in one bound he sprung at her hindquarters, digging in his claws. Nicu and Titu, as to the manner born, leapt at her shoulders and, biting into the neck, brought her down in the shallow water. The young deer lashed out frantically with her hoofs and Louis realised there was no time before scavengers would attack their spoils. Ravens were already cawing and swirling above the trees. He ripped out the heart and lungs and intestines; the three wolves raced off into the woods with their prize feed. It took minutes only to devour their succulent portions. Louis led them deeper into the forest to rest.

'Remember,' he solemnly reminded his boys, 'we wolves kill only to survive; that is the cardinal rule of our species. Wolves do not slaughter sheep; a pack will take only the one or two beasts that it needs.' Louis was inwardly amazed at his cubs' combined success in felling such an excellent animal. It made him feel secure as a potential hunting force. He knew that a wolf could exist for three weeks without feed, but that would take some explaining to Nicu and Titu; a young wolf's appetite for adventure and feed was the basic prerequisite to wild life. Still dozing in the late afternoon, they heard a cart rumble past. They were well hidden in bushes and listened in on the two wardens.

'Wolves have been here. They left the roe-deer in the river and scarpered. They say the 'Big Cheese' plans to shoot chamois this summer. He won't want wolves around. We must watch for trouble; any preliminary attacks on sheep or the rye, potato and maize crops, and we must step up the snares and traps.'

'Have you seen the Big Cheese?' asked the other.

'Once. On a bear shoot. Cherubic, plump cheeks, full lips, thick, dark, greying hair. A good shot – not too greedy. He has not done badly by us. Today, only three years into his rule, and it is a cheap time; free water, full employment. He was born a peasant and has worked his way from eleven years old, when he was apprenticed to a shoemaker in Bucharest. He understands the land and he likes his sport.' The warden paused and added reflectively: 'He is a good fellow, excepting if he gets to be a bad fellow.'

The bones of the savaged carcass were tossed lightly into the cart.

'My good woman could make a tasty broth out of them knuckles,' claimed the younger warden.

The three wolves stepped out into the evening. The forest reverberated with thrushes and wood warblers, and the summer nightingales joined in.

'Let's howl again,' urged Titu, and in a thin reedy voice, attempted the swell and swoop of a meaningful call. Nicu and Louis linked voices and a bout of tolerable howling took over. They paused. It was as if even the birds had hushed; a moment of acute anticipation. And then, an answer; the cry of a lone wolf; a she-wolf with a weakened voice, asking for help. She howled once more. Louis was intrigued to seek this frail caller; he and the cubs loped down through the woods. She had sounded so vulnerable, a point of empathy between them all.

'Father! Father!' Louis turned to see his cubs hovering by a deep earth tunnel plunged into a grass slope. A circle of rocks added protection to the den, and branches from the logging covered the approach. Standing beside his boys, Louis could hear the pups inside, whining and fretting for food. Through the leaves he detected four young, their eyes still fast shut from birth. They licked and nuzzled each other feverishly. Louis could see fleas on their little sunken bellies. It was apparent they had been abandoned. Indeed they were ravenous, dehydrated and on the point of death. The wolves crowded into the litter's den. Louis demonstrated to the boys how to regurgitate their own substantial feed to the pups. An exercise, which led to much general licking of lips and sniffing and feeding. Louis asked the boys to look for water and within yards they found some, pocketed in the bole of a beech tree. One by one, the pups were carried by the wolves to the cache of rain water. Louis showed Nicu and Titu how to open their jaws wide and transport the pups from the middle of the back and not by the scruff of the neck. When all were fed and re-settled, Louis proposed another howl. Their call was answered immediately. It appeared that the weakened she-wolf with the tentative voice was close to them. And again she called, on a high and stronger timbre. Louis and his cubs sat rigid and expectant by the den. They were consumed with curiosity.

She soon arrived; a little diffident and undeniably anxious over her pups. Stirring from their post-prandial, they had sensed and smelt their mother; a reunion of yelping and licking and nuzzling snouts ensured that after an absence of two days and two nights all puppy love was intact. The she-wolf extricated herself from the fusty warmth of the den to face her benefactors.

Louis knew he had seen her before. It was the night they had found the wolf lunging against the wire noose with the ratchet tightening on her neck. It was she. How had she recovered so fast and effectively? She intimated that first she needed water. They led her to the bole of the beech tree and found her fungus beetles and lichen. She had a desperate story to tell.

She had been hounded, she told them, by an evil and murderous she-wolfer. The little menace had been seen stalking the area, picking her moment to shoot the newborn pups. The she-wolf mother was seriously distressed with the story she had to tell. Louis and his boys sat quietly. Two evenings ago the killer had pounced. She had advanced brazenly on the she-wolf and her alpha mate, as they sat quietly beside the wolf den. The killer's sniper rifle was ready, poised to thrust through the den first and then at the alpha couple. Suddenly, and in a wild fury, her alpha mate had leapt at the wolfer and, clawing on her shoulders, had brought her down. Unfortunately her rifle went off and caught the wolf in his hindquarter. He lashed at her again with such ferocity that, seizing her gun, she escaped into the woods. But the shock of the whole evil incident had done for the she-wolf's mate. When she reached him, to lie in love and comfort beside him, he was dead. His tongue had slid to the back of his mouth, blocking the air passage and had suffocated him. The she-wolf shook with fright and misery at the near memory of it all. In fear of her own life and in wild despair for her pups, she had run through the woods for help. From where she knew not. The sharp undergrowth tore at her belly. Then she had been cruelly caught; tripped by the wire noose looped around the tree trunk. A dead faint came over her. In a last feat of survival, she clung to consciousness, leaning against the trunk; one slip to the foot of the tree and she could have been strangled. The night was still early; lowering herself carefully she could rub her body up and down against the trunk. It soothed her and kept her awake. She was totally and dangerously exhausted. The moon was high and it was then she howled and growled and bark-howled for attention. 'The foresters came.' There was silence as the wolves digested these appalling events.

'And we came too,' Louis assured her, remembering her appalling shrieks of pain.

The she-wolf crunched on her mashed fungus beetles as Louis, with a surge of elation, realised that he was effectively now in charge. A slender contingent of four pups, still birth-blind, a severely traumatised she-wolf, a pair of gangling young wolves could hardly denote a clan; but for Louis, Nicu and Titu it spelt promise and communication; a shared survival and all the fun of the lair.

The first essential was for Louis and his boys to make up a den close to the she-wolf, with their mutual security and protection in mind. A small rock cave within yards of the she-wolf was found, and the boys pummelled out an earth hollow beyond. An air of insouciance fell over the two dens and the disparate little clan. The relief of a joined dependence lessened the fears of the

203

forest; its abrupt and bitter blows. Louis was primarily concerned with the she-wolf's health; her vocal cords had been severely damaged by the wire lasso. Some days she could do little but open and shut her jaw to emit a pathetic squeak; until one day she joined in a howl with gusto. Her fur was mangy and her hind muscles weak. But Louis and the boys frolicked with her; dashing off with invitations to a chase soon developed her buttocks and thighs. When the pups' eyes opened a pale blue, and milk teeth appeared, her mask was wreathed in joy. As the she-wolf regained her spirits and her pups grew bigger, an ambience of happy pride enveloped the clan.

An interim month of peace and integration had benefited them all. Louis and the obliging Titu and Nicu had garnered the feed with field mice, trout and rabbit. A month old, the four pups, two a fluffy black and two gold, pushed out their snouts to the daylight of the shaded green forest. Their grunting and first stumbling steps were shielded possessively by the she-wolf. Louis and the boys stood by, coaxing and encouraging. With the cubs now venturing into the outside world, they had become the clan's whole responsibility. As they grew stronger and more adventurous, the more games were played. Louis and the she-wolf, Nicu and Titu were perfectly enslaved with such *jeunesse dorée*.

Louis reflected on the parlous state of the pups a mere month before: half-starved, dehydrated, seemingly abandoned, their mother lost and sick. It was clearly a close margin between surviving and thriving. But despite these days of fun and order and the happy preoccupation with the pups and their rapid progress, a notion of foreboding hung over Louis. He sensed the familiar miasma from the wolf-killer. In the early evening when the light was low, he felt it strong and close. Not every evening, but when it was there, there was no denying that it was there: a clinging cloud that curled round his throat and compressed his larynx. Louis and his cubs would ingratiate themselves to any foresters or wardens that passed by; fawning, tail-wagging and flashing their bellies. The men knew about the dens and the pups and gave the clan their implicit protection. But still Louis felt the danger. One evening it came; a bolt out of the blue. A wounded bear; but who was wounding these bears? It hurtled out of the trees in pain and fury and charged the dens. Louis, the she-wolf, the boys and the pups were sprawled languidly on the grass, nibbling and crunching pleasurably on red grouse and mountain goat. The she-wolf seized the pups, dragging and kicking them inside her den. The bear was one hundred yards from them. Louis, Nicu and Titu had no choice but to attack the roaring beast. Louis flung himself at its neck and shoulder. Nicu and Titu galloped up and clawed and bit into the hindquarters. The beleaguered beast rolled to the ground and, with its great paws, lunged at the two young wolves. The gasping and hollering from its tragic plight reached the ears of the wardens. They rushed to the scene with hypodermic rifles. The bear had been shot, once again full frontal, and clearly the work of the wolf-killer. The wardens put the young beast to sleep. They yelled up at the trees:

'Are you there, you murderous little nincompoop? This time we report you to the Big Cheese.'

The bear was slumped in peace. A large cart was brought along with two more men. Finally the beast, with his fur in its prime, was humped on board. 'He is worth saving,' said one of the wardens, 'the vet will attend in the morning.'

When night fell, Louis listened intently for snapping branches and crackling undergrowth for signs that the wolf-killer was lurking still. And then a profound relief stole over him, as though his fear had been lanced. He knew that this evil and incompetent killer would be removed.

The early summer passed peacefully; it was a somnolent time for wolves. No voracious appetites to appease, no chase, no predation on crops or livestock, no hunger. But Louis had instilled in his cubs an innate curiosity and a natural thirst for lupine lore and the ways of the forest. There was one predator that Titu and Nicu had not yet tracked: the sinuous lynx; feline, with leopard-like dark spots and a formidable deer stalker. It amused them to keep their eyes skinned for this well camouflaged creature. The lynx favoured steep and rocky areas, with fresh water creeks, where it kept cool in summer. The young wolves found such a place. One early evening a streak of spots flashed past them. It was clearly on the forage. The wolves hung back, they neither heard nor saw any more and loped home. The next afternoon they took up their post in the trees, when two keepers halted their cart. They carried a metal cage with trap doors on either side. The box was placed beside a known lynx trail, running through the woods. They put in two small mirrors in order to reflect light and the movement of leaves; bird wings and feathers were next heaped in the centre.

'Where is the skunk oil? And the wolf scat?'

The keepers sprinkled the objects liberally and shut the trap doors.

'I have never seen a skunk,' said the young man.

'They are not from these parts; American carnivores they are. Nice little beasties, black with white stripes, bushy-tailed and the stink from their anal glands is to die for. Drives their fellow predators mad with desire.'

Titu and Nicu hardly breathed for fear of betraying their cover.

Finally the keepers left and the two wolves took up their stance further away. They waited in captive anticipation. Evening was coming on; father would fret. A wolf howled. 'Father!' They answered him and he called back closer. As he reached them the lynx sprang up to the cage. It backed and reared elegantly in a provocative dance and was maddened by the pile of bird wings. Assuming elegant postures, she sniffed the skunk oil from every angle.

'She is a young lynx,' hissed Louis. 'Her curiosity will kill her.' She stepped on the whipping board. The trap doors snapped open slamming back on their pretty prey. There was a miaow of surprise, an eager pounce at the feathers and the traces of skunk, much cleaning of whiskers and a reclining position of studied ennui.

'I like skunk,' ventured Titu.

'That's not skunk, that's lynx.'

'I know, father,' Nicu jumped in, 'it's the stink of the skunk Titu likes.'

'Sssshh, boys. Somebody comes.'

It was the keepers again. They talked softly as they neared the cage trap. There had been a deal of lynx poaching. An illegal hunter in the foothills was found with lynx pelts hanging out all over his living room and the jaws and skeletons from the deer killings. There had been too much loss of lynx; never a high productive breed, its population was sinking.

'Hi there!' They rounded on the cage. 'Aren't you just a beauty?' The lynx stood snarling, her mask to one side, her lovely eyes narrowed and glinting. She glared at her uninvited visitors with disdain. The keepers talked to her in slow, quiet voices.

'Gently, gently, we won't hurt you. Just a little prick and a sleep. No pain, no pain.' And deftly, as the lynx fixed her eyes on the one keeper, the other slipped his jab-stick through the trap door and stabbed the needle and syringe into her rear. The wolves watched with intense interest from their eyrie. This sort of exercise could happen to them. The keepers soon returned and, checking that the pretty beast was totally insensible they effected tests on her blood, her faeces, her eyes, her teeth; her thick shining coat and tail was found free of all lice. The report was later to be sent off to Bucharest for analysis, said the keeper. And next the moment that the wolves most feared. What would the keepers do next? An identity tag was clipped to her ear and she was fitted with a small radio collar.

'Weighs light, about two hundred grammes – like a packet of the wife's salt.' It was the first collar the younger keeper had seen fitted.

'What will result from the collar?'

'It will transmit her movements, her habitat, her hunting; the lynx is a vulnerable species, a favoured prey of both legal and illegal hunting. Radio collars are a good communication between wild life and field work research.'

The young keeper looked dubious. 'But from the moment she wakes, that lynx will never be free again.'

The wolves strained to hear his words.

'That lynx is now a marked being; her howl, her hunting, her whelping will all be recorded by some invasive camera and transmitted. To what valid effect? Please don't you ask me to radio collar wild life.'

The senior keeper stood up tall and agitated. 'Stop this talk, young man. It is muddled thinking you have. The lynx will come to no harm. The collar is her protection. It could save her life.'

They lifted the beauty from the cage and rested her in a soft clump of grass. She stirred as they walked away. The wolves watched her, fascinated. She half stood and fell clumsily. She collected herself with little steps. She stopped and sniffed the darkening air gingerly. She detected the wolves. Turning slowly she fixed on them her blazing amber eyes. What have they done to me? She seemed to ask. The wolves trotted back in the twilight to the she-wolf and the cubs. Wild and free, their own ways and wishes unheeded by a collar and man's intrusion. Squeals and bark-howls greeted them as they neared the den, and loud, rapacious squawking. The she-wolf was leaping frantically at a spruce tree in a frenzy of fear for her cubs. Zwei and Drei had climbed ten feet up the trunk. Settling themselves on a branch, they had been smothered by the unexpected beating of black and blue feathers. Clinging fast to each other, they saw a fearsome, flapping fan-tail and bushy red eyebrows. Instinctively they shielded their eyes from the white beak and screeched to their mother below. The bird, a mountain cock, flew off for easier prey. The cubs slithered down to safety and rolled trembling to the demented she-wolf. It was clear to Louis that the increasingly active six-week-old cubs needed constant vigilance and that he and Nicu and Titu must enable the mother to have some freedom. He ambled up to her as she sat by the den and nestled down alongside. Their relationship had stemmed from need rather than romance; a robust partnership glued with shared responsibilities. They rejoiced at the antics of their united cubs: their growling and jumping on each other; burying their snouts in the ground, swiping sticks and mammal bones from Titu and Nicu, to race off gleefully to hide them.

Louis noted with approval how the she-wolf's body had spread under her fine gold coat. She was in her sitting position of strict surveillance. Would she not find a late evening solo stroll a pleasant distraction? A welcome change of scene? Louis-Loup took up his proprietorial role at the entrance to the rock den and listened out for trouble. He heard Nicu and Titu burrowing away in the woods and reflected on the six cubs he had assimilated. There had been a marked development at six weeks. He peeked into the den. They were still amusing each other, teasing, patting and copying their elders in acts of domination and submission. Everything now revolved around the cubs and he remembered how he was fussed over and loved. But he had been in a strange and singular position; quite different to this clan; Ein, Zwei, Drei, Vier and Nicu and Titu. He wondered how the six cubs would survive the rigours of the world outside: the harsh winters and search for food; the heat in summer and the diseases. Dog distemper; when they would become listless and emaciated with twitching muscles and yellowing teeth; their lovely eyes sore and dulled. Such hazards took their toll of cubs in their first two years. Sixty per cent never reached adulthood. 'Pray for the puppies,' he had been warned. Two of Louis' little charges were female: Zwei and Vier, identifiable from their slender build and more delicate throats. He heard a loud crashing through the trees; too heavy-bodied for Titu or Nicu. It was the she-wolf. She had been gone a good two hours. Louis detected she had had an incident; a good and rewarding incident, her mask implied. She drank long and deep from the bole of the beech tree and flopped down beside him.

'I saw her,' she began breathlessly, 'that beautiful, agile creature, the lynx. She was stalking through the woods. Her gold and slanted eyes showed no fear. She swayed through the shadows, safe in her camouflage.'

'And you smelt her?' asked Louis eagerly.

'I was quite close. We confronted each other obliquely and advanced slowly. She was fretting with this collar around her neck, pawing it and shaking her head, throwing her neck on the rough forest floor. I walked slowly towards her, as she sat and faced me with pleading eyes. She lay on her side and I bit hard on her cumbersome collar. The leather was thick and pliant. She lay still and expectant. It soon broke apart and she danced off, leaping high in the air.'

'What became of the collar?' enquired Louis.

'The lynx – she ate it. She then buried the transmitter and urinated on it.'

The outing had cheered the she-wolf. She looked bright and refreshed from her experience. They called in Nicu and Titu from the woods.

'Beware the wolf-killer,' Louis reminded them, teasingly. 'Would you like a story?' The little cubs trotted out from the den. 'The wolf-killer is being punished by the "Big Cheese"!' they all chanted.

'Yes please! A story!'

And Louis began: 'Man sleeps by night – the appointed time for his rest. Well restored, he goes about his business by day. But we wolves rest through the day and come alive at night. We guard our territory and we hunt with our clans. Like all nocturnal animals we are suspected of bad behaviour. But you must remember that we wolves are guided to kill by our need to feed.'

'What about the wolf-killers and poachers?' Nicu and Titu asked accusingly.

'There are good species of man and evil species.'

'Can we smell the difference?' asked Ein.

'A good question, Ein. We wolves have a powerful olfactory system.' Louis lowered his voice. 'And we have the power of extra sensory perception.'

'Who is he?' Drei put up his paw.

'ESP we call it; an intuitive sense of discovery that leads to an acute awareness of good and evil; in man, mammal or circumstances.'

'Tell us some evil,' called Zwei. 'Tell us about bad wolves.'

Louis sat tall on his haunches. 'This is an ambivalent tale,' he warned. 'At the end you may not judge the wolf good or bad. Through the dark ages of the world there have been wars and famine. In such times wolf packs would follow the armies and devour the bodies of dead soldiers. They would leave few human remains except for the equivalent pairs of feet. Remember – wolves never eat the feet of men. Bayonets were abandoned with the blood frozen thick on the blades and scraps of spinal bone stuck to the points; gnawed belts and army buttons were scattered in wide areas of stamped-down snow, frozen crimson with blood.'

'Stop! Stop! Father.'

'Go on,' urged the younger cubs.

'When there were no army marches, the famished wolves would repair to the towns to prey on corpses. It was difficult to bury the dead at such times. People lost their courage and left defunct bodies to the wolves. But there was a conspiratorial sense in this procedure. Can you understand?' Louis flopped on to his stomach. The cubs gazed at him blankly. 'You have, in this story, which is based entirely on truth, a dichotomy. The savage wolf scrounging on death is simultaneously defying death. The open putrefaction from these human corpses – whether military or civilian – was tantamount to wholesale disease. With their natural instincts, those wolves purged such plagues. They saved whole battalions and citadels.'

The cubs crept into their dens, bemused and not a little befuddled.

20

The four cubs, exulting in their new strengths and sensibilities, had induced an aloofness in the older siblings. Nicu and Titu felt a need for more freedom, for their own superior self-development, a desire to exploit and exert their muscle power; to pitch themselves against their adopted habitat. Louis, with the memory of his own bid for independence and his subsequent run through the mountain gorges, sympathised with his boys. A code of safety strictures was struck between them on lines of communication; regular howl practice, to include Ein, Zwei, Drei and Vier was encouraged.

Nicu and Titu would stretch out in the shade overlooking the alpine meadows, exchanging views on hunting and derring-do. The hot, breezy summer days passed in talk and sleeping and a growing absorption in the sheep herds below. The grass on the meadows was turning tough and dry and the odd intrepid sheep and cow would stray into the forest for fodder. Titu and Nicu would size them up in wistful respect. And they admired the rhythmic order of the herdsmen; their vigilance of the munching livestock and the milking three times a day with the sheep passing through a little shack door, their tails kept long for catching hold. Every three days the shepherds would move their enclosures;

moving their fir fencing to fresh grazing, to rest and repair the old. When the wind and the heat of the sun combined favourably, the two wolves could smell cheese. The shepherds would warm the milk in cauldrons, with a dash of rennet to curdle, and then hang it up in muslin cloths to drip from a ceiling beam. And Nicu and Titu detected a stronger make of cheese. Matured and preserved in fir bark and salt, and rested in a dark room, it reached them in great waves of enticement. They watched avidly as the shepherds ran to the horse carts to deliver their prized bundles. With the final milking over at dusk, the flocks were penned in their enclosures and the shepherd dogs, lapping furiously on their boiled flour and whey, took up their ground. Nicu and Titu knew it was time to head for the den when the huge, black, long-haired dogs set up their aggressive station. Their ferocious reputation was feared through the forest; the shepherds' casual attitude towards copulation between the livestock-guarding dogs had led to bastard breeding; and any stray wild dog sucked into this muddied complex threatened lethal diseases.

As night fell, the young wolves felt even more drawn to the scene below; they were fascinated by the ritual performance of bedding down. The sheep lay in docile white lumps in their enclosure and their shepherds repaired to the assembled wood cabins close by. The guard dogs, with a coterie of pups sent out to learn the job, ringed the pen; even from their high vantage in the surrounding trees, Nicu and Titu felt a high voltage vibration from the dogs below; poised to pounce on any predator, barking ferociously to alert the sleeping men, they would amass in a body and hound all trouble away. The wolves could appreciate these tactics and would confer with Louis on the possibilities of mounting their own attack. Looking on the venture as experience and self-reliant sportsmanship, Louis agreed to lead his boys into a proposed kill. If not starving, they all felt diminished from the tedium of their summer diet. A rich, fleshy ruminant would clearly revitalise the clan.

Declared Louis, 'It is important that we attack on a night of rain and storm, or heavy winds, when the guard dogs are under shelter. We will charge from the mountain ridges.' The next few days were spent in discussion, with the aid of sticks and stones, on the art and craft of attack and recovery. Ein, Zwei, Drei and Vier, listening in on the fringe of the plot, had suggestions on the choice of weather. Rain could impede with mist and mud; a storm with lightning could flash their position to the enemy; but wind could be to their advantage, drowning all noise except for crashing branches, and sweeping their scent away. It was agreed that a high wind was an essential asset for the confusion of the enemy.

The specified evening came; windy, capricious, with every bird folded in its wing. It was early September; any day now the shepherds would be moving the herds to the valleys. The three wolves, ensconced in their bosky look-out, waited impatiently for the camp and enclosure to settle for the night. An ominous guard dog sniffed its way up the hill. The wolves sat rigid and the monster wandered back to its post. The wind ruffled their manes and whined through the branches. The rising moon was boxed and chased by scudding clouds. Cold and fear crept in to the two young wolves. Suddenly Louis yelled, 'Off!' A starting pistol could not have shocked them better into action. They hared down the hill and, with their preconceived precision, put their plan in action. Louis separated and, reaching the west corner of the enclosure, yelped frenziedly and bark-howled. Guard dogs and shepherds gave chase for some distance, deserting their station. Nicu and Titu swooped on the abandoned, panic-stricken herd, seized and killed their prey and dragged it back up the hill, to a limestone swallow hole. They sat proudly guarding their trophy and watched the return of the dogs and shepherds below. The few drops of blood in the pen were snuffled and licked, but there seemed no curiosity in chasing after more predators. And then Louis, skulking low with care, returned to them, exhausted, relieved and not a little vindicated. They lay quietly and, when the moon had slid behind the mountain, they retrieved their prize and gorged; next they tore out the choicest chunks for the den and finally burrowed the remaining portions into the soft earth of the forest floor. The wind had dropped, Louis was anxious to reach the den under cover of dark. First they urinated over the buried meat, with a quick return in mind and loped back through the trees. Louis howled to the she-wolf as they neared the lair. There came no reply and then a fake rendition of a howl; then another; he knew it was the wolf-killer.

The three wolves speeded back with dread and foreboding. Had there been a killing of the cubs? A murderous plunder on the den? The woods were limp as though concealing danger and sinister secrets. They trotted in silence, their jaws clenched on the meaty parcels. Rounding a corner, they saw her. Alert and expectant, the she-wolf fell on them with pleasure and relief. She stirred up the cubs to feast on the first red meat of their lives. Louis' alarm was unfounded; yet he knew the wolfer had been near.

A few days later, the three wolves returned to their consignment of meat. The clean scent of hay was swept up to them as they loped through the wooded tracks. The swish of scythes and the steeling of blades, gave rhythm to their agile stride. Louis halted with Nicu and Titu, to see the hay stacked round the central pole and pitched up on a fork by a pretty woman; higher and higher to a young man up top who raked the down-sides to a sturdy, conical shape. But as they approached their ground, they sniffed the poison; the most deadly poison of all: strychnine.

'Nicu! Titu! Go no further! Some evildoer wants to kill us.'
Titu and Nicu wrinkled their muzzles. What was it from? An animal? It was from a flower, explained Louis, a deadly, beautiful white flower with black poisonous berries. Or it could have been a purple flower with bright red berries. It was known as deadly nightshade.

October stole upon them; the summer sun and shade had dwindled to a thin light and a hint of mist. Titu and Nicu had another request to make of their father. 'We would like to see more men,' they announced to the startled little clan. 'To compare the life of the wolf with man; to note their disciplines and order in the family unit, their loves, hates, failures and successes and, above all, their reactions to wolves.' Louis and the she-wolf had never heard anything more louche. Louis, especially, who had seen more of the vagaries of humanity in his formative years than any young wolf. But the originality of the request was recognised. 'There is a rummy old place I might take you both . . .'

He was thinking of a fortified church and all its complex nooks and crannies where remains of food could be rummaged. 'An ancient fortress that still has stale crumbs in the corners and rotting hams hung on hooks and cheeses green with mould. An old wolf traveller once told me; the stench astonished him. Or there is another man site, closer and easier to reach. It is the celebrated garbage tip on the outskirts of Braşov. Children and mothers meet there to watch the bears feed on their discarded pies and cakes and apple cores. A few wolves join in but it is more a bear's play-pen. Wolves do not fancy feed second-hand. The bears get close to the mothers and children in these feeding sessions and take food from their hands.'

'Ugh!' exclaimed Titu. 'We don't want to see that smelly place!'

217

'Let us go to the old church,' chimed in Nicu. 'And smell the stink of the peculiar food crumbling on the hooks.'

It was arranged they would be away for two or three days before the weather turned. They would take the Eastern flank of the Carpathians, higher and higher up through the forest. The she-wolf was more than pleased not to join them and again made her solo sorties in to the woods before they set off. Louis led his two consorts through the new territory. The ground was brittle with pine needles and the grass seared from the hot summer winds. Louis called a halt by a stream to cool and rest their paws. Nicu smelt gum, which was tracked down to resin seeping from an old fir trunk; the perfect lubricant for sore pads. There were footprints in the pale lime sand that edged the water. Nicu and Titu studied carefully the distinctive imprint of the firm heel and four toe and claw marks. They compared their own smaller paws alongside.

'It is a big wolf, father.' Louis reminded them of their mission to see more men and they continued up the mountain. He explained they would see more beasts in the higher mountain forests and on the rocky ridges. More bear, more wolf, more boar and deer. But the chamois was considered the most delectable feed. The trees were thinning round the alpine zone, when they heard strains of music and singing. In the near distance they saw a wooden hut mounted on blocks of limestone with a roof of shingled tiles. It positively burst with conviviality.

'Let us howl,' yelped Titu, and before Louis could plan a more tactical introduction, the two young wolves were in full throttle. Windows burst open with a flurry of exclamations.

'There! Over there! Aren't they just darling! Three real live wolves! Just look at that!' The excited lady was pulled back for others to take a look, when a moustachioed saxon commanded from the doorstep:

'No shooting now. Just remember, we are guests in wolf territory.' Lowering his voice, he added, 'mind you, it is rare to see wolves so close. They have no law protection. It is the brown bears the Big Cheese preserves for his favoured hunting. And the trophies are a lucrative asset for the forest authorities.'

The three wolves stretched out under a sycamore tree. And complying with this unexpected audience, the singing party resumed. As the guitarist strummed and twanged, the voices rose and swelled.

'What are they singing?' asked Nicu and Titu in wonderment.

'Opera,' guessed Louis from his vague memories of the Comtesse's wireless vibrations. The wolves listened intently.

'Oh, vision so charming . . . Her eyes so alluring . . . Ah, my love, forgive my madness'.

'We like opera,' confirmed Titu. 'You need a mate, father, to give your heart to – and have more pups and become an alpha wolf.'

Louis was startled. The romantic music had stirred him also. Smells of kindling apple wood and barbecued boar flesh and deer stole across the grass. Lights went on in the cabin. The autumn light was shrinking fast, as the wolves gazed at the silhouette of heads framed in the window. The endemic shyness of the wolves and the constraint of the hunters had evolved in a *juste milieu*. They bounded off and bedded down in a village graveyard. The grasses were tall and inviting and mice scuttled between the mounds and monuments. One grave was so heaped in white roses, with its headstone so streaming with ribbons, it resembled a bride rearing from her bed, suggested Louis. The three wolves clamped up close; there was a dank and mournful feel about, as if the restless spirits of the dead were settling on them like parasites. Nicu and Titu heard whispering and knew it was a dirge from the skeletons pleading to be free of their coffins. Could they go and sleep somewhere else? The light footsteps of a girl were heard and her live presence warmed the entire graveyard. They crouched down as she sat on the smallest gravestone of all. Throwing back the hood of her cloak, with her flaxen hair flying in the breeze, she sang in a low lament:

> 'Bonny sweet Petru is all my joy.
> He sleepeth ever and he is not dead.
> He is gone and will never come again.
> His blue eyes came from the sky.'

Nicu stood and stretched and caught the girl's eye. She shrieked and clasped her cloak round her slim body, running screaming from the tombs. The wolves fled from the roused village, glad to put the sinister gloom behind them.

Gaining a vast and seemingly deserted plateau, Titu spotted a shrine by the side of a grass ditch, a quaint little temple with an onion dome. They approached cautiously and noted a cross fixed to the finial.

'This is a holy place,' said Louis. Black spike railings penned it around. 'We cannot enter. It is a holy refuge for men travellers; to defend them from the evil night spirits and bad wolves.'

Nicu and Titu looked confused. 'But we are good wolves,' they wailed.

'Man's fear clouds his vision,' explained Louis. 'We are dangerous. We eat his women and babies. And when we starve we eat his sheep and his goat. But it is we who fear. We fear man for his stupidity and his judgement; his vertical stance and his gun. Dear Titu and Nicu – let us now sleep beside this protected shrine. And let us hope that in years to come our fine species will be protected by man.'

The rising moon threw sharp shadows on the undulating plain of rough grass. The few oak trees stood like sentinels by the shrine. In the far distance a horse and cart swayed slowly towards the mountain foothills. The hunched driver, with his load of hay topped with a curved blade and long, crooked pole, made an eerie outline. 'He is headless!' screeched Titu. And the horse and buggy vanished.

Louis reminded them that Transylvania was an uncharted land of weird mystery and threads of evil; a land that captivated with its wild beauty, its plateaux hugged by dark, impenetrable forests; a land of secrets, locked and guarded by its sheer mountain ridges; and a land overrun with ghosts, bemoaning their torturous deaths, their bloodied bodies flung into wells, their spiked skeletons holed up in dungeons, their warnings of the swinging blade that slices through bodies like butter. As he spoke they heard howling from the mountains. Two wolves had let out a low, plaintive call; a pause of some minutes and then a swelling throng of howling.

'They have seen us,' guessed Louis, 'and have grouped themselves to show their strength. They are marking their territorial claims. They acknowledge us but do not want to know. They may even think we are phantoms and will vanish like the horse cart.' Mindful of the cross on the finial, clearly reflected in the moonlit ditch, Louis urged they try and sleep. 'Ghosts and goblins are wary of crosses. We will not be disturbed.'

By next noon the wolves were approaching Prejmer; the saxon village, set in a wide and fertile valley with collective crops and trout farms, was formidably defended by its centuries-old fortified church. The outer walls of the fortress were said to be four metres thick and twelve metres high. Louis selected some higher

221

ground to observe their quarry. He noted the church was constructed in a cross formation with steep shingled roofs and turrets. He pointed out to the young wolves the slim buttresses: 'a way to slide down in time of trouble. In days of old this country was under siege from Turks and then Germans, to be plundered and annexed. The local peasants were housed in this fortress. They were well fed and went to the fields in good heart to battle with the enemy. The subsequent infiltrations of our frontier lands; the Greeks, Hungarians and Russians have enriched this culture. In those days of siege, the peasants hurled boiling tar on the enemy, from the turrets and the water shoots.'

'We want ham, not history,' complained Nicu and Titu ungraciously and warned that they were hungry.

After a surreptitious snatch at trout, idling in an unattended vat, Louis led them on a skulking prowl around the fortress boundary; the motive was to find a crumbling spot that they could widen or even tunnel beneath. But the massive turreted wall was unfathomable. Darkness was needed for a foray. Louis took stock of the intricate layout of courtyards and arcaded passageways. He particularly noted the rackety wooden staircases on the inner castle wall, leading to the tiers of 'meal' rooms. Here the peasants had staked their refuge and their food stores from the sieges. The wolves heard grunts and snuffles and a cacophony of barks. The village dogs and stray dogs were racing over the hay stubble and rounding on them in a circle, like a flock of famished birds. Louis feared for their lives; they were too many, too fast and too savage.

'Full speed to the village,' he yelped and the three of them tore down the cobbled streets and frightened the horses. They leapt into a wagon-load of hay piled high and dug in up to their snouts. Their tormentors were corralled by furious villagers.

'What a madness! What a tumult! You verminous curs!'

Along a narrow road, lined with poplar trees, the wagon trundled. Suddenly Louis gave the sign to leap to the grass verge; to run for their lives.

As they waited for twilight, Louis explained again about the fortress 'meal' rooms that branched off the wooden stairs. They were kept empty these days of peace but Titu and Nicu – not to be discouraged – were convinced they would find an old ham or lump of cheese lurking in some forgotten corner. It was a moonless night as they neared the fortress. Louis suggested they should first step in to the Gothic church. They breached the ancient citadel through the front courtyard and slipped in through a side door. The towering white limestone interior gave a damp chill to the wide aisles.

'This is real history,' said Louis and prodded his boys with his muzzle. 'These walls are seven hundred years. Can you imagine the men and the happenings they have seen?'

Said Nicu: 'I don't expect many of our kind have wandered in.'

Candles blinked from every corner; some red, some white and all welcoming. Louis sat and studied the vaulted stone altar ceiling and roof; the fine ribbed and webbed moulding reminded him of thigh bones with their femoral heads and of knee sockets. In a distant courtyard he heard a clock tower chime; it was nearing midnight. He herded the boys out into the silent darkness. It felt warm after the church and they felt secure beneath the velvet black arc of the stars. Nicu smelt bread. There was once a baker's courtyard, remembered Louis, from his huge accumulation of wolf-lore; used in the times of siege when the village families would store loaves in readiness. They heard snoring and, looking round sharply, saw an old watch-keeper, his head dropped forward over the bread rolls in his lap.

'No!' prompted Louis, knowing too well the temptation of an opportunist snatch. Through to another courtyard they were confronted with the flights of wooden stairs, each leading to a different set of rooms. Nicu and Titu bounded up a flight and then another, higher and higher. The linked landings of narrow wooden planks were bouncy. The wolves revelled in the ups and downs of this new exercise. Louis called them to a corner; they must explore the low, square storerooms. These rooms would have been packed solid with families, their dogs and hens, their food stuffed in cages and cupboards.

'Go and look in every room, on every floor, up every stair, and see if you can't find smelly old hams swinging on hooks from the ceilings.'

Titu and Nicu tore off gleefully, every olfactory nerve twitching. They soon returned to Louis; they had neither seen nor smelt anything. But – they sat beside him; there had been something of interest: a heavy wood door; it looked secret and . . . perhaps there was something good inside. They scampered ahead of him to the highest tier to a small recessed door. An iron ring threaded with cord was an open invitation to enter.

'It needs to be pulled,' hissed Nicu, dancing on all fours. They all pulled in turn and then Nicu suggested a tug, each holding on behind the other. The door creaked ominously; Louis feared it might even fall and flatten them. At the next attempt it flung open and sent them flying. Louis and Nicu fell into the secret room and, in their excitement, failed to hear the snap of splintering wood from the balcony. Inside they were confronted by a stuffed wild dog, a stuffed boar and a pair of embalmed wolves in the howling position. Musty mould clung to the small damp room. Nicu poked his snout into a hole in the wall and retrieved a brick. Louis identified it as bread;

fossilised for one hundred years. All four walls were recessed with food storage lockers; some still harboured old green hams as hard as rock, and bread and bottles of beer and wine, long dried out and blackened.

'Where's Titu?' Louis and Nicu started in surprise and, leaping to the doorway, they saw the shattered balcony. Had he crashed with the tug? They peered down to the dark stone courtyard and could neither see nor smell Titu. They separated and loped round every tier of rooms. Titu had vanished like a true Transylvanian phantom. The trip had been a disaster. Titu gone – perhaps even dead – no ham, no cheese. A fit of guttural coughing came from the front courtyard; it was the watch-keeper. As they streaked past him, he half rose like an avenging ogre, brandishing his nightstick and hollering obscenities. Louis and Nicu once more sped away from the suspicion of danger. It was every wolf for himself in trouble. Racing across the steppe in the early dawn, they plunged into the woods, loping up the gentle slope to the rock cliffs. They collapsed by a deep pool with a waterfall tumbling from a ravine. Nicu's narrow thorax was throbbing after the long run. He stared at the crystal clear liquid and the white lacy froth teeming down the rocks. The early sun rays sprinkled the slim cascade, silver and gold.

'It is a girl in white,' he exclaimed and made to jump in. But Louis leapt on him.

'No! There is danger here, Nicu. It is not our territory.'

But the young wolf had already slipped into the ice-cold pool. He gasped and felt his limbs stiffen.

'Father, I can't move well.' Louis hurled himself at a willow branch and snapped it for Nicu to grab. Nicu grasped it with numbed clumsy paws as Louis pulled his boy to the rock side. Louis grabbed the pelt on his back, and with every ounce of his strength, hauled him up. He rolled him in moss and lichen and warmed him in the sun. Nicu slept an hour, twitching and stirring until he woke to tell Louis: 'I fear this pool. While I slept, I sensed some presence, persuading me to jump in again.'

'Let's move on,' agitated Louis. They stalked up through spruce and birch to the ravine and nibbled on beech nuts and raspberries and soft, juicy mushrooms. 'We must be careful,' said Louis, 'this is bear feed. We may be trespassing on their fief.' As he spoke he saw a deep bear bite in the soft trunk of a spruce and the higher tell-tale gash of a claw. In the early evening, they found a peaceful clearing and stretched out. Nicu questioned his father fearfully on Titu's fate. Louis explained to him how in the pragmatic tradition of lupine ethics there are tough rules to keep. 'A clan large or small survives as a solid unit; to engage in the hunt and in the share of feed. If a member of the clan, young or old, drops out, the pack is diminished and weakened in its capacity to hunt and to survive. It might happen that a clan sets out on a long hunt. If the younger and less strong cannot keep up, they are left to fall behind. The prey must not be forfeited for the care and survival of the few. If the pack should halt and attend to the few it may not survive. We wolves have to learn to adapt, to play the game and live to survive.'

'You think Titu hurt himself when he fell off the balcony? What has happened to him? Was he killed and kicked into a corner and bundled away?' Nicu's mask crumpled with his love and fear for Titu and his sorrow. He stood and stretched and sniffed convulsively, with his tail hung low between his legs.

'I am hoping,' murmured Louis, 'that our Titu is not seriously hurt. Perhaps he was winded as he struck the stone; or he broke a foreleg, or a hind leg, a shoulder, or he could have cracked his ribcage. Any such possibilities would have badly damaged our return to the clan. I think he made the decision to leave us, to save us the hard decision of leaving him.'

'So you think he is alive?'

'Again, I am hoping. He must have escaped the empty fortress. We saw no sign of him. The watch-keeper was undisturbed. He would have hid in a hedge, assessing his damage and soon started on his return journey. By dawn the village dogs would have unearthed him.'

'A good peasant might have carried him home and tended his broken bits?'

'Unlikely,' Louis assured him. 'Let us hope that Titu is now slowly on his path, that he has adapted to his circumstances and understands the demeanour of an adult wolf.'

The wolves loped slowly through the night and by dawn were snuffling at the she-wolf's den. It was empty. But the scent was strong and fresh. They drank from the tree bole and waited, panting and exhausted. Could the she-wolf have taken the cubs out on a food search? But now she stood before them. She and the cubs had taken to sleeping in Louis' den. She looked around for Titu. Louis, allaying all concern, claimed that he was on his way.

Was he dead? He could not remember. His body felt paralysed, numbed; it did not exist for him. His snout twitched; so he was breathing. And he could see blackness, solid, with no clue or signal of what or where. His head was moving and his neck; his snout had now stirred his scent glands. He was cocooned in damp hay. He smelt rain, wet stone, and rotting wood, and was lulled by a clouded dawn. What had happened to him? He squirmed in the hay and pain shot through his ribcage. In an involuntary spasm he struck out with his legs and forearms. He could move again and he began to remember. The balcony had snapped. He had hurtled through the air and landed a fair crack on the cobbles. His immediate fear was discovery. He had dragged himself in excruciating pain to a hole in the wall where hay was heaped. He had now woken with the early morning. Snatching water from the puddled stones, he hugged the massive fortress wall and escaped this time-honoured house of refuge.

Louis and Nicu would have set off hours ago. By the law of lupine conduct, Titu knew they would not have waited. He counted on their prayers for his continued survival. In unremitting pain from his thorax, he limped past the village outskirts, through the steppes of maize and rye, tearing at the crops as he passed. He rested on the foothills of the mountains and at sundown stalked deep into the forest. He had never felt so alone, so apprehensive of the night to come. Perching on a mound, he took deep and painful breaths and forced a howl. What could it have conveyed other than the truth? Pain and fear, a need of sympathy, companionship. And he was answered; an evening call has a certain credibility. Near and nearer, down from the mountain, the caller approached him. He howled back, crouched by his mound, in all his shyness and shame. It was as though he had proffered himself for provocative behaviour. Or could his weak call have been interpreted as an offer for a shared feed? He listened to the murmur of a sloping stream and felt comforted. And then, through the silver spindly birch trees, she came trotting. Ears pricked, her mask expectant and amber eyes darting and eager. Titu stood shakily. He could tell a she-wolf: that elegant allure, that slender chest balanced upon the long legs of a mannequin. She was black-haired, her pelage long and lustrous.

'I have come,' she said simply and sniffed Titu's anus appreciably. He was astonished and sat down sharply.

'Why are you black?' he asked abruptly.

'My forebears came from North America,' she replied. 'What is your name?' she asked.

'Titu. I have a brother, Nicu, and a father, Louis-Loup. What's yours?'

'Seara – in the evening . . .'

'I like Seara. It's a soft and tranquil name.'

'What's your trouble?' she asked him and wedged her fluffy rump firmly up against his abdomen.

'I had a bad fall,' Titu coughed and whimpered with pain.

With a soft paw Seara gently probed his ribcage. 'You have broken some flat curved bones that shield your heart and lungs. They are mending already. Do you want a mate?'

Titu ducked. 'My father may need one,' he said as a conciliatory afterthought. He was tiring of her familiar talk. They walked companionably through the night, resting, drinking and snatching at vermin. They rounded on the dens as the sun came up. Nicu was sniffing the air and leapt and whelped with joy as Titu stole out of the woods. He was followed closely – almost possessively – by a black she-wolf. Louis, the cubs and their mother, roused by Nicu's excitement, gathered to welcome Titu. But who was his companion? Titu rubbed muzzles with his father and Nicu.

'I have a mate for you, father. Her name is Seara. She has guided me safely through the night. Isn't she a wonder?' Seara swayed slowly towards Louis, swinging her hips flirtatiously, her ears flattened and her lovely tail folded between her legs, the picture of submission. There was a sudden snarl and howl from behind as the she-wolf leapt in a fury at Seara, the black beauty; her claws and teeth were poised for attack. With one bound the cub contingent pulled down the tormented she-wolf and calmed her with licks and nuzzling.

'You must go,' commanded Louis to the bewitching Seara. 'This mother member of our clan will kill you.'

21

It was the lull before the storm, with the days passing in a hush of expectancy. What next? whispered the oak woods as their leaves shivered and floated from them. The streams, swollen with equinoctial gales, flowed purposefully down the mountains. But those days of capricious wind and ferment were now well past. It was the storm mounting in Louis-Loup's ordered frame that threatened to topple his composure. The speed and demands of a wolf's life had left him few moments to reflect. The balance of things had always provoked and challenged him; to hunt or retreat, to gorge or starve, to love or despise, to lust after or to exercise restraint. In his position as a quasi alpha wolf, he had been monitoring the clan's exits and entrances rather than his own. Titu's prompting to seek romance had jolted him.

Naturally a wolf should move on and get out of the light of those coming up behind. With over population deemed a cardinal sin in the clan, no coupling between younger members could be tolerated. Any sibling incest or paedophilia was instinctively taboo. Louis-Loup knew these things; it was inherent in any wolf to know how to behave, or indeed how to misbehave. And there was the rub. He, Louis-Loup, had to find a mate; to couple with her and have more pups, to start the ball rolling for Nicu and Titu, to forge their way through love and litters and the whole tyrannical parade of progeniture. Louis sighed sanctimoniously. Did man do better? Pretending he was asleep in the quiet of a dead-end afternoon, he burrowed his head in his thick mane and went back in time. He thought of Venus; that fierce desire, that lusty thrusting. Such a hasty tryst and yet so vindicated in his precious cubs. Girlie . . . he sighed and moaned afresh with his acute misery at her death. And then all the joyful times they had shared flooded back. He pondered also on the cub he had never met: the captive little male who had followed in his own childhood steps with Madame Veuve. Louis rolled over to see Ein, Zwei, Drei and Vier standing over him; looking on quizzically, they poked his neck and abdomen with soft little paws.

'I will take you fishing,' he said and the she-wolf joined them.

Louis led them through the woods to the mountain ridge beyond. The late autumn sun lit up the sky, to reflect on a lake in brilliant blue below. A village was clustered with rosy roofs and thatch and a church with a red, pointed tower. They watched a sturdy, kerchiefed peasant, propped four-square on a stick. Her winter logs were neatly stacked in a corner of her mud yard, where she stood proudly surveying a heap of golden pumpkins, and baskets over-spilling with sweetcorn. The cubs saw fishes leaping from a distant rock river. Louis guided them to a shallow stream where they splashed over the limestone bedrock. And then Zwei was distracted by a field mouse and Vier found a frog. Ein and Drei were left to chase a rabbit. Louis collected them to return when the she-wolf yelped in warning. A cavalcade of hunters was crashing through the glade; horses and wagons, hard-shouting men, silence, and then a fusillade of guns; roars of pain and yowling. Louis headed his party deep into the woods. Through the trees, they caught sight of chamois leaping over the stream. The wagons swished past with the dead beasts, their elegantly curved horns pointing up to the arched tracery of trees. And next, the gleam of a long, black motor car snaking its way down the valley, crackling through the splintered forest tracks.

'The Big Cheese on his chamois shoot,' noted Louis. 'We must watch out for his guns; keep well away.'

As dusk fell, the sky was streaked an angry blood red and bruised with purple.

The peace of the dying autumn days was over; an air of dread suspense hung over the forest. It was the season of man's quest to do or die, his dice with danger and his conquest of a bear, a boar, a stag; anything to assuage the desire to shoot well to the kill, to secure his beast, his trophy and his honour. But this was the prime time of the bear. The beasts of the forest were alerted to the preparations for man's redeeming sport; binoculars bristled from rocks and ledges and swung slowly over open ground to locate the bears' feeding grounds. Traps were assiduously checked; box traps, log traps and the torturous leg-gripping traps. When those double spring jaws jammed on skin and muscle, it was a struggle to the death for a bear's escape. Louis and his clan, stalking the woods for trouble spots, would overhear chance reports of beleaguered animals from the hunters and keepers.

'The bear tore and chewed his paw free; pieces of his teeth were broken off and scattered with his gnashing on the trap. You can see decayed molars and ground away teeth on many a beast.'

'And I have seen some that leave parts of their feet in steel traps. They sever their own feet and toes; the raven soon feeds on these little parts.'

The wolves saw the bears on their harried race to gorge themselves for their long winter hibernation; and the hunters watched them become slower and more obese with their scoffing on bilberries, blueberries, roots and drowsy insects.

'Never mess with a bear,' warned Louis. 'They are clever and agile and not the clumsy furry fools they appear. See how strong they are, their short legs close to the ground, with their tiny tails and large heads. And their long coat has a thick, fleecy underfur, to protect against an archer's arrow.'

'Are bears cuddly?' asked Ein.

The she-wolf whispered: 'You think a bear looks a friendly, safe and furry toy, but he is quiet and likes to be alone. When he is surprised or angry he is a danger to man and beast and roars like a lion.'

Louis, wary of the keepers and foresters laying their traps, kept his young clan close. At the first sign of dusk they would repair to the dens. It was then that the bears were most active: feeding, sniffing and defecating through their stride. A faint stench of putrefaction now wafted through the forest; feeding sites to bait the bears were being set up in specially prepared log dens. Lined with wood chips and grass, a short tunnel would open to a narrow chamber. Pigs' heads, road-killed ungulate and offal were laid down to entice the bear. When the spring-activated foot snare toppled the beast, he was powerless to turn or move in the restricted cavity. The hunt trail dogs would soon locate him. Immobilised by the keeper's syringe, his fate would be considered; a radio-collaring for the field records or his hide and head for the local hunters' trophy.

Louis motioned the she-wolf to head the clan for the last lap. It was a calm, soft evening and he felt the need to linger, to be solitary and to breathe in the last scents of autumn. He sat erect on the edge of a clearing, his ears pricked for man's sport and trouble. Immediately he sensed a presence; an undeniable force. It was neither evil nor especially agreeable; an amorphous, indefinable and teasing presence. He sniffed above and around him; a faint whiff of damp fur. A huntsman in his steaming deerstalker? A dead cub secreted in his game bag? Something stirred. Louis glanced through the slender birch trees as the sun slanted its dying rays. One ear, one amber eye and one half muzzle gazed on him from behind a silver trunk. He gazed back, as though electrocuted and then, as suddenly, he was earthed. Louis and Seara were rooted from their toes to their eyes. He watched the black hair of her mane separate, elongate and waver like a mobile. He fell on his mask, overcome with surprise and strange emotion. Seara knew her moment had come. She stalked over to him, with all the taut elegance she could muster and flounced down beside him. Their warmth mingled and their blood welled up between them. The sense of complicity was sweet and their minds were entwined in unspoken promises. Louis breathed hard and fell to dozing and sleep. When he woke, his dream companion had faded into the night.

The days became colder and the forest rang to the sounds and savage calls of hunting. The archery hunters, the muzzle loaders and the distinctive ratatat of shotguns, sniper guns and pistol shots chased the wolves to their dens. But Louis would take out his older boys. It was a time of learning from the pursuits of man. The bear had no quarrel with the wolf, and the hunters were intent only on the bear.

'The hunter,' explained Louis, 'keeps his scent from the bear. Man is the bear's enemy number one. The hunter must leave no trace on the ground, on bushes or branches. When possible he should wade in water and always be aware of wind and air currents. They say a bear gets the scent of man twelve feet away.'

What if a bear ambles towards a man? Nicu and Titu wanted to know.

'You must remember a bear has bad eyes. When first he sees a man, he thinks him another bear. Whether the man is friend or foe, he does not know. The man should stand firm and never run off.' They were interrupted by two old foresters walking through a stream.

'We must avoid the bear trails,' said one.

'Human scent hangs around for two days,' said the other.

'I told you the time I was savaged by a bear?' They sat on a grass knoll; two wise buffers reminiscing on their action days.

'It was a dark night up high in the mountains. I was hurrying down home when a wounded bear jumped up from behind a rock. He pounced on me. I cocked my gun. He felled me with one paw and grabbed my other arm. Tearing at it, he dragged me some twelve feet. It was my heavy coat sleeve that saved me being bitten to the bone. Look here! He took this hunk of flesh.'

His mate peered in awe at the exposed and mangled limb; noble scars, long and jagged, had carved up the muscles.

'Never try to escape from a bear,' he continued. 'Lie there so he believes you dead. And you know something? That there Theodore Roosevelt, the old president of USA, now he was a right lover of nature. He believed that a man with a gun, intent on his target, loses his enjoyment of the wilderness. He misses the beauty of the trail and learns little of the animal. To track a grizzly without a gun; that was the true joy of the hunt, so he thought.'

'But he was a rich man,' intervened his mate.

'Yes,' sighed the other, 'it's now the Big Cheese will be hunting with the first fall of snow.'

The forest was soon in the grasp of winter's harsh tentacles. The freezing winds and air cut through the wolves' fur and bit deep into their skin and bones. The young cubs hardly stirred from their mother's flank. Nicu and Titu hunted long for the meanest rodents; rats, mice and squirrels were brought to the den in hard-won triumph. Everywhere the din of men cursing, as they hammered stout boundary posts into the iron-hard hunting ground; and the swish and snap of the young, low branches, beaten down to clear the trails. The forest was alive with expectation and the united accord of man and beast to step into the breach. Horses and sleighs and wagons were drawn up from the valley to shelter sites with hay, and cabins for the handlers. The unaccustomed activity and barrage of scents from the general mêlée intoxicated Titu and Nicu. Wafts of man's sweat and hair, lathering horses and slavering hunting hounds made an appreciable start to events.

'The beating up will begin any day,' warned Louis, and Nicu thought fleetingly on the palpitating fear of the hidden bear and boar. Young men were building up pyramids of long logs for roaring fires; to warm the sportsmen in their breaks for food and rest. The forest had become thickly dunked in snow and the beaters lashed out at the fir trees to release the white mass from the splayed branches. It was from one of their early afternoon observation posts that the three wolves caught sight of the black beauty. Foraging for food she had no spare attention for any admirers. But Titu, in his excitement, gave a whelp of recognition. Seara stood erect and then lay flat on the snow, her long black pelage fanned around her. Her amber eyes devoured the concealing bushes.

'Go,' cried Louis. 'Go and get her.' Nicu and Titu complied eagerly. It was demonstrably clear to them that Seara and their father had forged a frontier; that somewhere, somehow, some romantic sensibility had taken hold. And they noted how Seara patted Louis on the neck and how he enjoyed it. Moving to another clump of shrubbery, they remained in clear view of the dominant couple.

Said Nicu authoritatvely, 'We male wolves are timid in love. It is usual for the female to make the first advances. If they fully engage, their union can be for ever.'

'Nicu, how do you know these things? Look! They are playing together and kissing muzzles and licking teeth.'

Titu and Nicu strode self-consciously past the amorous bower and set off for the den. Louis caught up with them in the gathering dark. Two boar had been shot. They were being disembowelled; the steaming blood was spattered like ruby gems and frozen in crimson slabs on the snow. They were yanked on to a horse-drawn sleigh. It hissed away over the thick crust of snow. A group of beaters stood together in the bloody detritus of death.

'They are two good boar,' declared the leader. 'The tusks half worn; thick coats of healthy dark fur. All of nine foot by seven foot; an hour's job to skin each one.'

Later that night, Nicu nudged up close to Titu. The clamour and upheaval of the hunting season disturbed him. He longed for spring already; the singing streams and birds, the fresh rustling leaves and tender grasses, the sun in his eyes – and a soul mate of his own. Each day the forest became more crowded with props and men in readiness at their post for the coming of the Big Cheese. The wolves' spirits rose as they cowered in a deserted rock den. The sun was climbing, leaving the snow patched with blue shadow. The young beaters, spread out wide, were easily spotted in their bright orange tunics; it was a change from chopping wood. The temperature was ten degrees below zero and a beater hollered, and then another and another, a chorus of urgent cries and shouting. The hunters, wrapped in heavy jackets and jerkins, their heads smothered in fur, flanked the forest drives, strategically positioned two hundred yards apart. Each trembling heart was bent on silence and waiting. Louis kept his boys on the periphery of the beating up; it was not unusual for wolves to appear on the fringe of these game hunts. A lad with a gun was stationed near to them.

'Scrape the snow from under your feet,' he was told. 'Always stand on solid earth; the scrunch of snow if you make a sudden turn could head a bear away. You might even topple, gun in hand, on a slippery pad.'

The wolves liked to listen and learn from man. A motley parade of footprints patterned the snow. Louis pointed out red deer, lynx, wolf, bear and boar. There was a sudden blast of horns in the near distance, and the muffled hum of a motor car drifted through the trees. Hearty cheers, and the reedy tones of a mouth organ, heralded an arrival.

'It is the Big Cheese,' exclaimed the beaters. 'He will be coming through this drive.'

And sure enough, the hero and his coterie were whisked along in a horse-drawn sleigh. He was padded in fur and high boots and breeches, his head and face almost concealed in a tweed cap and ear flaps. His full lips were smiling and his narrowed eyes keen. The beaters again set up their spasmodic hollers and the hounds raced and rooted through the undergrowth. Two bears lumbered from the trees and charged into the clearing. A bullet smashed the ribs and heart of one colossus. Rearing up, it coughed blood and bellowed. Pacing forward on its hind legs, pawing the air, it fell to the ground. The second beast was clumsily shot in the abdomen and careered off on a blinded course through the forest. In a dying spurt of venom, it clutched a trunk, shaking it with all the strength of its final death throes.

A keeper muttered: 'It is the wolf-killer he is after. He knows her scent anywhere.'

There was a single shot and the slight, hunched figure running through the trees dropped dead. Nobody knew who had fired but the Big Cheese was reported to look well justified as he lay down his rifle; wiping his brow, he turned up his ear flaps and tied them on the crown of his head.

For seven days the shots and shouts and the stench of sulphur and explosive cordite engulfed the forest. Sleighs were drawn swiftly through the freezing air to the wide avenues and fire breaks and drives. In each hunter was the overriding desire to shoot his bear. It was do or die. Wine, women and song – forget it! Louis would lead his boys on a skirmish for offal, left scattering in the snow where the carcasses had been humped on the wagons. They crunched on crimson frozen snow and lapped up chance pools of blood. When the hunters hoved to for the midday meal, the wolves withdrew to the trees, watching avidly the jovial scene in the clearing. There would be food enough when the Big Cheese led his party on to the next drive. The beaters had built up fires of oak and pine and fir, stoking the spicy logs in a pyre. The orange flames blazed and the snow wept at their hearth. The men rubbed hands and noses and stomped their feet. They hung out their socks and gloves and boots on sticks, to toast in the glare. Gallons of hot red soup, hunks of bread and sausage and beer and ţuică put the guts back into men. And they were soon off again. Each day was dark by four o'clock, when the wolves would scour the deserted food sites.

239

One late afternoon when the guns had ceased and a curtain of calm had fallen on the forest, there happened a horrific incident. Rooting for nuts and carrion and rolling sensuously in the snow, a bear was unexpectedly surprised. He smelt the sweat and lather of horses and the breath of men; the loaded carcasses of blood and bone and soaking fur completed the whole gamut of death. The bear felt threatened and charged from the trees to the forest track. The pair of horses neighed frantically and plunged forward, their gruesome cargo twisting and lurching.

'A bear can run thirty-three miles an hour. We are done for,' groaned one wagon-driver and aimed his pistol at the beast's head. But, advancing with one Herculean thrust of his paw, the bear smashed the jaw of the first horse and caved in the ribcage of the other. The bear, huffing and snarling, was shot dead as it swayed back to its cover. Forest wardens and keepers were alerted and raced to the distressed scene in tractor-driven vans. The horses, slumped in their harness, were close to death with fright and loss of blood. Released to the ground, they were put to their last sleep with a hypodermic rifle. The shocked wagoners were hustled into a van with a bottle of plum brandy to blabber their story. The wolves had descended to the woods and sniffed quietly on the rising vapours from the atrocious slaughter. The wardens and keepers joined the drivers in the van to wait for the carts home and the removal of the fatalities. The party soon became voluble on snorts of brandy.

'There was a fourteen square foot cabin through them woods,' remembered one. 'A bear was set scratching his back on the window sill. The hut shook like a quake and when he got to climb in the window, he was shot and killed. The bear has a bad deal; misunderstood, myopic and protected for the Big Cheese.'

'I have heard say that if a bison should stick out his tongue, the bear will hang on and rip it off.'

A third sporting man relayed his own account: 'The buffalo and the bear are the worst of enemies. I once saw a buffalo pitch a bear on to its back and sink his horns into its ribs. What does the bear do? Digs its canines into the old ox's nose, and wrenches the head to one side. The wretched beast's spine is snapped and his forefoot torn off for the bear's dinner.'

'So be it,' said the first. 'Beasts are our livelihood; bears especially. Bear grease is now a valued cure for aches and rheumatics; for softening leather and for shortening biscuits. Bear fat for cooking and for men's hair-dressing; bear meat, bear butter, bear broth. And what animal can rival those furry rugs with head and claws complete?'

There was a rumble of carts and engines and the men stood ready to hoist their dead.

The wolves stretched and skulked off through the ice and dark to their lair. Louis again assured Nicu and Titu of the wolf's standing with the bear.

'We two species of the wild have always existed in close proximity. We run faster and are more agile than the bear, but he is huge and stronger. We respect each other's strengths and differences. Despite the wolf's curiosity to understand more of the bear, he knows his own limitations, and the bear is too tough to quarrel with.' They reached the dens, exhilarated and exhausted, having picked up scraps of flesh and bones, left lying from the day's hunting. The cubs fell on them with all the pent up craving and energy from another day spent sheltered. The she-wolf looked disconsolate. She had seen the black beauty loping nearby. Louis' thorax throbbed; he guarded his mask and turned away with no comment. Had Seara been looking for him? Straining for a glimpse? She wanted him? He resolved to get up closer.

The hurly-burly of the shooting party was receding. The rhythm of endemic wildlife was reinstating its claim on the forest. A bracing tally of twenty-four boar dead and fifteen brown bear had headed the sportsmen off home to their habitats. The horses and hounds and carcasses and trophies; the heads and horns and hides. Each to be styled to the desires of man. In the aftermath, Nicu was stretched out on a boulder, away from the den. The morning sun shone hard, raising steam from the melting forest floor. The blood and mud of the past week was being exhumed. The birds had recovered their calling; he could hear the sparrowhawks and crested tits and the nutcracker's timid tapping. Trout were idling on the stream's surface and the scurrying of mice and rabbits was a pleasing antidote to the gunshot and turbulent agitations of the hunting party. He was jerked out of his reverie by the four cubs. Could Nicu take them fishing again? The worst conditions for fishing, he assured them. But it was the outing they craved with their guide and elder sibling. They loped well along the tracks when Nicu remembered his recent nightmare plunge in the ice-cold pool.

'It cannot be, boys.' Nicu halted abruptly. 'No swimming or fishing. We will die of cold and drowning. How about an insect hunt? They are crawling out from all the woodwork and we can feast on them. Off you all go!' As he diverted their attention, the familiar black mask of Seara, shielded by a distant trunk, had caught his eye. He stalked up to her. She asked tenderly after Titu and his ribs; next, lowering her head and lying in submission, she moaned of her love for Louis, the shy hero of her heart. She and Louis had an affinity, she impressed upon Nicu, to last to the end of their days. The four cubs were squealing and yipping excitedly through the trees. The she-wolf had arrived and was sharing in their insect hunt. Nicu detached himself sharply from Seara.

'Watch out for the jealous she-wolf. I will tell father that you need each other,' he hissed and was gone.

Repairing to his boulder in the early afternoon, Nicu felt a need to climb higher up the mountain. He called out to Titu to join him, to make a plan. The reawakening of the forests and the mountain ridge to the sounds of the wild was a revelation, a benediction. Titu tried to dissuade him from any mountain adventure. Why not wait for the spring and the flowers and the birds in the nest?

Louis trotted briskly past. Said Titu: 'He is off to check out Seara. Good luck to him.'

In their intuitive complicity the two wolves followed. They had a suspicion that Louis and Seara had delved deeper into a romantic attachment than might have been conceived; certainly by his sons. They stopped with a jerk; Louis and Seara could be seen half-concealed by a rock enclosure. Seara had taken dominance over her timid swain. As she patted and licked and rubbed, Louis lay in a subordinate daze of infatuation. Seara stood and backed her pretty anus on to his snout. Louis leapt up, charged with shock and the impetus of desire. Mounting Seara clumsily he clasped her haunches with his forelegs. With his penis lodged in the narrow passage of her vagina, the first stage was accomplished. Nicu and Titu looked on, transfixed from their hide-out. What would happen now? The two mating wolves were locked in an irrevocable tie. Nicu said their coupling could last another twenty minutes. They watched in consternation as Louis dropped his forelegs from Seara's rump and, with a cunning twist of his hind legs, his penis still firmly ensconced, the two performers were placed comfortably back to back. Nicu impressed on Titu to stay especially still during this second phase when the ejaculation took place. The fertilising element, the spermatozoa, would become

243

weaker with each thrust. And then it was all over and Louis and Seara fell apart. Nicu and Titu loped further up the mountain. It was growing dark already, with low cloud bursting with the threat of more snow. Nicu was still troubled with his nagging ambition to climb the mountain ridges, to ponder on life, his life and Titu's, their father's destiny and their own.

'It is dangerous to continue upwards in this dark,' declared Titu. 'We climb your mountains tomorrow.' Ever the adoring brother, he would up-sticks and follow.

The next morning, they had talked exhaustively; their last together. The clear blue ether had lured them higher and higher. They gazed up in awe at the sheer vertical drop of the dazzling white massif ridge.

Said Nicu: 'This limestone ridge is dangerously deceptive. It is made up of limestone steep walls, pierced with narrow crevices and a mountain to die for.' A hare raced by and another. The two wolves brought them down; rolling them in the snow, they demolished the heart and lungs. Warmed and invigorated, they continued up the mountain on a rough stone path. They saw bear and elk in the trees and pastures below and sheep and goat sheltered by villages. And they heard intermittent gun shots. In a cave hollowed out by wind and crumbling decay they took a rest.

'Let's talk about father,' suggested Titu.

'More pups on the way,' was Nicu's rejoinder. 'Louis-Loup and Seara – the alpha couple. They will lead the clan for two or three years and then be superseded. Or they will hand over voluntarily to you or to me and we will fight each other for supremacy; our one chance of leadership.'

'We will never fight each other,' exclaimed Titu.

'The privilege of mating is not given to all,' reminded Nicu. 'Our species retains its distinctions by rules and restraints. Too many wolves would demean the system, all running amok with muddled genes and blood and no idea of clan doctrine.'

'But we all need a mate, Nicu, to play with, to lie beside, to share a life and an affinity.'

'If destined never to couple with our mate we can wait and hope; it is a fact that a beta couple can eventually gain alphadom. Father, you and I could all be alpha males, increasing and strengthening the clan in turn . . .'

They jumped as the line of guns came closer up the mountain, in a steady, focused offensive.

'It is chamois they are after,' noted Titu from the opening of the cave. And a count of several beasts, their black spinal markings and upturned horns, flashed past and streaked ahead.

'We must stay sheltered; the gun dogs are also to be feared,' said Nicu as he snuffled round the cave's skirting for any signs of escape. The mountain fell quiet again and the wolves emerged cautiously into the pale camouflage of grey stone and snow. Passing through a thin line of trees, they came to an unexpected narrow ledge overhanging a deep gorge.

'Let us sit,' said Nicu, eyeing the fatal drop with morbid fascination. Titu pulled back to the wider rock mass.

'I don't think I will make old bones,' ruminated Nicu. 'Are you there, Titu? When we wolves find our soul mates we join together to the end of our days. And we will be good to each other, Titu – you and I.' Titu opened his mouth to give his undying allegiance, when a violent whip of air caught Nicu on his recumbent side. He leapt up dazed, an arrow swaying in his spine. He fell one thousand feet. Titu saw the archery hunter across the gorge; he was crouching to aim again. Racing for his own life, he heard the yowl of dogs, yanking his brother apart.

*   *   *

On the same morning of Nicu's dramatic death, *Toulon Matin* had announced a more tranquil demise:

Madame Veuve, domestique fidèle de La Comtesse de Beaucaire à Porquerolles . . .

'FINIS'

A month later, when the passing winter afternoons stayed lighter longer, there was a yip outside Louis' den. Titu roused his father. It was a young wolf waiting there with a thick reddish-brown coat. His tail was folded, his mask apprehensive, waiting for acceptance. Louis came out to him.

'I am your third son. Rufous is my name. Madame Veuve, our foster mother is dead. Gustave and Philomène have brought me to you.'

Louis, still overcome with his grief at the death of Nicu, lay before his long-lost son. He extended his forelegs and wept. Titu and Rufous stretched out beside him.

'Do the walls still talk?' he asked.

So long have the grey bare walls lain guestless,
Through branches and briars if a man make way,
He shall find no life but the sea-wind's, restless
Night and day.

> Algernon Charles Swinburne
> 'A Forsaken Garden'

BIBLIOGRAPHY

Adlington, Mark *Lost Beasts* (2001)

Boia, Lucian *Romania* (Reaktion Books, 2001)

Burton, Robert *Carnivores of Europe* (Batsford, 1979)

Carpathian Large Carnivore Project (Reports, 1997)

Carse, Robert *The Age of Piracy* (Robert Hale, 1959)

Comşia, A M *Romanian Game* (Meridiane Publishing House, Bucharest, 1968)

Evans, Nicholas *The Loop* (Bantam Press, 1998)

Fabre, François *La Bête du Gévaudan*

Fiennes, Richard *The Order of Wolves* (Hamish Hamilton, 1976)

Fournier, Le Ber, Lélia *Porquerolles, Une Ile en Cadeau de Mariage*

Fox, Michael W *Behaviour of Wolves, Dogs and Related Canids* (1971)

Frank, Harry (Ed) *Man and Wolf – Advances, Issues and Problems in Captive Wolf Research*

Ganne, Gilbert *Alfred de Musset, Sa Jeunesse et La Notre* (1970)

Gosse, Philip *The History of Piracy* (Longmans, 1932)

Holzworth, John M *The Wild Grizzlies of Alaska* (1930)

Jahandiez, Emile *Les Iles d'Hyere* – Histoire – description – géologie

Klinghammer, Erich (Editor) *The Behaviour and Ecology of Wolves* (1975)

Luret, William *L'Homme de Porquerolles* (1996)

Marsden, Simon *The Journal of a Ghosthunter* (Little, Brown, 1994)

Marsden, Simon *The Haunted Realm (Echoes from Beyond the Tomb)*, (Little, Brown, 1998)

Marshall Thomas, Elizabeth *The Hidden Life of Dogs* (Weidenfeld & Nicholson, 1994)

Mech, L David *The Wolf – The Ecology and Behaviour of an Endangered Species* (Doubleday, 1970)

Ménatory, Anne *L'Art d'être Loup* (Gründ, 2004)

Mivart, St George *The Monograph of the Canidae*

Ormerod, Henry A *Piracy in the Underworld* (Hodder & Stoughton, 1924)

Roosevelt, Theodore *The Wilderness Hunter* (NYC G P Putnam's Sons, 1905)

Schonmaker, W J *The World of the Grizzly Bear*

Schullery, Paul (Ed) *Spectacular Predator – The Yellowstone Wolf*

Zimen, Erik *The Wolf* (Souvenir Press, 1981)

Newspapers and Libraries

Le Figaro La Princesse des Iles d'Or – a review by Henry Bordeaux (7 Juillet 1908)

British Museum Library

Zoological Society of London Library

Redwood Library, Rhode Island, USA

National Sporting Library, Virginia, USA